Jonny Nexus is a Lancashire-writer in his spare time. When his wife, daughter, and dog; occasional work of theatre; and plays ...

Jonny began his writing career by launching the cult gaming webzine *Critical Miss* (criticalmiss.com), before moving on to write regular columns for the roleplaying magazines *Valkyrie* and *Signs & Portents*, as well as penning the *Slayer's Guide to Games Masters* for Mongoose Publishing.

Sticks and Stones is his fourth novel. His first novel, *Game Night*, was shortlisted for an ENnie award in 2008.

Sticks and Stones

WKPDA Book II

By Jonny Nexus

ISBN 9781661796419

10 9 8 7 6 5 4 3 2 1

Web: www.jonnynexus.com
Email: jonny@jonnynexus.com
Twitter: @jonnynexus

Wild Jester Press
Littleborough
Greater Manchester
United Kingdom

www.wildjesterpress.com

Cover image / artwork by Neela Jackson
www.thestartreestudio.com

Cover design by Henry Hyde
henryhyde.co.uk

Thanks to Jules for the love, encouragement and support she gave me throughout the writing of this book;

to Amanda and Lin for their help shepherding this book into the world;

to Jean, Angela, David, and Richard for the kind words and encouragement;

to Caffè Nero and Verona Lounge in Brighton, to Mooch in Hebden Bridge, and to Rebecca's, the Wine Press, the Cherry Tree, Veggie Vixen and Busy Beans in Littleborough, for the rocket fuel;

and to Violet, for being the best daughter a man could have.

Chapter One

Rav was a half hour into a dream featuring Phillip Schofield, a talking bear, heavy drinking, and — for reasons that had not yet become apparent — the entire England cricket team, when Gillian Anderson entered, dressed as Agent Scully and accompanied by the X-Files theme music. Up until now, this had been something of a three-stars-out-of-five type dream, worth watching if it came on the telly, but not something you'd actually go to the pictures to see. But it sure as hell wasn't three stars now, not now that the woman who'd been his not-so-secret crush since the age of ten had decided that of all the dreams in all the world, she was going to walk into his.

All Rav had to do now was ditch the cricketers and the talking bear, who, frankly, was already getting on his nerves, and think of a devastatingly witty line to open with. (Schofield could stay, provided he confined his role to buying drinks and bigging Rav up by claiming to be a mate).

Rav planted his elbow on the bar beside Anderson, waiting for her accompanying theme tune to fade out. But instead of fading out it was increasing in volume, louder, and louder, and loud—

He woke up.

Dammit.

On the bedside unit beside him, his phone was vibrating its way across the laminated top, its screen lit and its X-Files ring tone playing loud and tinny. He sent a groping hand out in search of it but succeeded only in knocking it off the unit and onto the floor, where it continued to ring. Who the hell was ringing him at— what time was it, anyway? He reached out over the side of the mattress, stretched, and then found himself rolling off the bed's edge, falling hard onto the floor. Fully awake now at — he finally found his still-ringing phone and looked at the time displayed on its screen — 03:58, he took a moment to consider the essential unpleasantness of the situation. 3:58 in the morning? And wasn't today Sunday? He looked back at the screen, which was displaying a number apparently unknown to his contacts database, paused a moment more, then thumbed the answer button. "Yes?"

The voice at the other end sounded desperate to the point of breathlessness. "Doctor Shah? Doctor Ravinder Shah?"

"Erm, yeah. That's me."

1

"Of the West Kensington Paranormal Detective Agency?"

On any other occasion, one in which it wasn't stupid o'clock and he hadn't just been rudely assaulted by his bedroom floor aided and abetted by its ruthless accomplice, Mister Gravity, Rav would have answered his phone more professionally. As it was, he merely filtered out the abuse and swearing his unfiltered reply would have contained, and went with: "It's four o'clock in the morning. Have you got some kind of emergency?"

"Yeah, I have." The voice paused for a moment, the breathing ragged as though on the very edge of insanity. "You've got to come over. I'm losing it. I can't handle this."

Rav had worked with enough troubled people to recognise genuine desperation when he heard it. He strongly suspected it was a mental health social worker his caller was in need of, rather than a paranormal detective — something he could say with a fair degree of certainty given that in his day job he was, in fact, a mental health social worker. But either way, the guy needed help, and what the hell — by the time he got back to sleep, Scully would probably be shagging Schofield. He gave himself the luxury of a brief sigh, then brought the phone back up to his face. "Fine, no problem. I'm on it. What's your name?"

"Ricky."

"Okay, Ricky. I'll come over right away. But you haven't actually said what your problem is."

"It's my tattoo."

His tattoo? It really was too early in the morning. "Okay. Right. And what exactly is the problem with this tattoo?"

"It's talking to me."

The address Ricky had provided was for a flat above a mobile phone shop in the Chiswick High Road, with instructions to go round the back and up a metal fire escape. The flat's front door was open, with a youngish man sitting on its step, smoking — nervously, if his shaking hand was anything to go by. He looked up as Rav approached him, his eyes twin pools of sunken desperation. "Doctor Shah?" He had dirty blond hair, worn shaggily, and looked like he might have been boyishly handsome had he not been so obviously near breaking point.

Rav nodded. "That's me."

"I couldn't sleep."

"Yeah, I got that." Had it not been 4:45 in the morning, Rav might have been in the mood for conversation, but given that it was, and he therefore wasn't, he decided to cut to what he figured was the chase. "So, what's this tattoo, then?"

The young man lifted up his t-shirt, revealing a strange spidery design across his left pectorals, shot through with what looked like hieroglyphic script. It wouldn't have been Rav's choice for the artwork he'd wear until the grave, but then again, he wasn't here as an art critic. "Nice. Where'd you have it done?"

"I don't know. I went out for a drink. First time in a long time. I… I don't know. I got separated from my mates, and then woke up in a skip somewhere in Hammersmith, with this."

"And you say, erm, you say, well—" Rav tried to tee the next sentence up in such a manner that it would appear neither sarcastic nor judgemental when it came out. "You say the tattoo talks to you?"

"Yeah." The young man nodded down at it. "Touch it."

Rav allowed himself an inward shrug, then reached out to tou—

Rav was somewhere else; he'd blinked out of one existence and into another. A screamed exhortation ripped through his soul like a diamond-tipped buzz saw. "SET. ME. FREE! NOW!"

He found himself scrambling backward.

The thing screamed again, each syllable hitting him like an individual bullet in a fully automatic burst. "RELEASE ME. NOW!"

Rav tripped, falling backward onto a hard, unyielding floor. Then the force, the presence, the whatever-the-hell-it-was, was upon him, snarling, probing; there, and yet at the same time, not there. Rav looked both at it and through it, seeing a worn wooden roof above him set on rusting iron girders. Rough walls of faded brick surrounded him on three sides; as he rolled desperately across a dirty concrete floor, he saw that where the fourth wall would have been was merely an opening, through which black water rippled under the moonlight. For an instant, a buried memory surfaced — he recognised this place. He'd been here before. But then the thing was upon him again, reaching into him, the cold sensation of its touch horrific and utterly overwhelming as its will flooded into his soul like acid dissolving through stone.

—ch the tattoo but found himself jerking his fingers away as his mind filled with memories, thoughts, and emotions. "What the hell was that?"

Ricky took a long, shaking drag on his cigarette before speaking. "You saw it, right? It talked to you?"

Rav took several moments to calm the screaming inner panic that was currently bouncing around his brain. It felt like every nerve in his body was pulsing, fired up by the adrenaline his body's fight-or-flight mechanism was currently dumping into his system in industrial quantities. Right now, keeping his legs locked and his frame standing was taking an effort of will. He'd been through some pretty scary shit in his time, but those frozen instants he'd just lived through were up there with the worst. Finally, he forced out a stuttering, breathless response. "Yeah. It talked to me."

The young man leaned forward and fixed him with a near-mad gaze. "I have that in my head, all the time. I can't make it go away."

Just then, a small figure appeared in the doorway beside Ricky. A blonde-haired girl, who couldn't have been more than three, dressed in Hello Kitty pyjamas and holding a small, fluffy bear. She reached out and touched the young man with a tenderness that spoke of harsh lessons learned at a too-young age. "Did Mister Tattoo wake you up, Daddy?"

"Yeah, he did, darling. But it's okay." He pointed up at Rav. "This is Ravinder. He's a special kind of doctor. He's going to help Daddy."

The girl looked at Rav with a gaze heart-breaking in its combination of innocence and pain. "Are you going to make my daddy better? Are you going to make Mister Tattoo go away?"

Rav knelt in front of her. Sixty minutes ago he'd had no concerns in life save keeping Schofield and the England lads out of trouble. But something about this situation, the girl, and the utter, total need that lay beneath her request had locked into his very being. This wasn't something he could walk away from, not if he wanted to remain the man he believed himself to be. He gripped her by the shoulders and looked her straight in the eye. "I'll make your Daddy better," he promised. "And I'll make Mister Tattoo go away."

Chapter Two

Matters paranormal are, by their very nature, elusive. It is the fate, therefore, of a paranormal detective to spend most of his or her time pursuing cases that prove to be wild goose chases of a very much non-paranormal kind. Since his last genuine case more than a year earlier, Rav had suffered several such outcomes. Red herrings had been chased down. Apparent impossibilities had, upon investigation, been revealed as curious, but ultimately explainable, events. Rav knew the truth was out there, but it had spent the last year in hiding. But not now. Not any longer. Not after a further twenty minutes of questioning had merely confirmed that this case was real, terrifyingly so.

It was time to pull in his resources and deploy the West Kensington Paranormal Detective Agency's three-person Lead Investigation Team. When he reached the bottom of the fire exit that led down from Ricky's flat, he pulled his phone out and hit a landline number from its favourites list. It was answered on the first ring.

"Ravinder?"

"How'd you know it's me?"

"It's quarter-past five on a Sunday morning. Who else would be calling me now? Should I take it that we have a case?"

"We do. There's a place we need to check out. An old abandoned warehouse on the Grand Union canal. I used to play there when I was a kid."

"And the purpose for investigating this warehouse is?"

"I just saw it in a vision. Look, I'll explain on the way. Be with you in half an hour."

"I'll be ready. Are you bringing Jess?"

"Yeah, I'm getting her. This is a big one, Prof. This is real. This is one for the full team."

Upon returning his phone's handset to its cradle, the Professor had washed and dressed, considering all the while what this new investigation might herald. Other men might have found such an unexpected interruption to their Sunday morning unwelcome, but not he. Quite frankly, his was a life in need of such interruptions.

It had been twenty-something years since the end of his academic career, following what he preferred to think of as a spot of unpleasantness, but which his NHS-appointed psychiatrist chose to describe as a "catastrophic, stress-induced breakdown" that had triggered "latent schizophrenic attributes". In many ways, the two decades between then and his recruitment by Rav as a member of the West Kensington Paranormal Detective Agency had been something of a personal interregnum.

Yes, it could be argued that this recruitment had been improper, given that they'd met due to Rav's assignment as his mental health social worker. And, as a former academic, the Professor very much understood the importance of professional boundaries and ethical behaviour, and would happily concede that as a technical argument, there was merit in this point. But, quite frankly, he didn't give a damn. He'd spent over two decades living in a fog of confusion and despair; his work with Rav, and the purpose and meaning it gave, had burned a path through that mist clearer than any route psychiatry had ever produced. He was, therefore, ready and waiting when Rav's car drew up in the gloom outside his retirement complex. He climbed gingerly in and managed to click his seatbelt home just as the car accelerated hard away.

The Professor generally found being driven by Rav a somewhat worrying experience, punctuated as it often was by erratic manoeuvres and an attitude to the Highway Code that could perhaps be described as "pragmatic". But on this occasion, aided by a near total absence of traffic, they made it to their destination without serious incident, parking up in a nearby side-street and continuing on foot along the Grand Union canal's towpath.

By the time they reached the abandoned warehouse, the sun had begun its ascent, illuminating this slice of post-industrial wilderness with rays of wan, slanting light. It was an early hour, and he'd not yet had his morning cup of tea, let alone any accompanying toast, but the Professor consciously forced awareness into his senses and alertness into his thoughts. The explanation Rav had given during the journey had been confused and fragmentary, lacking in salient details because there were no salient details. But it was clear, to use a somewhat clichéd expression, that evil was afoot.

As they crunched across the gravel and advanced carefully through the open maw that lay at the warehouse's frontage, he pulled on the latex gloves Rav had given him.

"It looks a bit different in the light," Rav observed, glancing around, a flash of fear in his eyes. "But this is definitely the place I saw in the vision."

At their feet, the third member of the West Kensington Paranormal Detective Agency's Lead Investigation Team sniffed warily at the cracked and dirty cement floor, before looking back up at them, her snout wrinkling in a manner that suggested a certain degree of wary suspicion. "Have a poke around, Jess," Rav said, waving vaguely at the warehouse's gloomy interior. The Border Collie gave the two of them a long hard stare, then resumed sniffing, working her way slowly across the rubbish-strewn surface.

Jess was apparently staying with Rav for several weeks for reasons he appeared to be disinclined to elaborate on. Regardless of what those reasons might be, the Professor was glad to have the dog on board. She had, in the past, saved both their lives on more than one occasion, and when venturing back into a realm of undeniable strangeness, it was good to have her with them.

The Professor took a slow, scanning glance, taking in walls made of worn red-brown bricks, dirty cracked windows set in rusting metal frames, and a wooden roof set on near-black iron girders. Aside from a scattering of random detritus and a glint that might have been discarded drug-related paraphernalia, it appeared empty. It was also quiet; eerily so, the only noise that of early morning traffic on the distant A4. "Unless my eyes are deceiving me, we appear to be alone here, Ravinder."

The younger man appeared confused.

"Is something wrong?"

"Yeah, maybe. I don't know. It's been a few years since I was last here, but, well… I remember it being bigger. Squarer. Deeper." He pointed at the far wall. "Like that wall was further away."

The Professor took a few paces forward and squinted at the back wall. Now that Rav had singled it out for close examination, some aspect of it jarred, although subtly enough that it took him a few seconds to realise what it was. "It's too featureless," he observed. "And too regular. It looks the same age as the other two walls, and is weathered to the same degree, but where their ageing and weathering is varied, its is consistent, marked neither by variation nor feature."

"Like a new wall maybe, faked to look old?"

"Perhaps."

Both Rav and the Professor began to walk towards the wall, but Jess — who was a few steps ahead of them — chose that moment to sniff up to it, and then, impossibly, go into it, leaving the rear half of a Border Collie extending out of the eroded brickwork. Then the rear half continued forward and she disappeared from view.

The Professor found himself rooted to the spot. He'd witnessed the impossible before, but even so, this — seeing a dog walk through a brick wall — was something beyond his previous experiences. Beside him, Rav appeared similarly dumbstruck. But then the younger man, perhaps braver than the Professor, or more curious, or perhaps simply more foolhardy, resumed his advance. He carefully approached the wall and, from a distance of perhaps six inches, extended a pointing finger. It reached the wall and continued, disappearing into an apparently solid brick.

"It's not there," Rav said, the catch in his voice betraying the degree to which his mind was clearly struggling to accept what his senses were telling him. "It looks like it's there, but it's not. There's nothing. No resistance. No sensation. Nothing." He slowly pulled his finger back out of the wall. It was, the Professor was relieved to see, still there. Jess chose that moment to reappear, her head and neck emerging from the wall like some kind of animatronic hunting trophy. She looked up at Rav with a quizzical expression.

The younger man glanced across at the Professor, a smile on his face that was presumably intended to be ironic but, in the circumstances, achieved only grim. "Guess I ought to see what's on the other side."

"Are you sure that's wise, Ravinder?"

"No."

And then, before the Professor could shout out a plea of caution, Rav plunged his head into the wall.

As Rav dipped forward into the apparently illusionary surface, his eyes instinctively screwed themselves shut. The stress and tension of what he was doing was almost unbearable. But as his head moved through the point he judged to be the line of the wall, he felt no sensation whatsoever. After a few seconds in which nothing happened save the pounding of his heart, he managed to talk his eyes into opening.

The view was something of an anti-climax, albeit one that replaced his previous confusion with a totally different confusion. His eyes were now telling him that he was standing in a squarer — though still empty — building, one whose proportions matched his memories. Some way in front of him stood a rear wall whose appearance matched the side walls, and which was in the position his recollection said it should be. At his feet was a whole Jess. And he himself was standing in an open area, leaning awkwardly forward. Of the illusionary wall, there was no sign. He took a step forward, then turned, looking back. The Professor was still standing where he had been, staring hard in Rav's general direction, but entirely failing to focus on him. He waved at the older man, but got no reaction.

He took a deep breath and plunged his head back towards the Professor. Again, there was no sensation, but as he looked around, he realised he could now see his own head growing out of a resumed, illusionary wall.

The Professor stepped back with a start. "Ravinder! You're back. Are you all right?"

"Yeah. This isn't a real wall."

"I had rather gathered that from the way your head is extending out of it. Some sort of illusion?"

"Must be. Come on in."

Twenty minutes of searching had failed to establish anything beyond the single, utterly impossible fact that an entire two-metre slice of warehouse had been somehow screened off by a one-way illusionary wall, visible from one side, invisible from the other. (As an experiment, Rav had tried placing himself such that the line of the wall bisected his head, with one eye on each side of the line, but the resulting, nausea-inducing scrambling of his brain's visual processing circuits had persuaded him to not repeat the test).

A thought occurred to him: what would his phone's camera see? He left the Professor and Jess searching in the hidden area and walked back through the wall, then took a photo. The image that appeared on the screen was consistent with his current, observed reality: the illusionary wall, with Jess and the Professor nowhere to be seen. He walked back through the wall and took another picture, and again the image matched what he was currently seeing, which in this case was merely a view of the warehouse and the canal beyond, with no intervening wall. This was weird heaped upon strange, albeit, he realised, a piece of weirdness — an electronic image of an illusion — that at least matched the underlaying strangeness — the illusion itself.

Then his phone beeped with a message, the caption on the screen revealing that it was from his cousin, Mindy.

Hey cuz cant sleep you up?

He quickly replied, attaching the first picture.

Yeah investigating this wall would you believe?

Her reply came back within a few seconds.

Nice oh well least youve got the prof and jess with you

What? How could she see them? He went back to the text he'd sent and examined the picture. Sure enough, it showed only the wall, with absolutely no sign of Jess and the Professor, hidden as they were behind the illusion. He hit call. Mindy answered straight away.

"Hi Rav, how's—"

"You can see Jess and the Professor in that picture I just sent you?"

"Erm. Yeah? Am I not, like, supposed to be able to?"

"No, yeah. Well. It's complicated."

"You okay?" she asked, a clear note of concern now in her voice. Mindy had been caught up in the events of the previous year. Alone of his friends and family, she knew where his moonlighting business sometimes took him.

"Yeah, yeah, I'm fine. Got a new case. Nothing bad."

"You sure?"

"Yeah." The Professor chose that moment to emerge from the wall, the sight still utterly staggering in its wrongness. "Look, I'll call you back." He hung up. "What's up, Prof? Found anything?"

The Professor held up one of the clear sandwich bags Rav had given him. At the bottom nestled a small gold object, shaped like a cross with a loop at the top. "It's an ankh," he said. "An ancient Egyptian hieroglyphic symbol often worn as an item of jewellery. I found it in the dirt in the centre of the shielded area."

Rav took the bag and examined the item closely. It was small, no more than an inch in height, with no markings or inscriptions. "Was there anything else around it?"

"Not that I could see. In fact, the area around it looks almost suspiciously tidy, as though it's been cleared of rubbish. I would conjecture that this item might have been accidently mislaid subsequent to that clearing."

"Okay. We've got an illusionary wall and an untraceable item of jewellery, and that's it. That's all we've got."

"We do have one other thing."

"What's that?"

The older man smiled. "A case, Ravinder. We've got ourselves a real, honest-to-goodness case."

Chapter Three

After dropping the Professor home, Rav had spent the rest of the day working on the case, save for a pause to watch Chelsea stuff Man U on Sky. He'd surfed and searched on illusions, ankhs, and tattoos, and even the history of the Grand Union canal, and while he'd learned much, none of it seemed in any way relevant. He tried loading the pictures he'd taken at the warehouse onto his laptop, but that, too, revealed absolutely nothing, with the images continuing to match what he'd seen with his own eyes. Baffled, he brought up the final picture he'd taken, which showed the Professor's upper torso protruding from the illusionary wall, took a picture of his laptop's screen with his phone, and sent that to Mindy with an accompanying message asking if she could see anything weird about the picture.

She phoned back almost immediately. "Rav, what's going on? Are you okay?"

"Yeah, I'm fine. Look, can you see anything unusual about that picture I just sent you?"

"No. It's a picture of your laptop displaying a picture of the Professor standing in the middle of a grotty-looking room, leaning forward and waving. Are you sure you're okay?"

"Yeah, I'm fine. Look, I'll call you later."

After he'd hung up, Rav re-examined the picture. It clearly showed the Professor's body protruding out of a wall. But whatever he was seeing, Mindy wasn't. More by random intuition than genuine hunch, he loaded the picture into some photo editing software and started playing with it. He turned it black-and-white, then made it into a negative, restored the colours, swapped them around, then put on a bunch of filters. But the image stubbornly continued to display the Professor's body emerging improbably from the wall, except now in random psychedelic shades. He was about to give up for the night when he tried a final random change, hitting the option to mirror the image, swapping left for right.

And then, in one reality snapping instant, the image transformed. The Professor was still leaning forward, with his left hand now waving rather than his right, but he was whole now, the real wall visible some feet behind him, the illusionary wall gone. For several long seconds Rav stared at the image, before a further thought occurred to him. He mirror-imaged the picture back again, but the wall did not reappear. He grabbed his phone and flipped through the images. Every single one that had previously shown the illusionary wall, now didn't. Whatever phenomenon had been affecting what he saw was now apparently broken.

This was getting weirder and weirder. The illusion was clearly not an effect that existed in the physical world, but was instead a hallucination of the mind, and one that worked only on those who'd encountered it first-hand — with its effect being limited to human beings only, if Jess was anything to go by. But nonetheless, it was powerful enough to persist even when looking at recorded images several hours later, and had finally broken only after the image had been manipulated beyond the hallucination's breaking point.

A chill ran down Rav's spine. What the hell was this?

The next morning, Rav phoned work to say he was running late, and then headed for a small terraced house that sat a little way past Hounslow bus station, shielded from public view by an overgrown garden and windows so unwashed that they had an almost leaded appearance. Since he was a small boy, his mother had warned him about Madam Clara. Not in the typical crazy cat lady sense, although that was a reasonable description given that her house was home to such a quantity of cats that she herself was unsure of their number, and that Rav had first encountered her in his professional capacity as a mental health social worker.

No. His mother's warning had stemmed from a far deeper fear, that Madam Clara was "one of them", who did "that". Usually, such a warning will prove, upon reaching adulthood, to have been related to certain cards placed in certain phone boxes offering personal services of a non-legal variety. But this was not such a warning. When people spoke of Madam Clara it was in hushed whispers. They said she was part-gypsy, that she possessed mysterious gifts, gifts that were perhaps not of this world. His mother's Catholic friends crossed themselves whenever they talked of her.

Once, Rav would have dismissed this as gossip and rumour, totally unfounded, and cruel to boot. After all, in his dealings with her, Clara had never been anything other than kind and considerate; if she did have a certain "not of this world" quality, that was not so much a statement of spirituality as a reference to a streak of eccentricity broad enough to have brought her to the attention of social services. But that was then, before he himself had seen things that were not of this world. He knew now that there were truths out there, truths beyond the comfy confines of conventional reality. He had a case that appeared to have little in the way of obvious clues, and if people said that Clara could see things, you know what?

Maybe she could.

Clara answered the door on the third knock, opening it just enough to peer round its edge. She stared at Rav with owlish confusion until a broad smile of recognition split her face. "Rav! Come in, love! Didn't think I was due a visit?"

She opened the door fully and waved him in. The interior was much as he remembered it: musty, dusty, and covered with cats. He followed her into the small sitting room, prodded at a furry cushion on the sofa to make sure it *was* a cushion, then sat down. "You weren't," he said. "I'm not here for social services. This is more of a… private matter."

Clara had an appearance that defied analysis or characterisation, her hair, makeup, and clothing such that she could have been almost any age between thirty and seventy. Alternative without being hippy, glamorous without being conventional. She raised an eyebrow. "A private matter?"

"People say you know things. That you can see things."

"People say a lot of things, most of which aren't very nice." She paused for a moment. "But you were always straight with me, Rav, so I think I can trust you. Yeah, I've got the gift. My mother had it, and her mother before her. Sometimes I can help people with it, and sometimes they pay me a little something as a thank you — though I'd appreciate you not mentioning that to the dole office. Do you need my help?"

Rav nodded. "Yeah. I think so. I've got something." He fished out the sandwich bag containing the ankh. "I need to know whose it is, where it's been, where it came from, maybe even what it is."

Clara gathered up her voluminous skirts and stood. "We'd better go through to the parlour." She led Rav to a small room tucked in behind her cluttered kitchen, in which stood a square table and two simple wooden chairs. A plain green tablecloth covered the table, and the walls were lined with tapestries. The curtains of the room's only window were open, but little light filtered through the dirt-darkened glass. Clara took the far chair and motioned Rav to sit opposite her. "That'll be fifty pounds, dear. You're a lovely boy, but I need to eat."

Rav extracted two twenties and a ten that he'd had the foresight to get from the cash machine on the way over and placed them on the table, then handed over the sandwich bag. Clara took it, then reached in to retrieve the ankh. She held it up, examined it, and then placed it in one palm before cupping her other hand on top of it. She closed her eyes, and her voice quivered as she began to speak.

"I sense power and corruption. I see a man. A white man, first young, and then middle-aged, and then finally old. There's a name."

Rav leaned forward, eager to hear, not wanting to interrupt.

"Mortimer." She paused for a moment, her hands starting to shake. "He fears, seeks revenge. There's another name I sense… the Hindustani."

"The Hindustani?"

Her eyes snapped open. "Yes, Rav, the Hindustani. Look — I'm just doing the bloody reading. Don't blame me if what comes out sounds a bit dodgy!"

Rav held up a placatory hand and waved her to continue.

"Mortimer is angry. Trapped." Her breathing was starting to come hard now, her chest rising and falling in halting shudders. "There is evil. Great evil. Wrong things. Terrible things. No, please! It's in my mind! Get it out! Get it out!" She broke into a scream — a long, unending cry of steadily increasing agony.

Rav forced her hands apart and flicked the ankh clear of her palm. The scream caught, choking, in her throat. She slumped forward across the table for several long seconds before looking up. "That's all you're getting, Rav."

"You can't get any more?"

"I don't want to get any more!" She pointed angrily at the ankh, which was now lying on the green tablecloth. "That thing is evil, tainted, cursed. I'd suggest tossing it into the deepest reservoir you can find, except I'm scared what it might do to the water supply." She grabbed the money and stuffed it into one of the folds of her outfit. "Please understand that I mean this with affection, Rav, but fuck off. And take that fucking thing with you."

Chapter Four

When Rav finally made it into the office, it was to find the usual bulging, Monday morning inbox, so it was lunchtime before he could consider the information Clara had given him. Tapping the name "Mortimer" and the phrase "the Hindustani" into Google bought up a result straight away, albeit one that seemed irrelevant. "The Hindustani" was a 1937 pulp science fiction novel by one Sir Edward Mortimer, apparently considered of no significant literary merit, but nonetheless regarded as a footnote in the development of the genre. He tried Googling the author's name, but that produced no further information; given that the man had lived nearly a century previously this wasn't surprising. All other avenues apparently exhausted, he fired up Amazon and found a second-hand copy of the novel available for a rather eye-watering amount, which — after a moment spent pushing thoughts of his bank balance aside — he ordered for next-day delivery, to be delivered to the Professor.

He then spent the afternoon visiting various clients, the last of whom was the Professor himself. Having filled him in and warned him to expect a visit from ParcelForce, matters turned — over tea and biscuits — to the question of what to do next. Two teas each and several biscuits later, they hadn't made much progress, although the Professor had filled several pages of his notebook in his tidy, neat hand.

"The question then remains," said the Professor, relaxing into his high-backed armchair, "what now? That there is a case to be investigated is a truth unchallenged, but in which direction that investigation should proceed is perhaps less apparent."

Rav thought for a moment. "We could go back to the warehouse. Have another look around. See if there's anything we've missed?"

"That would seem a sensible course of action." The Professor paused for a moment. "And such a course would allow us to address a curiosity I have about one particular aspect of this illusion, or hallucination, or whatever we should call it, which is the question of how long might we expect it to persist? Would it still be there now, some—" the Professor checked his watch, "—thirty-six hours later?"

Rav finished dunking his biscuit, took a bite, and chewed as he pondered for a moment. "Yeah, that's a good question. Only one way to find out, I guess. Come on, car's outside. We can pick Jess up on the way."

They parked in the same seedy residential street as the day before and set off down the towpath, their way lit by the slanting light of a summer evening's sun. The warehouse was darker, in shade now. And the illusion was gone, the Professor realised immediately, the interior volume back to its correct, near-square proportions.

"It's gone," Rav grunted, somewhat redundantly.

"That was probably to be expected," said the Professor. "It was already impossible enough as it was, even as a temporary phenomenon. You and I both know that this world contains things considered mythical, but which are nonetheless real. But there must be limits to how big a truth can be and still remain hidden in the shadows."

Rav nodded. They walked over to where they'd found the ankh and squatted down, both sharing the same unspoken hope that somehow, a second search might reveal something they'd missed. Then Jess let out a low, warning growl. The Professor looked up to see a man standing on the section of towpath that faced the warehouse's open front, staring straight back at him. He looked to be a not-quite-handsome individual in his early fifties, with black hair worn slightly long, and clad in a long frock coat just this side of pretentious. It was not a casual glance. It was instead clear from his body language that the sight of them there, at the place where they'd earlier found the ankh, disturbed him. Then, with a clearly forced nonchalance, the man turned and began to walk slowly away.

Beside the Professor, Rav took a step forward. "Hey, mate. Wait!"

For a moment the man paused, as though in the grip of a mental dilemma, unable to resolve his next course of action. Then he broke into a sprint.

Several months earlier, Rav had adopted as a New Year's resolution a commitment to increase his level of fitness, and having joined a gym on a fixed twelve-month contract, he attended a full eight sessions over three weeks before giving up. As his pursuit took him from the warehouse's cement floor onto the crunching gravel of the towpath, it occurred to him that continuing with his fitness programme might, upon reflection, and taking hindsight into consideration, have been a good thing. But since the man — who he was chasing for no reason other than he apparently didn't want to be chased — was sprinting hard away from him, Rav put his concerns over his fitness aside and continued the pursuit.

The first section of towpath was lined by bushes set against a chain link fence. Rav found himself settling into a rhythm, neither gaining on his quarry, nor losing him. Then the path switched to the other bank via a high humped-back bridge, for reasons which would presumably have made sense to its Georgian builders but which were utterly incomprehensible to a twenty-first century Rav.

The man took the bridge first, scrambling through the ninety-degree turn and onto its sharply inclined surface, followed several seconds later by a similarly scrambling Rav. Back on the level, they sprinted past a slowly moving narrowboat, over a stretch of path that was littered by broken glass, and then underneath an ugly cast-iron road bridge. The man whipped his head round for a moment to check on his pursuer, but stumbled in the process, falling onto his knees and collapsing in a heap perhaps twenty metres ahead. This was his chance, Rav realised, pressing on.

The man looked up, a cold mixture of fear, determination, and anger showing in his eyes, then lifted his arm and spoke whispered words inaudible at that distance. Like a bad dream the night before a job interview, Rav felt his body seize up, every muscle frozen, every joint locked in place. He tumbled to the ground like a lumberjacked tree, bounced hard, and rolled across the towpath and off its edge, falling into the cold, dirty water with a splash. For a moment, he floated, more helpless than he'd ever been; then the weight of his waterlogged clothes caused him to roll onto his front and sink slowly beneath the surface. In all of this he was, from the neck down, utterly paralysed, unable to do anything save clamp his mouth and eyes shut and try desperately to rein in the panic and terror surging within.

And still he sunk, deeper and deeper into the cold, clammy water, until terror and panic began to break through the fragile dam his conscious mind had strived to erect. This was it.

This was the end.

Border Collies are famously pack-oriented animals, and if there's one thing that pisses them off, it's their human masters choosing to split the pack, leaving them with the dilemma of which pack faction to stay with. When Rav had set off along the towpath, Jess had chosen to remain with the slower moving Professor, reasoning that at least this way, she could keep the missing portion of her flock, Rav, in sight. As a result, when he'd abruptly toppled, frozen, into the dark waters of the canal, she'd been some way back, having only just made a claws-scrabbling turn off the hump-backed bridge and back onto the towpath.

Rav was not the best of masters. Had he been a shepherd, she would have obeyed him grudgingly and to the minimum extent necessary; had he been a sheep, he'd have been first in line for a warning nip at the ankles. But nonetheless, according to the deep, wolf-inherited subroutines encoded into her doggie read-only-memory, his occasional acquaintance with her did qualify as pack membership, he had disappeared beneath the waters without any consequent reappearance, and she didn't need to be in possession of tool-using levels of intelligence to know that this was not good.

Jess switched up a gear, from fast trot to hard sprint, the gravel hard beneath her padded toes. Disturbed water marked the spot where Rav had rolled into the canal.

She dived.

Rav was not enjoying the process of death. Some men might die calm, happy in the tranquillity of a life well-lived and an acceptance of an inevitable end, but such men are generally meeting death from the comfort of their beds, rather than by drowning while fully conscious, but paralysed. Then, from somewhere above, he heard a splash, followed a couple of seconds later by the feeling of something grasping hold of the waist band of his suit trousers. He felt himself being tugged upward, his back breaking the surface, and then something else, something cold and metallic, was digging into his jacket, pulling him up further, enough for him to feel his face emerging from the water.

An old man with a kindly, rugged face reached down and grabbed hold of him. A woman joined in, and together they pulled him over the railing of the narrowboat he'd sprinted past seconds earlier. His rescuer put down the boat hook he'd used to snag Rav and reached back to pull a very wet Jess into the boat. The dog gave Rav a pained look then shook herself dry, showering him in droplets of canal water.

The man looked down at Rav. "You all right, lad?" he said, speaking in a thick Northern accent. "You went straight under! Good job your dog dived in after you, or I'd never have been able to get you out."

Rav tried to respond, but found himself still paralysed, unable to move a muscle.

The man peered at him in concern. "Is it drugs?"

It took several minutes before Rav could move, and several minutes more before the full effects of whatever the hell it had been wore off, long enough for the old man and his wife to tie the boat up and welcome on board the Professor, who'd been following along behind Rav, close enough to see what'd happened, but not close enough to do anything about it.

Now, in the boat's tiny galley-cum-living space, Rav had his hands wrapped round a mug of hot, sweet tea, trying to stop himself shaking. He felt more than upset, more than angry, more than scared. He felt violated.

Later, as they walked slowly back to the car, Rav still shivering even under the blanket the old couple had given him, still finding the act of simply putting one foot in front of the other a strain, his shattered brain finally managed to verbalise the question he'd spent the last twenty minutes unable to ask. "What the hell happened?" he said. "I mean, like, what in the name of Christ was that?"

The Professor rested a kindly hand on his shoulder. "A man waved his arms at you, spoke some words, and then created an effect not possible according to the scientific theories by which we have come to understand the world. Improbable as it might sound, there is only one word that fits what we've just witnessed. Magic."

"Magic?"

"Yes, Ravinder. That man cast a spell on you."

Chapter Five

Rav didn't go to work the next day, choosing instead to spend the morning under a duvet shaking, with what was either delayed shock, the onset of rat-borne Weil's disease, or both. He eventually roused himself enough to take Jess on a short walk around the block, before heading back under the duvet — this time on the sofa — to watch a few old film classics from his pre-Netflix DVD collection (sticking entirely to non-horror, non-fantasy films from the eighties and earlier, for fear that anything outside of that safe envelope might trigger some latent PTSD). He was eventually interrupted in the early evening by the ringing of his flat's entry phone. He staggered over and found its tiny grey screen filled by the concerned faces of Mindy and the Professor. He wasn't particularly in the mood for conversation, but pretending he wasn't in would have required a meanness he didn't have in him.

He thumbed the button. "Hi guys. Come on up." He left the front door open and retreated under his duvet.

From the sequence of looks that played across her face, Mindy had been about to launch into a bollocking, stopping only when she saw how bad a state he was in. She sat down on the end of the sofa, the Professor bustling past her into the kitchen, presumably to make some tea. "You okay, Rav?" she asked. "I heard you fell into a canal."

On the telly, a One Show guest presenter was enthusing on a subject he most likely didn't give a damn about. Rav picked up the remote and muted him. "Yeah."

"And you haven't been answering your phone."

"That would be because it was in my pocket when I fell into the canal."

"Why the hell did you fall into a canal? I asked the Prof, but he went all mysterious and said it was best if you explained."

The Professor poked his head out of the archway that led to the kitchen. "I was somewhat worried about you, Ravinder, so I took the liberty of phoning Parminder, and she suggested we visit you. I hope you don't mind."

Rav waved away the apology. "No, that's fine. I appreciate it."

"The canal?" prompted Mindy, her tone managing to split the difference between concern and exasperation.

"Would you believe that some bloke I was chasing along the

towpath cast a spell that paralysed me?"

She smiled a grim, tight smile that spoke of unpleasant memories. "A year ago, no, I wouldn't. I'd have told you to stop bullshitting me and tell me the truth." She shuddered for a moment, as though shaking herself back to the present. "You look terrible. Have you eaten?"

Rav hadn't, and he was — he realised — hungry. He shook his head.

Mindy pulled her phone out of her handbag. "Pizza?"

Unlike Rav, the Professor had not allowed his day to slip away. While his colleague had been spending his waking hours using a fifteen-tog bed covering as a psychological shield beneath which he could hide from reality, the Professor had taken advantage of the Amazon package that had arrived shortly after breakfast, to fill his day productively. He waited until Rav had finished his pizza, during which the two of them were able to fill Mindy in on the essential facts of the case, and then raised the subject of the package's contents.

"The book you ordered arrived today, Ravinder."

Rav had now started on the garlic bread. He took a chew, then swallowed. "The Hindustani?"

The Professor nodded.

"Have you started reading it?"

"I have finished reading it. It's one of the reasons I wished to speak with you tonight, other than to check on your general health and wellbeing, of course."

"Did you find anything in it?"

"Yes, in a sense." The Professor paused, unsure of how best to launch the discussion. He eventually decided to lead with a disclaimer. "Now, you have to bear in mind that it is a very curious work."

The Hindustani was indeed a curious work. It was poorly written, its use of language clumsy and its imagery weak, and it suffered from a plot that managed to be implausible, illogical, and ultimately unsatisfying. Its fourth wall was regularly breached by an overly bombastic narrative voice whose admiration for authoritarianism could only be described as quasi-fascist. And its entire text was shot through with persistent racism, sexism, and homophobia. A more prejudiced man might have written it off as a work of pulp science fiction typical of its time, but the Professor was not such a man, and knew that such a casual dismissal would be an insult to both that genre and that era. It was indeed a very bad book, but that said far more about its author than it did about the cultural space within which it had been written.

"Curious? In what way?" Rav asked, in between bites.

"Well, the book, which was written in the late-nineteen thirties, remember, is set in an imagined England of the early twenty-first century, an England in which people commute to work by vertical take-off rotor-planes, and travel to Europe and beyond in rocket powered airships."

"Rocket powered airships?"

"It's not a very good book. Can I continue?"

"Yeah, sorry. Go on."

"It is a world that no doubt reflects the worries and concerns of its author, this Sir Edward Mortimer. The somewhat brief biographical entry at the front of the book states his year of birth as 1877, so I suspect that by 1937 he was already something of a man outside his time. The society depicted in the story is essentially one of genteel decay, decadence, and corruption. In one of the book's few insightful predictions, a network of television screens in every home allows fringe cults and degenerate individuals to broadcast poison to the masses. The Britain of the novel is still a great power, but one overshadowed by a resurgent Germany. It is in some ways a re-imagining, albeit not a particularly skilled one, of the decline of Venice in the eighteenth century."

From her perch on the arm of the sofa, Mindy interjected: "What, all decadent aristocrats and masked balls and general— what's the word?" She clicked her fingers. "Debauchery?"

"Exactly, my dear. Exactly."

Rav took a swig of his Diet Coke. "Okay, this is super interesting and all, but is there a point?"

"Yes. The protagonist, the hero if you will, is a young man from the ranks of the aristocracy who rejects the privilege granted to him by the class of his birth, and joins an underground group who, to avoid a pointless degree of explanation, are essentially Nazis, although the book never states this explicitly. I should also point out that this protagonist, the Honourable Percy Munkton, does appear to be a somewhat idealised character, one who I suspect is the author's subconscious projection of himself."

"Okay, this would all be great if we were writing an A-Level English Literature essay, but since we're not, can we fast forward to the end?"

The Professor felt himself sighing. "You really do need to learn some patience, Ravinder. Deduction requires not facts alone, but the context from which those facts have been drawn."

Mindy jabbed an eager finger. "Like in archaeology, right? You can't just dig the stuff up, you have to take notes and pictures of where you found it, first."

The Professor nodded. "Quite, my dear. That is an excellent analogy." He gave her an appreciative smile and received a dazzling grin in reply.

Mindy turned her attention to Rav. "If you stop interrupting him, he might actually be able to finish the story."

Rav put up his hands in mock surrender. "Fine, fine. My lips are zipped."

The Professor waited a moment, and then continued, "Young Munkton faces various obstacles, chief among them being the eponymous Hindustani, a relatively young policeman of Indian ethnicity and origin, bought to Britain to serve in some sort of vaguely unpleasant secret police. The Hindustani is portrayed in quite viciously unpleasant terms, as both dim-witted and yet sly, lacking in both moral fibre and principle, and a traitor to not only his own people, but also those he has found himself dwelling alongside. The Hindustani is aided in his quest to thwart Munkton's plans by an older white man, who comes from some sort of academic background. But it is when we come to the third member of the Hindustani's team that things start to become a tad strange."

Rav stirred. "Why? Who is the third member of his team?"

"It's not so much who, Ravinder, as what." The Professor paused. As serious as their situation was, he still found himself enjoying reaching this, the climax of his findings. "The third member of the Hindustani's team is... a Border Collie."

"A young Indian guy, an old, white ex-academic, and a Border Collie?"

"Yes."

"In a novel written in 1937?"

"Yes."

Rav was shaking his head. "You've got to be kidding me."

"To use what I believe is the modern vernacular, I shit you not."

Mindy stifled a giggle. Rav, meanwhile, appeared unable to find any humour in the situation. "So we've got a wizard who can cast spells, who's connected in some way to a piece of jewellery, which is itself connected to some bloke from eighty years ago who wrote a novel in which he was the good guy and you, me, and Jess were the bad guys. Oh, and apparently, he feared me and wants revenge. And if that wasn't enough, there's also a poor bastard who got drunk and woke up with a telepathically talking tattoo with a serious anger management problem."

"That is a reasonable summary of the case."

"It's a bloody stupid case."

"I fear ours usually are, Ravinder. The question is, do we wish to continue, and if so, what is the plan?"

There are times in a man's life where circumstances force him to choose between two paths diverging in a wood: either the well-gravelled path that leads to a visitor's centre stocked with coffee, cake, and souvenir tea towels; or the narrow, muddy path that will lead to an illegally blocked right-of-way and an unpleasant encounter with a shotgun-toting farmer. For Rav, this was such a decision point. The previous night, he'd come within a hair's breadth of death. Only luck, a Border Collie, and a passing Northerner with a boat hook had saved him. The sensible thing right now would be to walk away. But one thing made walking away impossible: a three-year-old girl whose single-parent father was being driven slowly insane. Rav had told Scarlet Fletcher that he would make her daddy better.

Failure was not an option. And neither was walking away.

He shoved the duvet onto the floor and sat up straight. "I'm not giving up. But I can't ask you guys to be involved."

The Professor smiled. "If you are resolved to pursue this case, then you shall do so with myself beside you. As I recall saying to you previously, our work grants me opportunities to put something back into the world; opportunities that are otherwise unavailable to me."

"And anything I can do, cousin, I will," Mindy added. "This bloke Ricky, and his little girl — they need help, and it looks like we're the only ones who can give it. So, I'm in, which makes four of us if you include Jess." Across the room, the dog stirred at the mention of her name, looked warily around, and then went back to sleep.

Rav was only going to have Jess for another five weeks, given that she wasn't actually his dog, and was only staying with him while her owner Brian was doing what he'd euphemistically described as a "security job" in Iraq. But given that within those five weeks, it was likely that either the case would have been put back in its box, or he would, that didn't seem worth pointing out. "Thanks, guys. I appreciate it. In which case, I guess the question is: what are we going to do next? Was there anything in the book that gives us a clue?"

The Professor shrugged his shoulders in a very awkward, pained manner. "Possibly. Perhaps. Maybe."

Rav leaned in. "Could you be a bit more specific?"

"The plot leads to a climactic struggle between Munkton and the Hindustani atop a communications mast, a mast which is a key part of Munkton's plan to trigger a simultaneous uprising across the Empire against key government installations and leaders."

"And?"

The Professor hesitated for a moment. "The Hindustani is thrown from the tower by Munkton and falls to his death."

"Nice."

"There's no reason for us to treat this as some kind of prophecy, Ravinder."

"Easy for you to say. You ain't the guy who's apparently going to go BASE jumping without a parachute."

The Professor acknowledged the point with a nod. Rav, meanwhile, felt a little of his new-found resolve dribbling away. It was a rather unpleasant feeling, one that he could only describe as the mental equivalent of that moment when you're busting to go to the loo, find a toilet, but then feel a little bit of wee prematurely force its way free while you're still fumbling at your trousers. He consciously forced his thoughts back to the situation at hand. "Okay, so in terms of the leads, we have the ankh, and from that Mortimer. But right now, that doesn't seem to give us any obvious further avenues of investigation."

"No obvious ones, no."

"Then we have the bloke who cast the spell at me. But all we've got there is an eye-witness sighting — ours — of his face. Other than that, no name, no picture, nothing."

"Also correct. Which leaves us with only one avenue of investigation."

"Which is?"

"The tattoo, Ravinder. Sir Edward Mortimer is long gone and, it appears, near forgotten, so we go back to where this all started: with the tattoo."

Chapter Six

Somewhere in Greater London.

Life in the twenty-first century was not panning out as Mortimer had hoped, dreamed, or planned. The bars of his cage taunted him, as they had done every day since his awakening. He took a sip of water from the bottle in the corner. In the first months of his return he'd often refused sustenance, daring his captors to either release him or watch him die. But their resolve had been stronger than his, and each time it had been he who'd backed down, revealing a weakness within himself that he despised. His captors had seized on that weakness, in turn depriving him of food, forcing him to divulge for free the information he'd wished to trade to them. In the end, they had everything they needed; he served no continuing purpose save being a source of amusement.

In the far corner of his prison was an exercise device his gaolers presumably expected him to use. He didn't. He might have found himself lacking the moral courage required to fast his way to death, but refusing exercise and growing fat, if not happy, as a result, was easily within his capabilities. He returned to his bed.

One of his two captors approached: the woman, wearing her usual silly, shallow smile. She smiled down at him, muttered a quick protective incantation, and then walked away.

It hadn't always been like this.

He'd had a life once, back when he had lived on the other side of the veil.

Richmond-upon-Thames, Surrey, 1937.

Overhead, a plane drones across the sky, no doubt on a slow descent to Croydon Aerodrome. Inside his flat, Mortimer crunches his knuckles before returning to his typewriter. His fingers dance across its keys, letter after letter appearing on the pristine sheet of paper loaded into it as the rods hammer home.

"It's over, Mister Munkton," screamed the Hindustani, his spiteful features contorted in rage. "You're under arrest."

"It's never over," roared Munkton in reply. "Not while I still live and England still needs me!" He pulled himself back onto the platform and launched himself at the policeman, the fury of his charge sending the man tumbling into, and then over, the narrow encircling rail. A long scream slowly faded as the

Hindustani fell to the ground a thousand yards below.

For several minutes more the rods thunder home, filling sheet after sheet, until finally, the words "THE END" appear. Mortimer leans back in his chair.

It is done.

Rav spent the next day working both smarter and harder, skipping coffee breaks, eating lunch on the run, and spending only enough time in the toilets to actually perform lavatorial-related activities rather than — as was usually the case — also check Twitter, Facebook, and his various email accounts. He was, as a result, able to get away around three o'clock, satisfied that all his work-related I's and T's were at least addressed, if not necessarily dotted or crossed. Having picked the Professor up and driven to Hounslow West station, it was then only a fifty-minute journey on the Piccadilly line to Russell Square, where the Professor had an old friend who specialised in the sort of hieroglyphic script that the tattoo looked to be written in.

Lord Jonathan Dene was waiting for them in the lobby of the School of Oriental and African Studies. A warm and enthusiastic man in his early sixties, he had a rumpled, burly appearance quite at odds with his studious and precise manner. 'Quentin, my old friend!" he exclaimed, in a BBC English accent with an underlying trace of Mancunian. "It's good to see you. And you also, Mister Shah," he added, giving Rav a friendly smile.

"The feeling is very much mutual, Jonathan," the Professor replied, taking Dene's outstretched hand and shaking it enthusiastically. "I hope we find you well."

Dene tipped his head. "Well, there is the never-ending battle against budget cuts and cultural barbarians and budget-cutting cultural barbarians, but that aside, yes, I'm well. I understand from our telephone conversation yesterday evening that you have a document you wish me to inspect?"

"Of sorts, yes."

The academic pointed at the lobby's main stairs. "Perhaps we should adjourn to my office, possibly via a stop at the regretfully limited facilities this establishment offers us in terms of liquid refreshment. If you would follow me?"

Once ensconced in Lord Dene's small and cluttered office, via a detour past a battered vending machine from which they'd extracted cups of something that wasn't quite tea, Rav reached into his backpack and pulled out an envelope. "This is what we'd like you to look at," he said, sliding the envelope across the academic's desk. "It's photos of a tattoo. We think it's some sort of hieroglyphic writing."

"A tattoo?" Dene asked, pulling the photographs from the envelope.

"Yeah."

The Professor leaned in. "It is a somewhat long and complicated story, but we have a suspicion that this tattoo is not simply a random design and are hoping that it may contain a meaning."

Dene nodded, spread the photographs out, and began to examine them. After a few moments, he spoke. "You are correct in thinking these markings are in an ancient Middle Eastern language, but they're actually a cuneiform script rather than hieroglyphs." He peered over his glasses. "Sumerian, not Egyptian, that is. You're familiar with Sumerian?"

The Professor waved his hand in a manner that was presumably the academic equivalent of an ambivalent shrug. "Not to any greater extent than the average man in the street, I'm afraid, given that my academic speciality was some fifteen hundred miles and three thousand years removed, and more concerned with matters cultural and artistic than linguistic. I know that Sumerian was the language of ancient Sumer, which was a civilisation during the early Bronze Age in what would now be southern Iraq, and that it has a particular prestige as the most ancient written language. My understanding is that it was eventually replaced by Akkadian as both a written and spoken language by the start of the second millennium BC, and was then largely forgotten until your nineteenth-century academic forebears began the task of deciphering excavated tablets. But that, I am thoroughly ashamed to admit, marks the extent of my knowledge."

Rav nodded in feigned agreement, wearing the expression that he liked to think projected an air of thoughtful calculation and deep understanding. The Professor had clearly been raised on better streets than he, ones inhabited by considerably more knowledgeable "average men", but he felt no particular compulsion to admit to an ignorance far outranking the Professor's.

"Good, good." Dene spent several moments examining the

pictures, before nodding almost imperceptibly. He spun his chair round, reached out to the over-filled floor-to-ceiling bookcase that stood behind his desk, and pulled down a fat volume from the fourth shelf. Flipping through, he finally settled on a page containing a large colour picture of a worn, stone tablet. After several seconds, he sat back, looking at nobody in particular. "Now that is interesting. Very interesting."

Rav put down his polystyrene cup of not-quite-tea and leaned forward. "In what way?"

Dene turned his attention back to Rav and the Professor with a surprised abruptness that was almost a start. "Ah, yes, sorry. I'm afraid I was lost in the academic implications. The text appears to be a variation of a passage inscribed onto a tablet known as the Mortimer tablet." He waved a hand at the open book. "Not a copy of the passage, or a translation of the passage, or even a mistranslation. An apparently intentional and skilled rewording of the text to give a slightly different meaning."

As he was speaking, a gong clanged somewhere in Rav's brain. "Sorry, did you say the Mortimer tablet?"

"Yes. It's so-called because it was unearthed in slightly mysterious circumstances in Istanbul, in 1922, by an otherwise obscure amateur Orientalist by the name of Sir Edward Mortimer, having presumably been previously dug up — looted, really — by illegal vendors of antiquarian artefacts."

Rav and the Professor shared glances. As innocent coincidences went, this was looking guilty as hell.

Then the Professor looked sharply back at Dene, in the manner of a man to whom a thought has but recently occurred. "Jonathan, you say it is a variation on that text. How do the two texts differ?"

Dene pinched his nose. "First you must understand that deciphering texts such as these carries a note of interpretation. One might be able to decipher a literal meaning, but as with all communications, to understand the deeper meaning behind the words often requires an understanding of the cultural context in which they were written."

The Professor nodded. "Noted."

"The Mortimer tablet is generally thought to be an incantation intended to protect the then-King of Sumer, Lugalanda, by compelling the demon Asag to act as his unwilling defender. Lugalanda being a corrupt and unjust king, this is the sort of thing he would do. But this text appears to have been rewritten to apply not to Lugalanda, but to those who…" He peered again at the photographs. "Those who bear the mark."

Once again, Rav and the Professor exchanged meaningful glances. You didn't have to be Sherlock Holmes to figure out what "the mark" might refer to. Hell, you didn't even have to be Doctor Watson.

Dene chuckled to himself. "This is most curious. Most curious. Having seen this, I'd love to go back and study the original tablet, but of course, that's not possible now."

"Why not?" asked Rav.

"Because it was stolen three months ago from a museum in Istanbul."

Chapter Seven

"On behalf of British Airways flight 678, we'd like to welcome you to Istanbul. The local time is thirteen minutes-past twelve, and the temperature is around twenty-three degrees. We hope you enjoy your stay, and we look forward to having you fly with us again."

Flying to Istanbul to investigate the theft of the tablet hadn't been a wholly obvious path to take. The justifications were flimsy and there were logistical challenges, namely how the hell to pay for the trip and who'd look after Jess while they were away. Not going would have been a cheaper, easier option, and one Rav had seriously considered. But when hard clues are sparse, a detective must, out of necessity, turn instead to suspicious coincidences; and as coincidences go, the theft of the tablet from which the tattoo was derived was suspicious as hell.

Rav solved the first of the twin logistical challenges by pushing his bank balance deep into the overdraft zone and then whacking the rest onto an already whimpering credit card. He addressed the second by dumping Jess on his parents, making sure to ignore his mother's sarcastic remarks about this probably being the closest she'd ever get to looking after grandchildren.

As soon as the Airbus A320 nosed into its slot at the gate, Rav was up and out of his seat, grabbing his and the Professor's backpacks from the overhead locker and taking his place in the aisle, where he then proceeded to wait the five minutes it was always going to take for the doors to be opened. After navigating their way through the badly signed chaos of the airport beyond, they eventually managed to find the taxi rank, where they hailed a cab with a broken meter to take them to Istanbul for a fare that Rav would later calculate was a little over four times the going rate.

Beside him, the Professor appeared to be drinking in the sights of the city, this huge metropolis of some fifteen million people draped across a rolling landscape, an urban sprawl broken only by the slim pillars of mosque minarets reaching skyward towards God. Rav, meanwhile, was more interested in the journey itself, which consisted in the main of periods of speeding interspersed with episodes of hard braking and random lane-changing. Those things alone would have been enough to hold his attention, had the journey not been rendered even more terrifying by the absence of seat belts. (To be strictly accurate, the seat belts themselves were present, but had been disabled by having their receiving sockets pushed down into the gaps between the seat cushions).

Rav eventually calmed himself by repeating a simple mantra he'd once heard on a late-night infomercial channel: today was not his day to die. Which — ignoring the possibility that tomorrow might be — was still statistically likely to be true, even given the lack of seat belts and the lunatic at the wheel. He reached into his pocket and pulled out the sheet upon which Lord Dene had handwritten a name and a title, followed by a phone number.

Mehmet Osman. Chief curator, Ancient Orient Museum.

More than forty years had elapsed since the Professor's last visit to Istanbul. He'd been something of a bearded hippy then, with the city being but one stop on a hitchhike that would eventually take him all the way to the Indian subcontinent, if not quite to the spiritual enlightenment he'd been in search of. A truck laden with polished, gleaming Germanic automotive engineering had taken he and his companion through the night from Belgrade, depositing them in the heart of the old town a little after seven o'clock. They'd spent the day exploring the Topkapi Palace and its surrounding museums before bedding down for the night in the nearby railway station, where they were awoken in the early hours of the morning by a squad of Bulgarian cleaners who'd given them a savage beating before forcing them to hand over their remaining funds as some kind of payment for services rendered.

His memories of that visit had until now been vague, save for the beating, which, being something of a Kodak moment, was preserved in full, glorious Technicolor. But now those recollections of the Topkapi Palace and its grounds were returning: the medieval archway that led from a busy, bustling street into a tranquil park, the magnificent vista of the old city and the Golden Horn beyond, and the elegant nineteenth-century buildings that housed the museums, with the centuries-old magnificence of the Sultan's palace behind them. And above it all, permeating everything, a sense of time and place so strong one could almost taste it. This was an ancient city, where history sat upon history like layers of rock.

A grand staircase led up to the entrance of the Ancient Orient Museum. A slim Turkish man was waiting for them at its base as they approached, no doubt alerted by the phone call Rav had made when the taxi had arrived outside. He wore a tieless blue shirt, open at the collar, with a pair of austere spectacles perched on the nose of his narrow face. Smiling, he approached them, hand outstretched. "Mister Shah? Professor Richardson?" At their nods and handshakes, he added, "Lord Dene contacted me and explained your interest in the Mortimer tablet." He sighed. "Perhaps I should begin by showing you where it was until three months ago."

Rav didn't need to be a detective to spot the crime scene. At the centre of an otherwise crowded room stood a conspicuously empty glass box from which one sheet of glass was missing. Attached to the box's wooden plinth were a pair of laminated sheets that explained, in first English and then Turkish, that the exhibit within was currently undergoing restoration. (At least the English version did — for all Rav knew, the Turkish one might have contained a promise of genital-based retribution upon all those responsible for the theft).

Osman gestured sadly at the empty display. "That's where it was. One of the finest examples of Sumerian ritual writing. Gone."

"When was it taken?" Rav asked.

"In the early hours of the morning, between 1 and 2am. Everything was normal when we closed up in the evening. It was there at 1am when the security guard made his patrol. When he returned at two, it had gone."

"But haven't you got a security system? Alarms, motion sensors, stuff like that?"

"Yes. But none of it went off."

"Any idea why?"

A voice spoke from somewhere behind Rav, low enough to qualify as a whisper. "That is something we think you might be able to help us with, Mister Shah." Rav spun round and found himself face-to-face with a man in his early thirties wearing a well-fitted suit and a sardonic smile. Beside him stood a uniformed policeman, grim-faced and silent. The man in the suit leaned slightly forward. "I'm Detective Captain Demir. If you'll come with me, please?"

"Sorry, what?" Rav stuttered. "I don't understand. How can we help you?"

The man held Rav in an unblinking gaze. "We'd like to ask you some questions."

This didn't sound good. "Why? Are we under arrest?"

"Not yet, Mister Shah, not yet."

Ignoring Osman's furious protests, the detective and his mute, uniformed companion led them out of the museum grounds to an unmarked white BMW, into which they proceeded to insert first Rav and then the Professor. Rav didn't resist, partly through prudence and partly through fear, but mostly because no preferable alternative had made itself apparent. Demir, who'd taken the driver's seat, spun the car through one-hundred and eighty degrees and set off through the traffic-choked Old Town, navigating the chaos by judicious use of the horn, shouted curses, and a clear willingness to carve into gaps that would be viable only if the other driver blinked first and swerved away. Sights, sounds, and the occasional smell assaulted Rav's senses, adding to the confusion caused by the arrest, turbo-charging the near-panic that was already causing his thoughts to swirl like dirty water in an emptying bathtub. He'd seen Midnight Express. He knew what happened in Turkish prisons.

The Professor, meanwhile, was soaking in the surroundings as though this were some kind of tour, turning first this way and then that, letting out exclamations of delight at regular intervals.

They drove past a rather large train station and a magnificent, quad-minareted mosque before heading over a bridge that the Professor informed Rav was spanning the Golden Horn. Once across the bridge they turned a hard left, cutting across three angry car drivers and a clearly enraged tram driver and diving into a confusing maze of narrow and sharply inclined cobbled streets, which Captain Demir navigated with the same casual contempt for safety that he'd exhibited in the previous portion of the journey.

Finally, they skidded to a halt outside a narrow, three-storey building with an open set of double wooden doors, above which was attached a sign that declared in white lettering on a blue background: "Polis".

The uniformed policeman got out, opened the rear passenger door on Rav's side, and then spoke his first word of the entire encounter.

"Come."

Uncounted hours had passed, and the interview room now smelt of Rav's fear and someone else's farts, with the main suspect for the latter being the uniformed policeman— if his repeated pattern of a sideways lean followed by a satisfied sigh was anything to go by. Other than the noxious emissions, the cop had contributed little to the conversation, limiting his role to bored stares broken by the occasional threatening glance. Instead, it was his boss, Demir, who'd been doing the talking. Never actually violent, but always insistent, always probing, each subtle insinuation followed by a barely veiled threat. The uniformed cop sat on one side of the battered wooden table, with Rav and the Professor on the other, and Demir pacing and prowling behind them.

Demir sighed once more, and then resumed. "Let's go through this again, shall we, Mr Shah? You claim to have no knowledge of the tablet, or its theft, and yet—"

He was interrupted by a loud thud at the door that sounded awfully like someone being pushed hard against its other side. There was a sharp outburst of angry Turkish, and then the door opened and a blond-haired man walked into the room, followed closely by an enraged looking local with thinning hair and glasses worn askew. Both men wore suits, smart and tailored in the case of the blond-haired man, and noticeably creased — possibly from being rammed up against a door — in the case of the local.

The blond-haired man gave Demir a smile laced with steel. "Detective Captain Demir, I understand?" His accent was English, of the posh-but-not-too-posh Home Counties variety.

Demir gave him a grudging nod before erupting into a stream of Turkish aimed at his creased-suited underling, interspersed with much pointing at the blond-haired man. Rav was no student of languages. His skill set didn't extend much beyond English, pulp movie-level Hindi, and the few bits and pieces he'd picked up at school. But you didn't need to be a genius to get the gist of what Demir had said, that gist being something along the lines of: *who the hell is this bloke, and why is he in my interview room?* After twenty seconds or so of what was clearly a full and frank exchange between Demir and the other man, an exchange that apparently ended in Demir's reluctant concession of defeat, the two of them left, followed by the uniformed cop, leaving Rav and the Professor alone with the blond-haired man.

"One moment please, gentlemen," the man said. He pulled a slim, wand-like object from the inside pocket of his jacket, flicked it on, and began to advance around the interview room, waving the wand across the peeling paint of each wall before moving on to check the desk. That done, he stared at the green light at its tip then slid into the chair previously occupied by the uniformed cop. "Always best to make sure no-one's listening." He put the wand back into his jacket, and then pulled out another device, a slim black box that he slid onto the table. He flicked a switch on its side and a red light on top glowed. "Combined jammer and monitor," he explained. "Just to make assurance doubly sure."

Rav leaned forward. "Sorry mate, but who are you?"

The man smiled, revealing a lined, middle-aged face slightly at odds with his boyish hairstyle. "Didn't actually say, did I, old chap? The name's James Fox, attached to the British embassy in Ankara, although I spend most of my time here at the consulate. Heard you'd been arrested. Thought I'd come down." He stuck out a hand, which, after a moment's pause, Rav shook.

"And you're here to offer support?"

"In a manner of speaking." He leaned forward, the expression on his face that of a man weighing up which of the possible explanations available to him he should deploy. "I understand through my sources that you arrived in Istanbul with the intention of investigating a recent theft from the Ancient Orient Museum?"

"Yeah."

Again, Fox paused to consider his words. "Her Majesty's government, at least that portion of Her Majesty's government that I represent, has a certain… interest in your investigation."

An understanding was starting to dawn on Rav. "Why do I get the feeling you're not a regular embassy person, and you ain't generally in the habit of visiting tourists who've got themselves arrested?"

Fox smiled a wry smile. "Well, yes, my actual role might not necessarily always match my official job title."

"Deputy Cultural Attaché?" asked the Professor.

"Something like that, Professor Richardson. Something like that."

Rav's mood was now somewhere between fear and annoyance. "Why exactly is the local head of MI6 spending his Saturday evening helping out two British investigators who've got themselves arrested? Why would you care about a stolen stone tablet?"

"Because we believe this tablet has certain… properties."

"Properties?"

"Yes. Properties powerful enough that the prospect of their use by persons unknown concerns us." He let those words sink in before resuming. "There's no need to be coy, Mister Shah, or act the fool. You and I both know that there are things in this world beyond the reality most would understand or acknowledge. I know who you are, and what you do. But here and now, you're in a big heap of trouble.

I'm sad to say you've poked your nose into something of a hornets' nest. For the moment, I've told Demir to go forth and multiply. But I could depart and allow him to resume."

"Or?"

"Or you could agree to help us."

Rav wasn't sure he liked the direction this conversation was heading in, but then again, he hadn't much liked the situation he and the Professor had been in prior to Fox's arrival. "Why do you need our help? What've we got that you guys ain't?"

"As I said, Her Majesty's government has certain interests. But we also have certain constraints. Not just the obvious ones of politics, legality, and capability, but those imposed by the assumed and accepted nature of the world. Put simply, Mister Shah, there are certain things that Her Majesty's government cannot be seen to believe in, truths we cannot be seen to acknowledge."

"Which is where we come in?"

Fox smiled; not hesitantly, or ironically, but not quite genuinely either. "Exactly."

"What's it you want us to do, then?"

The smile was replaced by a serious expression now, as Fox leaned forward on his elbows and spoke in a whisper that was presumably for effect, given the carefree manner of his previous speech. "The precise identities of the persons responsible for the theft of the Mortimer tablet is a matter of some confusion, but we have reason to believe that subsequent to the theft, said persons purchased an item from an antiquities dealer here in Istanbul, at the Grand Bazaar. Like the tablet, this item is understood to have certain properties, which we fear may be used to unpleasant ends, perhaps even more so than the tablet. We'd like you to find the persons involved and retrieve the item. Do we have a deal?"

After a moment's awkward pause, Rav nodded. His case was spinning out of control, with vague clues leading to suspicious coincidences that in turn led to interesting — yet quite possibly tangential — developments. But on the other hand, it didn't seem like they had much of a choice, and besides, this looked to be the only half-way genuine lead they were going to leave Istanbul with. "You haven't said what this item is."

"It's a skull, Mister Shah. The skull of St Horace."

Chapter Eight

By the time Fox had busted them out of police custody, a process that had involved the deploying of barely veiled threats by him and the delivery of a grovelling apology by Rav, it had been too late to get anything else done. So after Fox had dropped them off at their hotel and departed with a cheery "good luck", having paused only to hand over a plain white business card with his name and phone number on the front, and the name of the antiquities dealer who'd apparently sold the skull quickly scribbled across the back, they'd got their heads down. Now, a few hours of not particularly satisfying sleep and a hurried breakfast later, Rav was advancing down a narrow winding street in the Old Town, accompanied by a guidebook-reading Professor.

"The Grand Bazaar," the Professor read, "whose Turkish names translate to either Covered Market or Grand Market, is one of the oldest and largest markets of its kind. Its sixty-one streets and over four thousand shops attract between two-hundred and fifty-thousand and four-hundred thousand visitors daily."

Rav wasn't really listening. Quite frankly, the city was unnerving him. Like the Professor, he'd only visited Istanbul once before, and while he'd not suffered the violence that had been visited upon his colleague, its threat had never been far away. When Rav and his fellow Chelsea supporters had landed at the airport for the away leg of a Champions League tie against Galatasaray, they'd been welcomed by banners proclaiming, "Welcome to Hell", and a reception committee doing their best to live up to that claim.

The Professor, meanwhile, was still reading from the guidebook he'd purchased at Heathrow. "In 2014, the Grand Bazaar's ninety-one million annual visitors saw it crowned the most visited tourist attraction in the world."

"Nice," Rav grunted in reply, hoping that it wouldn't be too busy, and consoling himself with the thought that Sundays generally weren't.

"Construction began during the winter of 1456, under the leadership of Sultan Mehmet II, shortly after his conquest of the city, and was completed four years later."

"Right." Rav couldn't help but think that if this place was as busy as the guidebook implied, then the street they were walking down perhaps ought to be busier. Somewhere in the hind portion of his brain, various semi-autonomous thought processes began to craft a nagging doubt, one dedicated to the proposition that this street didn't lead to any of the Bazaar's various entrances.

"The Grand Bazaar of today is one of the major landmarks of Istanbul, employing more than twenty-six thousand people."

Ahead of them, the gently curving street straightened out to reveal an impressive arched gateway currently blocked by a set of stout-looking doors.

"The Grand Bazaar opens daily from 9am to 7pm, except for Sundays and public holidays."

Bugger.

Five minutes of furious knocking on the door produced no result save to conjure forth an agonised throbbing in Rav's now cut and bleeding hand, at which point he took a step backwards, both metaphorically and literally, and noticed that there was a small entry-phone type unit beside the door.

"Perhaps we should try the entry-phone," the Professor suggested.

Rav bit back a reply and trudged over. Call button thumbed, he waited.

And waited.

And then waited some more.

Eventually, several presses and further waits later, a muffled response that was presumably in Turkish emerged from the small speaker grille set above the button.

"Do you speak English?" Rav asked, experiencing the habitual agony of an embarrassed, largely monoglot Englishman consciously suppressing the instinct to lead with a Hugh Grant-like rambling utterance of, "Now, I'm terribly sorry, it's awfully embarrassing, I feel bad even asking, and I know it's a huge imposition given that I'm a guest in your country, but I was wondering if perhaps, maybe…", due to the knowledge that the aforementioned ramble is not actually the best way to initiate a conversation in English with a non-English speaker.

"No."

"Sprechen sie Deutsche?" Rav tried.

A long stream of what was presumably German erupted from the speaker, at which point Rav realised that while his unseen Turkish co-conversationalist might be able to speak German, he — several years on from his Grade D GCSE — couldn't.

The Professor eased in alongside him. "If I may?"

Rav gave him a "fill your boots" wave of the hand.

Several exchanged lines of German later, the Professor straightened up. "He says someone's coming down."

After a wait of at least five minutes, a man appeared through a small side door. He was dressed in a security guard's uniform, with a neat peaked cap to match his neat moustache.

"We were wondering if perhaps—"

"I'm afraid the Grand Bazaar is closed on Sundays," the man said. "It will be open tomorrow."

Rav had never been very good at delivering bribes, with it not being the way things were generally done in Hounslow, but he thought he'd give it a go. "Perhaps you could make a special exception for us?" he asked, holding out a hand which contained a tightly folded one-hundred Turkish Lira note.

The guard looked at the note, and then signed, "No." Rebuff delivered, he took a step back through his side door and slammed it shut behind him.

Rav let out his breath, kicked at a random pebble, then turned back to face the Professor. "You think we should try sneaking in?"

The Professor shook his head. "I think not. I suspect they take security quite seriously, and the whole complex is built to be secure." He lifted the guidebook and began to read. "The concentration of trade into one location offered security against theft, fire and uprising. The gates were locked at night, and guards, paid by the merchants' guilds, patrolled the interior. Theft was extremely rare, with the most serious case being when thirty-thousand gold coins were stolen in 1591, an act that so scandalised the city that the Bazaar remained closed for two weeks while suspects were tortured. After the money was found hidden under a floor mat, the culprit was revealed to be a young Persian seller of musk who was executed by hanging, rather than by torture, only after the personal intercession of the Sultan Murad III."

"So maybe not try breaking in, then?"

"I think that's for the best."

Rav thought for a moment more, then remembered the business card in his pocket. He took it out. "Maybe now's the time to tell Fox we need a favour," he told the Professor.

Fox answered on the first ring. "Mister Shah? How can I help you?"

"We're at the Bazaar. Where the antiquities dealer's based."

"Ah yes. And you've found that it's closed?"

"You knew?"

There was a slight pause. "Well, I could call it an initiative test that you've passed by calling me, but the truth is, old bean, that in all the excitement it completely slipped my mind. However, somewhat fortuitously, I have a contact there in the security department. Hold where you are."

The line clicked dead. Rav looked back at the Professor. "I think he's going to get someone to come down."

Fox did indeed get someone to come down, that someone being an unshaven, monosyllabic man with a bad haircut, who, after grunting a vague greeting that appeared to include the name "Fox", ushered them through the doorway and led them down a maze of covered streets, finally depositing them in front of an arched opening festooned with artefacts and antiquities of every description, and which led to a vaulted chamber beyond, similarly stacked with wondrous items.

Silently, their guide departed, leaving them alone in this still and gloomy tunnel of shops. Most of the shops were shuttered, but a good number, like this one — which presumably belonged to the dealer they were looking for — had their shutters up. Shutters up, but not open, Rav realised, noting that the various objects before them seemed to be in the process of being rearranged. A pile of discarded paper and cardboard extended out to the front of the shop. As Rav appraised the scene, a man appeared from behind a standard lamp that looked to be carved out of solid marble. He nodded at Rav, the nod pitched just this side of friendly.

"Can I help you?" the man asked.

"We were hoping to ask you about an item," Rav replied, figuring that it was probably best not to mention Fox.

"I'm not open," the man replied. "It's Sunday. I'm doing a stock-take."

Rav held up a hand. "It's okay, we're not looking to buy. Well—" he paused, realising that this might not be the best course of action to take with someone of a mercantile disposition. "Not right now, that is. Not today. But we were interested in an item we heard you might have for sale?"

"Yes?"

"A skull."

The man shrugged. "Were you looking for something in marble, or brass, or gold, even?"

"No, no, not an ornament. A real skull."

"A real skull?" The relaxed attitude was gone now, replaced by a wary caution bordering on suspicion.

The Professor chose that moment to break in. "It's the Skull of St Horace."

"The Skull of St Horace?"

"Yes. It's the skull of Horace, or Horatius, of Antioch, a ninth century saint famous for his aid to the poor and disadvantaged of the city of Antioch. When he fell sick, members of a local church gathered outside his dwelling, ready to harvest his corpse for relics as soon as he died, the body parts of saints being highly prized in those times. However, when word arrived that members of a larger church were on their way to do the same thing, the local church panicked, stormed his house and hacked poor Horace to death. Of all the various pieces of him that they carried away that day, the most prized relic was his skull, which they housed in a box made of cedar wood inlaid with gold and rubies. It was held in various churches around Asia Minor, being stolen several times, until eventually being lost in the chaos following the fall of the Byzantium Empire." The Professor paused for a moment. "We were wondering if perhaps you might have sold it recently?"

At some point during the following several seconds the Professor noticed that Rav was now staring very hard at him.

"I'm afraid I took the liberty of taking your iPad this morning and having a little browse on the Internet."

"Right." Rav gave him a few seconds more staring, before turning his attention back to the shopkeeper.

"I did not sell your skull," the man said, his voice now chilled down to a point where it would cause gases to assume liquid form. "I have never heard of this St Horace. And I do not sell skulls. That would be illegal." He turned and waved a hand at the back of the shop. "Kemal!" A young boy peered out from behind a vase the size of a telephone kiosk. The shopkeeper spat a long stream of Turkish at the boy, interspersed with various hand gestures that appeared to indicate that Rav and the Professor were leaving and that he, the boy, was required to escort them off the premises. The young boy scuttled forward before being stopped by a further stream of Turkish, and more pointing, appearing this time to indicate that he should take some of the paper and cardboard rubbish with him.

The boy gathered up a stack in his arms, then approached Rav and the Professor. "Come!" he said, indicating with a flick of his shoulder that they should follow him.

He set off, the two of them trailing in his wake. Now Rav had got a better glimpse of the boy, he realised that he was older than he'd first taken him for, a lithe, slim, and boyish looking teenager rather than the child he'd earlier assumed him to be. He waited until they'd rounded a couple of corners, then quickened his pace enough to draw alongside him.

"Do you speak English?"

The boy stopped, looked warily up at him, then waggled his hand as best he could, given the several flattened cardboard boxes clutched against his chest. "A little."

Around them, the deserted streets stretched away, looking so much like a George Lucas film set, that had a couple of jazz-playing aliens emerged from one of the openings, they would not have seemed out of place. Rav fought down the urge to wave his hand in a circle and declare, "We are not the people you're throwing out of this complex" and instead bent his knees slightly to bring his face level with the boy's.

This might have been a last roll of the dice, but it was a calculated roll rather than a desperate one. Rav would never have claimed to be a Derren Brown when it came to mind-reading, but he figured himself to be a pretty good judge of body language. Certainly, when it came to the Friday night poker game with the lads, he was never the proverbial fool at the table. And, surprised as he had been by the Professor's unexpected regurgitation of St Horace's Wikipedia entry, he'd made sure to keep at least half an eye on the shopkeeper.

And he was pretty sure the guy had been lying when he'd claimed to have never heard of St Horace.

"We're interested in something we think your father might have sold in his shop."

A look of fear flickered across the boy's face. "We not talk about what we sell. If you want buy, come back tomorrow."

Rav put on his best smile. "Whoa, hey. It's okay. This is between you and me."

The boy looked across at the Professor.

"And him."

"I still know nothing."

Rav held up a finger. "Hang on." He pulled his backpack off his shoulders, unzipped its main compartment, and took out his brand-new iPad. "You want this?"

From the gleam that appeared in the boy's eyes, it was clear that he did.

"Your father sold something recently. A skull. A skull that might have been in a— what was it again?" He looked across to the Professor.

"A cedar-wood box inlaid with gold and rubies."

"Yeah. That. Do you remember that skull? Can you remember who you sold it to?"

Conflicting expressions played back and forth across the boy's face, as though his greed and conscience were rival combatants in a side-scrolling video game.

Rav indicated the iPad with a tilt of his head. "You can get some wicked cool games on that thing."

"He was Russian. Rich."

"You got a name?"

The boy looked around, and then bent forward to whisper. "I write it down." He fished a pen out of the back pocket of his jeans, then ripped a packing label off one of the flattened cardboard boxes he was carrying. He quickly scribbled on it, then handed it over to Rav.

Rav read the scrawled writing. "Menshikov. That's all you got?"

"Yeah. Yeah." The boy held out a hand. "iPad?"

Rav handed the tablet over. The boy pointed down the corridor. "Exit that way." Then he scuttled off down a side corridor, both iPad and cardboard clutched to his chest. Rav carefully folded the slip, then put it into his wallet.

"Do you think he's telling the truth?" asked the Professor. "He might have made that name up."

Rav thought for a moment. "Yeah, he could. But I don't think he'd have looked so guilty if he had."

Chapter Nine

After a return flight delayed by the usual, undefined problems, it was well into the early hours by time Rav tumbled into bed, only to be rudely awakened a few hours later by his phone's alarm — which was set to wake him on weekdays at 7am in order that he could fulfil the dictates of a harsh, capitalistic society through the sale of his labour.

Actually, on most occasions, Rav was something of a small-c conservative. Show him a media clickbait story about a permanently unemployed man with three "wives", seventeen children, and a combined benefits bill sufficient to power a medium sized commercial enterprise, and he'd be spluttering outrage with the best of them. But unlike, say, his Uncle Raj, who was happy to rise at five each morning to ensure that each one of this three shops opened on time, Rav's small-c conservatism varied somewhat according to current circumstance. (Basically, while his spirit might have been happy to talk the talk of personal self-reliance, his flesh was often less eager to walk that walk. Especially on the Monday morning after a late Sunday night.)

This was one of those Monday mornings.

He switched off the alarm, turned over, and went back to sleep, falling into a dream that involved Russian oligarchs, Nordic-looking blondes draped with both diamonds and attitudes, a frankly gratuitous cameo by Roman Abramovich, and for no obvious reason, a MiG 31 Firefox (Clint Eastward model, not to be confused with the actual MiG 31 Foxhound produced in the decades since that film's production, a plane that, non-plane spotter as he was, Rav would only have been able to identify in the fighter plane equivalent of a police line-up had the other "suspects" been an Airbus A320 and a Boeing 777).

He was eventually reawakened not by his phone's alarm, but by its X-Files ringtone, and while that abrupt wakening wasn't great, it got worse when a cursory examination revealed the caller to be his boss, Fenella. He hit answer, grimacing as he did so. "Erm, yeah, hi?"

"Erm, yeah, hi indeed." Her voice had an almost amused tone to it, which could sometimes be a good sign, but in this case, most likely wasn't. "It's half-past ten. Were you planning on gracing us with your presence at some point today?"

When discussing his work with friends and family, Rav would

often claim that Fen was an awful boss. Deep down, though, he knew the truth was that she was quite a good boss, stern but fair, and that it was he, the employee, who was awful. His brain, which was slowly stuttering into life like an old car engine on a cold day, ran through a variety of possible excuses, every one of which failed the basic, "Is this so clearly bullshit that a sniffer dog could detect it even after said sniffer dog's death and subsequent cremation?" test.

"I overslept."

There was a long pause. "You know what, Rav? I almost appreciate the honesty, and the time you've saved by not attempting to bullshit your way out of this. Please be aware that the only reason you're still employed is because last year, after whatever it was you got yourself involved in, certain people pulled certain strings on your behalf, very hard. They made a large deposit into your account of excuses, but that account is now, once more, overdrawn. Do you get my drift?"

Rav did. "I'll be in the office in twenty minutes."

There was another pause. "You'd better be. And I'd appreciate you allocating five of those minutes to a shower. I don't mind you turning up looking hungover but I'd rather you didn't smell that way."

Unlike Rav, the Professor had no need to fulfil the daily demands of a harsh capitalistic state. So, after a civilised breakfast of tea, toast and cereal, he'd adjourned to his care home's lounge and recreation area and made a beeline for the facility's Internet workstation.

The Professor was no expert on things online. Quite frankly, a year ago, he'd viewed the whole shebang in much the same way as a Palaeolithic ape-man might have viewed a banana-chip vending machine transported back through time: as a magic box whose workings were a mystery beyond comprehension. But over the past twelve months, he'd worked hard to enhance his skills as a member of the West Kensington Paranormal Detective Agency's Lead Investigation Team, and had undertaken a self-directed course of study, aided by fellow resident Joe, who used to work for the GPO and thus knew about these sorts of things, and Mrs Singh's seven year-old grandson, who'd apparently learned to use the Internet at about the same age as a Polynesian learns to swim.

Fingers cracked, second cup of tea sipped, the Professor had dived in.

And found nothing.

Which is to say that he'd failed to find the particular something he was looking for by finding, instead, everything. One of the things the Professor had learned in his studies was that the problem with the online world was rarely that of having too little information, but of having too much. When small needles nestle within multiple haystacks, the art is to filter, sift, sort, and order. Sets must be reduced to subsets. Chaff must be stripped away from wheat. Qualifiers must be applied, and the answer zeroed in on.

But on this day, the Professor's hard-won expertise had expended itself fruitlessly against the glacis of what had proved to be an opaque and intangible search task. There were many Russians named Menshikov, but nothing the Professor could find that might indicate which one of them was their man. He'd tried adding first antiquities and then Istanbul to his search terms, and then followed that up with half a dozen synonyms for each one of those two terms, but each time the data sifted and sorted to reveal the same essentially random list.

Eventually, after taking a break for lunch (overcooked beef and soggy vegetables, followed up by a bland sponge in lumpy custard, but then one mustn't grumble, especially when it is at the tax-payer's expense, one's own funds having long since been exhausted) before resuming his search only to hit the same metaphorical brick wall, he retreated to his room to call Rav.

"Hi Prof, what's up?"

"I've been attempting to Google our Russian friend, but I'm afraid to say that I've been unable to make any progress whatsoever. I was wondering if you perhaps had had more success."

"No. I tried at lunchtime but came up with zip."

"What would you suggest as our next plan of attack?"

"Don't know. Hang on— I've got another call coming in. I'll call you back."

The line clicked dead. The Professor thought for a moment, then picked up that morning's copy of the Times, whose crossword was still very much unsolved.

Might as well address the day's other tasks.

The caller ID on Rav's phone was that of Jenny Seagram, one of his colleagues at Hounslow Council's Social Services department. Rav hit the button to answer. "Hi Jenny? What's up?"

"This is sort of a heads-up, yeah?" She sounded unsure. "Unofficial like, yeah?"

"Yeah, understood. What's the situation?"

"I've just had a guy sectioned. He went into a cosmetic clinic on the Chiswick High Road, demanded that they remove some tattoo right away, then lost it big time when they said that wasn't how it worked."

This wasn't sounding good. "Ricky Fletcher, right?" A bright spark of guilt flared within him, fuelled by the knowledge that, reduced to chasing tangents as he was, he was nowhere near solving Ricky's clearly worsening problem.

"So you do know him then? He mentioned your name, over and over. I wasn't sure what to do. Client confidentiality and all that."

"No, you did right. Where is he now?"

"West Mid. I'm here now, getting him checked in."

Rav took a look at his watch. "Can you hang on a bit? I'll come over. Be with you at— four?"

"Yeah, that's fine. I'll be a while anyway."

The West Middlesex Hospital was a rambling and chaotic affair typical of a modern NHS hospital, where an original Victorian complex has had so much ad hoc enhancement applied to it that an expert on signage can take their best shot at making its interior navigable and still fail so miserably that porters pushing trolleys will have to weave their way past lost visitors and people who've been looking for Outpatients for the last ninety minutes. The psych unit was tucked away around the back, in a modest nineteen-sixties building, a relatively short walk from a car park whose fortuitous obscurity ensured that it usually had a parking space free.

Rav found Jenny at the reception desk, working her way through the stack of tedious paperwork that, notwithstanding the Human Rights Act, constitutes the average citizen's best defence against an unjustified sectioning. She motioned him over to a small seating area in the corner.

"How is he?" Rav asked her.

She shook her head. "Not great. He's not lucid. The doc had to sedate him just so the police could get him into the car. Now he's babbling away about nonsense. Only thing that made any sense was when he asked for you. Is he a friend of yours? I did a search and he's got no history with us."

"More of an acquaintance than a friend, but yeah, it's personal, not professional. You know he's got a daughter, right? Scarlet? Aged about three, I think."

She nodded. "Yeah, I went through his wallet and found a card for a nursery. Called them up, and they filled me in. Said they weren't aware of her having any other relatives. Her dad was the only one who ever picked her up and they've got no other numbers on file. So I've arranged with them to keep her in until home time as normal, and then some guys from the children's department will pick her up and drop her off with emergency foster carers. Unless you know of any relatives?"

"Not that I know of. No, I think you've done the right thing." For a moment, Rav considered asking to go and see Ricky, but quickly decided against it. There was nothing to be gained, it probably wouldn't help the poor guy, and it would likely raise questions in the minds of the psych nurses, which, given that Jenny had gone out on a limb by filling him in, was a bad idea. Instead, he thanked Jenny, asked if she could keep him up to date on any further developments, then walked back out into the sunshine.

This case was going from bad to worse. He'd always known this was a ticking bomb situation, but he'd hoped it might tick a little longer before going bang. Now he had a client who was in a psych unit, legally sectioned, and medically sedated. And a three-year-old girl whose life was about to be turned upside down by the arrival of two complete strangers telling her that daddy couldn't pick her up, so they were going to take her somewhere else instead.

And he had nothing. Two people had put their trust in him, placed their lives in his hands, and he'd made no progress save a one-word surname that might have no connection to the case whatsoever. He could have cried, and quite possibly would have, had he not been standing outside a building full of medical professionals for whom blubbing adults are a sign of possible future trade.

And then his phone rang.

Mindy.

He hit the answer button. "Hey Mindy, what's up?"

"You know your tattoo?"

"What about it?"

"Well, while you and the Prof were in Istanbul, I was spending my weekend pounding the pavements of West London, and seeing as I happened to have today off, I carried on today as well." From the tone of her voice, Rav could tell she was smiling. "Ask me what I found."

"What did you find?"

"I was going into every tattooist I could find saying I was interested in something with hieroglyph type stuff and seeing what artwork they offered me. Anyhow, there's a tattooist in Shepherd's Bush called Danny Killen. And when I asked about hieroglyphs, he showed me a picture that was your bloke's tattoo exactly. I told him I'd think about it and left. Did I do good?"

Rav felt a weight starting to ease. "Yeah. You did good. You have no idea how good. You free tonight?"

"Yeah, I'm free."

"How about we meet at the Bear, about nine, and you tell me everything you can?"

"Yeah, long as you're buying, cuz."

"Course. Oh, and Mindy?"

"Yeah?"

"Thanks for this. I really appreciate it."

Chapter Ten

Danny Killen's joint was located down a scruffy side street off the Uxbridge Road. Across its top stretched a sign that singularly failed to match the window below by virtue of the fact that while the sign was new, the window — with peeling paint on the frame and battered putty securing dirty glass — was not.

"Killers Tats!" the sign proclaimed, the missing apostrophe introducing a presumably unintentional ambiguity as to whether this was an establishment run by someone going by the nickname of "Killer", or an establishment run for people who regularly practiced homicide, on either a professional or recreational basis.

Rav ducked through the open door into an interior rendered gloomy by the plastic transfers affixed to the window's inside surface. On an easy chair inside lounged a powerfully-built man, with a look that was halfway between hippy and metalhead, like a Special Branch undercover cop who's nearly, but not quite, got it. Long hair drawn back into a ponytail; brass, pirate-style earrings in each ear; a set of wraparound sunglasses worn high on the forehead; a leather waistcoat worn over a bare chest; and a cigarette that was presumably unaware that it was no longer the nineteen-seventies smouldering casually in his right hand, filling the tattoo parlour's tiny interior with smoke.

Rav prided himself on being a non-judgemental, unprejudiced, progressive, live-and-let-live type of guy, but as his brain's indexing system filed Danny Killen's picture away in his brain space with a tag of "tattooist" it couldn't help but add a second tag of "wanker" based purely on looks alone.

Killen, assuming that was who it was, remained seated, but pointed an open hand at the chair opposite. "Take a seat, brother. I'm Danny Killen, but my friends call me Killer. How can I help you this fine morning?"

It was actually afternoon, a little after one, that being the earliest Rav had been able to get away from the pile of casework on his desk. But he decided to let that go. "I was looking for a tattoo."

"People who visit me generally are," Killen replied with a smile.

"Something that's sort of ancient Egyptian, like." Rav was purposefully not mentioning the word "hieroglyph", figuring that for two people to come in on consecutive days and ask for the exact same thing might set alarm bells ringing, especially if there was something dodgy about the tattoo — which, given that Ricky's version was linked to a very angry Sumerian demon, seemed highly likely.

Killen ambled over to a shelf laden with folders, searched along the spines, grabbed one, and then started flicking through the designs encased within in neat plastic hole-punched protectors. "How about this?" he asked, holding one out to Rav.

It showed a picture of a Hollywood style animated mummy, flanked by palm trees, with a pyramid beyond. Rav shook his head. "No, I was thinking something more... Mystical? Archaeological? Like something Indiana Jones might find in an abandoned temple, you know?"

Killen grinned, and pointed a finger. "I think I do, my friend." He put the folder back on the shelf, pulled open a drawer in the battered desk that stood to one side, and retrieved a simple card folder. "How's this?" he asked, revealing a design identical to the one Ricky had on his pectorals, complete with the spidery pattern and the cuneiform script.

Rav leaned slowly forward, examining it as though for the first time. "Yeah, yeah. I think that's the sort of thing."

"Funnily enough," Killen said, sitting back down in his chair. "I had one of your lot come in yesterday, looking at this design. Said she'd think about it."

Rav added a third mental tag of "racist", but managed to restrict his reply to a disinterested sounding, "Yeah?"

He could leave now, make his excuses as Mindy had done, and depart to continue trailing Killen from afar, like a submarine commander running silent with active sonar turned off, relying on passive sensing alone. But then if that had been the plan, he needn't have come here at all, could have trusted Mindy's judgement on the design she'd been shown. No, this wasn't the time for passive shadowing, or circuitous digging, not when he had one of his clients gibbering in a secure unit and the other in emergency foster care. It was time to go in for the kill, for the jugular, trusting that Killen was merely the blustering bullshitter his appearance indicated him to be, and not the dangerous psycho his nickname might suggest. He put the folder aside and leaned forward. "Actually, I've got a mate who's got a tattoo exactly like that."

"Really, well—"

"Right here." Rav patted his chest. "I reckon he got it done by you, here."

"Well look, it's a common design—"

"Yeah, sure. That's why it's in a card folder in a drawer in your desk, rather than one of the display folders on the shelf, right?"

"Look, I don't know who you are, mister?"

"Smith."

"Mister… Smith?"

"Yeah."

As fake names went, Smith was pretty implausible, given Rav's ethnicity, but that was the point he wanted to make to Killen. He wanted to throw him off balance. Rav had the feeling you sometimes get at a poker table, when some sixth sense tells you that someone's trying to bluff their way to victory with a hand full of shit, and that they'll fold if you push them hard enough. And Killen would fold if he pushed him hard enough. Rav took a deep breath and continued.

"My mate came in here drunk."

"Now, look—"

"There's laws about that. Could lose your license. All it takes is one phone call. Young guy, sort of good looking, shaggy blond hair. Came in a few months ago, plastered, late one night."

Rav was gambling. Even if this was the place, it might not have been Killen who did it. Maybe he had other guys working for him. But from the nervous swivel Killen's eyes made when Rav gave his description, it was pretty obvious he was the guy.

Killen gathered himself up, putting a look of defiant bravado on his face. "So what if I did give him a tattoo? People often have a drink before they come in, don't make them drunk. Ain't like I'm supposed to breathalyse everyone. What's his problem? Changed his mind? Looking for compensation, is he?"

Rav shook his head. "This isn't about compensation." It was time to go full bullshit now, he realised. Time to light the afterburners on his previously veiled threats. "And this isn't about having your license taken away." He paused for a moment to deliver a fake thousand-yard stare past Killen at the flat-screen TV mounted on the wall, then turned his attention back to the tattooist. "You ever heard of the Kolkata Knight Riders?"

"The Kolkata night… What?"

The Kolkata Knight Riders were actually an Indian Premier League cricket team, but it had been the first thing that had popped into

Rav's brain, and rather than risk disrupting the flow, he'd gone with it. Hoping to God that Killen wasn't a sports fan, he ploughed on. "Let's just say these guys are pretty handy with a cricket bat." Rav tapped the back of his head, at the base of his skull. "You get my drift?"

Killen nodded.

"One phone call to Southall, that's all it takes to make your license be the least of your concerns."

"Look, I'm sorry about your mate. I'm sorry if he's changed his mind. If you want me to try to change the design, I will, free of charge."

Rav shook his head. "I only want to know where that design came from. Who gave it to you?"

Killen looked genuinely fearful now. "I can't. It's a private design. I wasn't supposed to use it for other people. But when your mate came in, and there was an old Indiana Jones flick playing on the telly, and he pointed at that and said he wanted something like that, and I…" His sentence trailed off into an awkward shrug.

"I need a name."

"You don't understand. The people who gave me the design. They're a bit weird. If they find out I've talked to you—"

"I'm not going to tell them you talked to me. Give me a name and I'll walk right out of here, and the only reason you'll see me coming back is if you've stiffed me."

Killen shrunk back in his chair. "The guy who gave me the design. He didn't leave a name. Paid cash."

Rav went for a probe in the dark. "Black hair, slightly long? Late forties, early fifties, maybe? Long, posh coat?"

"Yeah. That's him."

Bingo.

Killen was still talking. "Gave me the design, told me he wanted that on his arm. Had the tattoo done. Paid cash."

"So why did he leave the design with you?"

"So I could tattoo the others, when they came in."

"Others?"

"Yeah. Did nine, ten maybe. Can't remember the exact number. I wasn't counting. Some men, some women. They'd come in, ask for the special hieroglyph tattoo. Pay cash, and then leave. Figured it was some sort of weird club or something."

"No one ever gave you a name?"

"There was one."

Rav raised an eyebrow, waiting for Killen to continue.

"She paid in cash, but she was chatty, told me her name. And then she came back a few more times, had more stuff done. Paid by card. Normal designs, you know? Talked a bit more."

"I need a name."

"India Ponsonby. She's some sort of life coach, she reckons."

Rav gave Killen a smile. "It's been good talking to you." He let the smile linger a few moments too long, then headed outside. He walked down to the main road, turned the corner, then pulled out his phone, retreating into a doorway, out of the sunlight. Thirty seconds of Googling produced the home page for India Ponsonby's life coaching business; a further sixty seconds on Google Maps' Street View established that the address of that business was a detached house in a nice part of Mortlake. Rav shut down the app and hit a name in his favourites list.

Three rings in, the call was answered.

"Prof?" Rav said, not giving his colleague a chance to answer. "I think I've got us a lead to check out. Place in Mortlake. Think we might want to head on over there tonight and take a sneaky look."

"Are you suggesting some sort of reconnaissance?"

"Yeah. Something like that."

Rav filled the Professor in, hung up, spent a few moments engaged in a certain degree of satisfaction, then remembered that he had about a day's worth of urgent social work currently sitting on his to-do list and only an afternoon in which to do it.

He headed for his car.

Chapter Eleven

After receiving the phone call from Rav, the Professor had spent the afternoon preparing for the planned evening's excursion, starting with some general background research before moving on to the question of what to wear. It being summer, he'd long since switched his daily wear from his winter outfit of a tweed suit, to his lighter, linen suit. But it now occurred to him that when the task in hand involves a certain amount of moonlit subterfuge, such a suit might be lacking both in utility and camouflage. He thus switched to the backup outfit he deployed on summer rambling excursions: stout but lightweight walking shoes, dark moleskin trousers, and a navy blue, wind and water-proof jacket, topped with a black beret. It was, he felt, an outfit that managed to combine a relatively low visibility with comfort and durability whilst managing not to look out of place in a civilised urban environment.

Preparations made, he waited for Rav, who picked him up at a little after ten dressed as some sort of ninja.

"You don't think you look a tad conspicuous, Ravinder?"

Rav pulled his balaclava off. "Yeah, maybe I should leave this off until we get into position. Anyhow, you getting in or what?"

The Professor climbed into the car, and they sped away. "No Jess?" he asked.

Rav shrugged. "I thought about it, but she'd probably smell a cat and start making a racket. You know what she's like. And I figure Ponsonby's probably already got a description of us from wizard-boy, so this needs to be an in-and-out, stealth job, like."

With the evening traffic light on the A4, they made it to India Ponsonby's house in less than twenty minutes. Rav pulled the car into a free spot a few houses down and killed the lights.

"Wonder if she's in?"

The Professor nodded at the silver BMW parked in the driveway. "Her car's there."

"How do we know it's her car?"

"Because three months ago she wrote a post on her life coaching company's Facebook page about purchasing a car, a post which contained a picture of a car remarkably similar to that."

"How'd you get on her Facebook page?" Rav asked, managing to sound both embarrassed and surprised.

"There was a link to it on her website. Do I take it that you failed to peruse the contacts section?"

"I was meaning to, but I was snowed under with work." Rav yawned. "Anyhow, did you find anything in her Facebook posts?"

The Professor shook his head. "Nothing that appears of any significance, I'm afraid. I was unable to get to her personal page, should she have one, only her business page. And most of the posts are related to that enterprise, special offers and the like. Other than concluding that she appears to be a somewhat shallow individual, I'm afraid I'm little the wiser. However, some of these things may prove to be significant later."

"Yeah. Like they say: first you collect the dots, and then you start joining them." Rav thought for a moment. "Okay, according to Google Maps, there's a path that goes round the back. How's about we head round there, get into the garden, and then maybe see if we can work our way into a side position where we can observe the front and the back?"

"And then?"

"Don't know. See how it goes, I guess."

Had India Ponsonby bothered to maintain the six-foot fence that lined the rear of her garden, it might have presented a formidable obstacle. But since its planks were worn and rotten, and the nails fixing it together rusted, it was a relatively simple job to push a couple of slats aside to make a gap large enough to squeeze through. Rav went through first, then turned back to help the Professor follow, before leading him into the wild and unkempt shrubbery that appeared to have colonised large areas of the spacious back garden. (Whatever attributes India Ponsonby might have had as a human being, dedicated gardener clearly wasn't one of them).

Beneath, as they were, a cloudy sky with only a crescent moon and distant streetlights for illumination, it was dark, and the progress was slow. A little way in, Rav dropped into a crouch and signalled a halt, using the hand pumping gesture familiar to anyone who'd grown up watching Vietnam war films. The Professor, who apparently hadn't grown up watching Vietnam war films, cannoned into him. Rav pointed at the house.

"Someone's in. There's a light upstairs."

The Professor whispered a reply. "From her posts, Ms Ponsonby appears to be a single woman who lives alone, save for her three-year-old son, Moonbeam."

"Moonbeam?"

"It might perhaps be a pseudonym created purely for Internet posts, to protect his current and future privacy, but given the language she uses to describe her life coaching philosophy, I fear not."

"Christ. Poor little bastard."

"Quite. Presumably, she has retired upstairs for the night, but has not yet gone to sleep."

Rav considered that for a moment. "Yeah. Okay, let's try to get a bit closer."

He set off through the shrubbery, aiming for a conveniently placed bush he'd spotted a little way to the side of the house, from which they'd be able to observe both the front driveway and the conservatory's side door. It was hard going, made more so by the low crouch he was attempting to maintain, and interrupted two minutes in by the sudden realisation that he'd left his balaclava in the car. He mentally shrugged that off — nothing he could do about it now — and continued his slow progress, stopping periodically to check that the Professor was right behind him. They wound round the rubble of what had presumably once been a rockery, edged between two apple trees, climbed up over a terrace that the Professor informed him was something called a "ha-ha", and then finally reached the edge of the shrubbery.

Between them and the bush was a ten-foot stretch of roughly mown lawn, across which stretched a path of round, stepping-stone paving slabs. There was nothing for it but to dash across. Rav checked left then right, and — seeing nothing — set off in a quick low run, easing his way into the bush. He waited for the Professor to join him, then pushed in deeper, probing between the branches, looking to find the perfect spot from which he could observe. Finally, he found it in a little open void with just enough foliage in front of him to shield him from view whilst still allowing a good arc of observation.

He settled himself down, at which point he became aware of the man who had already been occupying this portion of the bush prior to his and the Professor's arrival.

If, when later questioned, the Professor had been asked to describe the events that then transpired, he would have found it a task rendered non-trivial by virtue of the confused manner in which those events had unfolded. It began with a totally unexpected outbreak of conversation between Rav and some other individual.

"Who are you?"

"Well, who are you?"

It then continued with a shout of "Run!" from a clearly animated Rav, who, not pausing to wait for the Professor, hurtled out of the bush, tripped over a branch, and forward rolled out onto the gravel that bordered this side of the house. The Professor eased after him and found himself face-to-face with a second shadowy, crouched figure. He was still considering introductions when the entire area was suddenly turned from night to day by an array of floodlights that had chosen that moment to turn on.

"Motion sensors," muttered the man the Professor was looking at.

"Yeah, maybe we should be leaving," muttered the man behind the man.

As one, they all scrambled to exit the area, the Professor making a quick dash across the lawn to the shrubbery, sensing the two other men following close behind. He took a quick look behind, seeing no sign of Rav, but then a crash and a scream emerged from up ahead, suggesting that Rav was already on his way out. (Having apparently not only reached the ha-ha, but having encountered it in a manner that demonstrated why that type of feature had been so named).

Forewarned — or more accurately, reminded — of the ha-ha's existence, the Professor eased himself over its edge, aided in his task by the considerable illumination of the security lights, and in the process caught up with Rav, who was midway through the task of picking himself up. Then the two other men crashed in. For a moment, the four exchanged awkward looks, until the younger of the two men spoke.

"How about we get out of here now, and do introductions later?"

After getting out of the garden, Rav had suggested that they all retire to Jack's, an open all-hours joint off the Hogarth Roundabout that he sometimes dropped in at after night-time call outs to the Chiswick end of the borough. There was no great plan behind this save that it was just over the Chiswick Bridge, and offered a grilled chicken sandwich that right now, he was ready to kill for. He wasn't sure the two guys would come, but a couple of minutes after he and the Professor had nosed into the first of Jack's three parking spaces, the two men eased into the second in a silver-grey Nissan bearing a Hertz sticker on its windscreen.

As they got out, lit by an adjacent streetlight and the interior lights filtering out through Jack's windows, Rav was able to get his first proper look at them. The first man, who'd been driving, was perhaps a little younger than Rav, mid-twenties, maybe, and boyishly handsome in a sort of teen idol kind of way. He had slightly wavy hair the colour of teak and was clad in jeans and a battered leather jacket, worn open to reveal a dog collar (of the clerical, rather than fetishist, variety).

He paused to appraise Rav for a while, before a wry grin snuck onto his face, and he stuck out a hand. "I'm Jackson. Jackson John. And I'm thinking that maybe you're Ravinder Shah?"

Rav took his hand. "You've heard of me?"

The wry smile morphed into a cheeky grin. "I've read your website. And an acquaintance of mine has mentioned some of your exploits in Yorkshire last year. Don't worry, Emma was very complimentary." He looked at the Professor. "And of you, too, Professor Richardson."

The second man chose that moment to move into the conversation. He was older, early forties perhaps, with close-cropped red hair topped by a skull cap that set off a neatly trimmed beard and wire-rimmed glasses. "Samuel Bronstein."

A chill wind blew across the parking spaces. "Shall we go in?" Rav suggested. "I'd say they do a wicked chicken toastie, but I'm guessing you'll be looking for something kosher, Mister Bronstein, and I'm not sure this is."

Bronstein smiled, allowing John to answer for him. "Yeah, I think Sam might have to pass on that. And I should warn you, it's Rabbi Bronstein."

Despite everything, Rav almost found himself laughing. "Sorry, you're a vicar and he's a rabbi, and together, you, well…?"

"Let's say we take an interfaith approach to battling the forces of darkness."

Chapter Twelve

John took a bite of his grilled chicken sandwich and chewed appreciatively. "That's pretty good, Mister Shah."

"Rav."

John nodded. They were sitting in one of the booths at Jack's, with three grilled chicken sandwiches, one salad sandwich, and four steaming mugs of tea spread across the Formica table. Other than them, and the Polish night chef, the place was empty. The young vicar put down his sandwich. "Look, since we're all in the same line of work, how about we lay our cards on the table about why we were both staking out Ms Ponsonby's house in the middle of the night?"

Rav finished his mouthful. "So, you're in the same line of work as us, then? I don't want to sound rude, but you seem to know a bit more about us than we know about you."

"Fair enough." John glanced across at Bronstein. "You want to take this one?"

The rabbi smiled. "No, you're good."

"Okay. What I'm about to say's completely off the record, yeah?"

Rav nodded, as did the Professor.

"Like I said, my name's Jackson John. I'm an ordained minister in the Church of England, but I'm employed full-time in the Diocese of London's Deliverance Ministry, reporting directly to the Bishop of London."

"Deliverance Ministry?"

The Professor touched Rav's arm. "They're the ones who do the exorcisms."

"What, like in The Exorcist?"

John held up his hands in mock protest. "No, no! Well, yes. Let me explain." He spread his hands out on the table before he began to speak, in an accent that Rav was now noticing as being working class South London underpinned by a more educated grammar. "So yeah, strictly speaking, Deliverance Ministries are the teams within the church tasked with doing things like exorcisms. Each diocese has one, drawn from regular ministers within that diocese who do this as an extra duty. But in reality, a Deliverance Ministry is really social work. When a regular minister encounters a problem that requires specialist care beyond spiritual comfort, involving someone with possibly deep-rooted psychological problems, they call the

Deliverance Ministry, and get someone who's received extra training in this area. We now know that when someone's hearing voices in their head, it's going to be due to a chemical imbalance in their brain, not demonic possession."

"Except when it isn't," added Bronstein, with a chuckle.

John sighed. "Yes. Except when it isn't. Because, as you guys know, contrary to what the majority believe, there is evil out there. Supernatural evil. And a city like London attracts a lot of it. Which is why I'm the only full-time Deliverance Minister in the C of E, and which is where me and Sam come in."

Rav looked over to Bronstein. "So you're like him, but in like, Judaism, then?"

"Yes, although unlike Jackson here, I don't have the luxury of doing this full-time. I have a synagogue to run. But I do have a similar role, albeit a bit more informal."

Rav took another bite of his sandwich. "So what was the deal with you guys and India Ponsonby?"

Jackson answered. "There was an incident in an early years' nursery in East Sheen. It's attached to a school we run, the C of E, that is. A few weeks ago, the children started talking about an imaginary friend they had, called "Monster", saying they had to keep him hidden so that he didn't get taken away. The staff didn't think anything of it. Kids are always having imaginary friends, and although it was a bit out of the ordinary for children to share an imaginary friend, it still didn't seem to be cause for concern. Then one day, one of the assistants opened a cupboard door, and found Monster hiding inside it."

"And Monster was?"

"A minor demon. An Imp, if you want the technical term. Anyhow, as you can imagine, there was lots of screaming and a fair amount of panic. They were scared to call the police for fear that they'd sound like lunatics, and then the Ofsted inspectors might have got involved, and that thought scared them more than the demon did. So they called the vicar of the church the school's attached to, and he called the bishop, and the bishop called me."

"So how the hell did a demon get into a nursery in East Sheen?" Rav asked.

"Well that took a little while to figure out. Our first task was to send Monster back where he came from, which was a bit difficult because he didn't want to go. He liked being at the nursery. We had to fake a problem with the water supply to get the nursery closed down for the day, then go for a full seven-hour ritual to banish him."

"And then," Bronstein added, "we had to call in a team of discreet cleaners to spend several hours cleaning up the mess that the little sod had created during this whole process."

"Bad?"

"Imagine a supernatural monkey, throwing poo tainted with elemental evil."

Jackson shuddered. "We had to do a full blessing afterwards just to get the place fit for human habitation. Anyhow, it was only then we could start investigating how he came to be there."

"Which is important," said Bronstein, tapping the table for emphasis. "These sorts of things don't just happen. The boundary between this world and Sheol is only breached when idiots play with things they don't understand."

Jackson leaned forward. "You understand we're talking about magic here, Mister Shah?"

"Yeah. We get that."

"And magic is dangerous. It's not some nice fluffy, hippy thing, tapping into the natural energies of the universe. It's about taking evil energies and giving them shape and form. It's corrosive, poisonous. Use it, and it'll do to your soul what radiation does to your cells. That's why sending Monster back was merely the beginning of the story, not the end."

"And this is where India Ponsonby came in?"

"Yeah. After we'd got the worst of the damage sorted out, we did a sort of scan of the place, trying to detect any hot spots that might give us clues."

"How'd you do that?"

"That's kind of a secret of the trade, but let's say that if you're attuned, and you're holding the holy book of your choice, you find yourself getting a sort of spiritual spidey sense when you're touching evil things. It was Sam who found it."

Bronstein took up the story. "You know those educational toys for toddlers where you have a five-by-five array of spinning blocks in a frame, with a letter on one side of the frame and a picture on the other? You know, A, Apple, B, Ball, and so on?"

Rav nodded.

"Well, we found one of those reeking of evil. Deeply possessed. We asked the staff about it, and they said that it wasn't one of the nursery's toys. Turned out one Moonbeam Ponsonby had brought it in."

Now it was Jackson who took up the story. "Our theory is that his stupid cow of a mother tried to enchant it to use it as some sort of Ouija board, to do some sort of divination, or talk to the dead. Then Moonbeam took it to nursery, the kids played with it, and managed to use it to summon a Type-V Demon."

"So that's why you decided to investigate India Ponsonby?"

"Exactly. She's clearly got herself involved in something dodgy and we'd like to know what it is."

"We might be able to fill you in on some of that," said Rav. "Let me tell you how we got involved."

Rav's story took a little longer to tell than John and Bronstein's, being a little more involved, and being frequently led down tangential routes by interruptions from the Professor, but eventually, he got to the end. John considered it for several seconds, his head tipping back and forth, then glanced across at Bronstein. "What do you think, Sam?"

The rabbi shook his head. "I don't like it, I can tell you that. What we had, a badly enchanted child's toy, wasn't great, but it could possibly sound like an amateur dabbling in things they don't understand. This, however, an ankh so cursed that a clairvoyant screams, a full-on wizard who can cast illusions and paralysis spells, a bound and captured demon, and some sort of religious relic skull, this is serious stuff. This is a group of people who've made a serious and determined effort to gain a very deep, albeit very misguided, insight into the occult."

Rav blinked away a flashback to his near-death experience in the canal. "As the guy who nearly got killed by that wizard, yeah, this is some serious shit."

The rabbi gave him a sympathetic smile, then continued. "They also seem to be following a plan in which later steps build upon earlier steps."

"Such as the tablet and the tattoos," added John. "And presumably, this skull?"

This seemed like a good time to ask a question that had been nagging at Rav. "But why did they need to steal the tablet to do the tattoos and capture the demon, if there's pictures of it in books, and they changed the text anyway?"

"Because objects have power," replied Bronstein. "An object can have power because spells have been cast on it, or have been cast using it, or because it has been the focus of worship or adoration. Or even simply through age, through maintaining the form it has inhabited for thousands of years. That tablet was not simply a surface upon which the spell was written, and I should point out that the spell itself would have been far more than merely the words on that tablet, which, properly speaking, are an input to the spell rather than the spell itself. The tablet was both a powerful focus in general through its history and previous usage, and a specific focus for having been used before to cast a variant of this spell."

"They knew what they were doing when they stole the tablet," said John, in between sips of tea. "This isn't people exploring. This is people following a set path. Which brings us to this Sir Edward Mortimer you mentioned."

"Have you heard of him?"

"No. And I don't recall hearing any stories of anything even remotely like this that came up with my predecessors."

"Predecessors? Like the church had magical types that came before you?"

John held up a warning hand. "We're not wizards, Mister Shah. Don't claim to be, wouldn't want to be. Like I said earlier, magic is more than dangerous. It's evil. Contrary to what modern lore might declare, magic isn't a harmless pastime. There's no such thing as white magic, merely people who haven't yet realised quite how deeply in over their heads they are. Magic's inherently corrupting. Popular culture has it that wizards manipulate the natural energies of the universe, and that those energies are essentially inert, with it only being the tasks they're put to that can be either good or evil. The truth is that magic involves the manipulation of evil. Evil energies, evil forces, evil beings. To cast magic is to quite literally do a deal with the devil."

Bronstein cleared his throat, a gentle smile accompanying his mock cough.

John's pointing hand segued into a waved hand of concession. "Okay, all right, the devil is a concept in Christianity used to personify evil. Point noted, Sam. But understand this, Mister Shah. Magic is evil. It cannot be used for good, and were you to attempt to do so, it would be like—" He paused, searching for a metaphor.

Rav dived in. "Like a Jedi attempting to use the dark side of the

Force for good?"

John considered that for several long moments, leaning forward, with several abortive replies making it only so far as the initial finger point, before sitting back and smiling. "Actually yeah, that's not a bad analogy. Magic's like the Force, but with no good side. Where the Force corrupts only if you use it in anger or hate, magic just corrupts, period. You might be a good person when you start down that path, but you won't be when you finish."

Bronstein put down his coffee. "We study magic to fight it, not to use it. We're like bomb disposal experts. We have to be experts in how a bomb works, but we'll never actually build one. And even then, we sometimes get closer to the evil than we would like."

Rav nodded, mentally removing "become a kick-ass wizard" from the spot at the top of his mental bucket list. "Okay, magic— bad. Got it. But if we can't use magic against these people, how can we fight them?"

John shrugged. "Find out what they're doing. Stop them before they have a chance to do it. Question is, where do we start?"

"We?"

"It seems to me we have common aims here. We both want to stop these people. I think we should team up. What do you say?"

Rav thought on this. He'd only just met John and Bronstein, and other than the fact that they apparently were acquaintances of his erstwhile compatriot Emma Reece, he'd no reason to believe they were on the side of the angels. But something deep in his gut told him they were genuine. He turned to the Professor. "What do you reckon, Prof?"

"I think joining forces sounds like an excellent idea, Ravinder. As the Reverend Martin Luther King Junior once said: 'We may have all come on different ships, but we're in the same boat now'. It would seem that the only question is the one that's just been posed. Where do we start?"

Rav thought for a moment. "I figure India Ponsonby's still our best link to this group, gang, cult, whatever they are."

"Agreed," said John and Bronstein.

"But maybe we should avoid sneaking round her house after dark. Especially now we know she's got some kind of security system. How about we just observe her? Try to follow her around. Find out where she goes, and who she meets."

John and Bronstein exchanged glances, then nodded in unison.

"Sounds good," said John, pulling a small pad out of a jacket pocket. "How about we draw up a rota?"

Chapter Thirteen

The rota was, out of necessity, basic. Sam — who was apparently a morning person — volunteered to take an early 3am to 9am shift, starting that morning. The Professor would then handle 9am to 3pm, followed by Jackson — who, unlike his colleague was not a fan of early starts.

That left Rav, the only one of the four in possession of a regular nine-to-five job, assigned to the 9pm to 3am shift for the foreseeable future. In hindsight, he probably should have suggested they try for a more flexible schedule, but he was so busy playing the role of a "can do" kind of guy that, like an anthropomorphic cartoon bunny making it several paces off the edge of a cliff before looking down, it was only sometime later he realised the sleep-crucifying nature of the schedule he'd taken on.

After dropping the Professor back home, he snatched a couple of hours' sleep before waking up early and heading to a car hire joint. He'd originally intended to get a car for the Professor, but after considering the difficulty of hiring a vehicle for a man with no credit history and a personality that could be charitably described as "eccentric", he realised it would be easier to hire the car for himself, and let the Professor use his. So after dropping into Hertz to pick up a budget Ford — making sure to not allow the full cost to permeate through both hemispheres of his brain simultaneously — he drove home, dropped the new car off, then drove his car to the Professor's and got the older man to drive him to his office at Hounslow's Civic Centre, a journey that doubled up as a useful driving refresher lesson for a man who'd driven a car only once in the past twenty-something years.

That done, he dived into the office, and into a day that turned out to be both distressingly busy and tiresomely long. He finally made it out of the office a little after seven, grabbing some chicken nuggets and fries at Micky Ds on the way home. By time he finally pulled up behind Jackson's car, which was parked a little way down the street from Ponsonby's house, he was already knackered. He walked up to the car, and let himself in by the passenger door, sliding in beside the priest.

"How's it going?"

"Quiet at the moment," Jackson replied, consulting a notebook filled with a list of times and notes. "She went for a jog a little after seven. Luckily, Sam's outfit from the night recon looked plausibly like leisure gear, so he was able to follow her on foot without standing out. She apparently did about five kilometres at a pretty good clip, returning at around seven-thirty."

It occurred to Rav that perhaps it was for the best that he wasn't covering the morning shift; had it been him attempting to jog after her, the report would have read that she'd left the house a little after seven, ran off, and then lost him when he'd collapsed in a heap. A further thought occurred to him. "Hang on, I thought she lived with her son? Is he not there today?"

Jackson consulted the notebook. "It looks like she's got a live-in nanny, or au pair, or something." He found the entry. "Early twenties, blonde, left the house with Moonbeam at around eight-thirty. Said something to Ponsonby when she was leaving. Sam didn't catch what it was, but it sounded vaguely Eastern European."

"Don't recall her mentioning having a nanny on her business's Facebook page."

The priest sniffed. "She's a life coach, trying to make out that she's discovered the secret to having it all. The secret in this case being to use her ex-husband's money to pay for live-in staff."

Rav chuckled. "So what happened next?"

"She left the house, in the BMW this time, a little before nine. Drove to a coffee shop in Richmond, where she met with a couple of friends. Sam and the Prof eventually managed to do the changeover in the cafe. Then she drove back home. Sam managed to get some pictures of the friends, which he'll email round. But he said his gut instinct was that they were just fellow ladies that brunch, you know?"

"Yeah."

"So then she stayed at home. I took over from the Prof at three. She had a couple of people come. A man who the Prof clocked arriving at two-thirty and I saw leaving at three-thirty. And a woman who arrived at four and left at five. I figure they were clients. The nanny, au pair, whatever, arrived back a bit after five with Moonbeam. She hadn't come back after leaving with him, so either she'd taken him on a trip, or she'd dropped him off at nursery and then pissed off for the day."

Jackson moved his finger a bit further down the list.

"Then she went out, in the BMW again, at a little after six. Went to the local twenty-four-hour Tesco, did some shopping, came back home. That was it." He handed the notebook over to Rav. "Okay, you're on. I'll see you tomorrow."

He offered Rav a fist bump, which Rav returned, before getting out and heading back to his own car.

Now if he could just stay awake…

By Friday night, after three successive nights of only a few hours' sleep, Rav was feeling like fate was about to deal him the fake chance card that his cousin Faz had once surreptitiously added to his family's Monopoly set — a card that read "It is your funeral, divide your entire assets evenly between the other players and exit the game", a card whose receipt by Faz's older brother had triggered off a row so violent that the Monopoly set had been put away, never to be played again.

Three days of twenty-four hours' surveillance had turned up precisely nothing. They had collectively tracked India Ponsonby through two dates, a hot yoga session, one dance class, five client sessions, a food shopping trip, two clothes shopping trips, and a pair of morning runs. They'd lost her twice, once for five minutes during clothes shopping, and then for a thirty-five-minute stretch of the second date that might or might not have involved her shagging her partner in an alley round the back of the restaurant.

Jackson's Fiat 500 was parked in a side street in Richmond, opposite a small bistro, exactly where his text had said it would be. Rav slid his hired Ford in behind the Fiat, parking at a crooked angle, which, had he not been so epically knackered, he'd have corrected. Feeling punch-drunk, he made the short walk to Jackson, opened the passenger door, and got in beside him.

"You look like shit," Jackson said.

"Thought you was supposed to be a vicar?" Rav mumbled.

"Sorry. You look like shit, my son."

Rav decided he'd better shift the conversation back onto the case while he was still awake. "So what's happening?"

Jackson nodded towards the Bistro. "See that table in the window? She's with the bloke with the goatee and the ponytail."

Rav peered at the window. "Oh yeah. I see them. Anything happened?"

"They haven't gone round the back for thirty-five minutes, if that's what you're asking," said Jackson with a wry smile.

Rav found his resulting chuckle morphing into a yawn, one of those yawns so primeval that once you've started, you can't stop.

"I think we need to change our strategy," said Jackson. "I mean, we need to change shifts, before you, like, die, but we need more than that. I'll take your shift, tonight, now. I'm feeling good, and you need the break, but I think we need to do something more active. We can't go on like this, and sooner or later she's going to clock one of us, if she hasn't already."

Rav would have argued about the change of shift, had he not been so exhausted. Instead, he sort of waved a thanks while his yawn entered its closing stretch, then — when it finally stuttered to a conclusion — managed to speak. "Thanks, I appreciate that. But on the doing something, what did you have in mind?"

"Don't know. One possibility would be to get inside her house, I guess. But that's high risk. Illegally so." He paused. "It's not like Sam and I have never done things that, strictly speaking, aren't within the law. My first allegiance is to Christ, and my first duty is to protect his people from evil, and if I have to break the laws of men to do that, then I will. But it's pretty much a last-ditch resort. Render unto Caesar, and all that."

"Jesus wasn't exactly obeying the law when he went into the temple and tipped all the moneylenders' tables over, right?"

"No. But I'm not sure my bishop would see things that way, if it all goes to pot."

Right now, Rav was finding it difficult to get his thoughts into any kind of straight line. He made his way past another several-second yawn, then shook his head. "Let's talk about it tomorrow. And thanks mate. I appreciate this." He attempted to give the priest a fist-bump, but somehow managed to miss, then hauled himself wearily out of the car.

His bed was calling, but there was somewhere he needed to be first, and thanks to Jackson's generosity, he now had a chance to be there.

The house stood a little way back from the road, its slightly faded nineteen-seventies frontage sitting easily in a row of near-identical dwellings. Rav checked the address scribbled onto the crumpled yellow post-it note he'd pulled from his pocket and walked down the garden path to the white PVC front door.

There was a doorbell, but he didn't ring it, not with it being well past nine at night. Instead, he knocked lightly on the door. He waited several seconds, and was about to knock again, but then a light came on in the hallway and the door was opened a crack.

A middle-aged woman peered at him from around the security chain, which was fair enough given that it was late at night, at one of the poorer ends of town. Rav was horribly aware that he was probably projecting a look pitched somewhere between serial-killer and fanatical evangelist, but he pasted on his best smile. "Mrs Henson? Jenny Seagram gave me your address. Hope that was okay."

A note of caution appeared on her face. "Is it about Scarlet?" She unhooked the chain and opened the door fully. "She's asleep right now, but you can come in if you'd like, Mister?"

"Shah. Ravinder Shah. I work with Jenny. I've been involved with Scarlet's father, Ricky." The door was open, but he didn't step inside. Truth was, he wasn't quite sure why he'd got the address of Scarlet's emergency foster carer from Jenny, and why he'd come here now, other than he felt as if common decency had compelled him to do so. "I don't need to come in. I just want to know if she's doing okay. It's been like five days, right?"

Mrs Henson nodded. "Yeah." She paused for a moment. "She's doing okay. She's sad, she misses her daddy, and I can tell she's worried about him, but she's bearing up."

"Thanks," Rav said. "That's good to hear."

"Do you know how her dad's doing? Is he any better?"

Rav shook his head. "Jenny said there's no improvement." He went to say something else but realised there wasn't really anything else to say. "Look, I won't take up any more of your evening." He nodded goodbye, then retraced his steps back to his hired Ford. He got in but didn't drive away. It was good to hear that Scarlet was bearing up, but that wasn't the point. He'd made a promise to her, and so far, he'd achieved damn all when it came to fulfilling it.

Instead, he had a multi-stranded case, where every strand was deadlocked. Following Ponsonby was getting them nowhere. The wizard was, well, out there somewhere. And where the hell Fox and his skull might fit into any of this was anyone's guess. He was working on the assumption that the various pieces would eventually slot together into one case, and that might then reveal a path leading to a cure for Ricky. But right now, this wasn't so much an investigation as an exercise in spinning plates. They weren't getting anywhere. He needed something else.

For several minutes he sat there, thinking. By now, Ponsonby had probably seen Jackson, Sam, and the Professor around. And even if she hadn't clocked them, seeing them face-to-face might bring a memory back to the surface. She might not have seen him, on account of him having been stiffed with the night shift. But the bloke who'd cast the spell might have given her a description. Hell, if they'd tracked down his website, he might have given her a picture. He shuddered at the thought. But then, despite — or perhaps because of — his knackered state, an idea began to occur to him. He fished in his pocket, pulled out his phone, and hit an entry in his favourites list.

She answered on the third ring. "Hi cousin. What's up?"

"I need a favour, Mindy. Have you ever fancied having one of those life coaching sessions?"

Chapter Fourteen

Once, a long time ago, when he was young, stupid, and still harbouring the mistaken belief that the way to attract women and impress men was to be both young and stupid, Rav had been involved in an unfortunate incident that involved the following elements: a car that was at least borrowed, if not quite stolen, a bloke who, it turned out, couldn't actually drive, and a flashy, high-speed traffic manoeuvre that ended with the car parked backwards inside Mrs Sharma's now wrecked launderette.

Rav and his three companions had managed to avoid entanglement with the police through the simple but effective tactic of running away very quickly. But the Asian community is tight knit. To say that word gets around would be like a declaration that light travels quite fast: correct, but somewhat missing the point. Word doesn't so much get around as force its way into every nook, crack and crevice. The four of them had, as a result, found themselves hauled up in front of what the Daily Mail would no doubt have described as a "parallel system of justice" enforced by "self-selected, so-called, community elders", but which was actually the mother of all bollockings delivered by Rav's Uncle Dev over tea in a back room at the temple.

It was some twenty minutes after breaking into Ponsonby's house via the window of the downstairs toilet — aided by Mindy, who had, as previously arranged, said she needed to spend a penny exactly seven minutes into her life-coaching session with Ponsonby — that Rav experienced a sudden flashback to that past event, a flashback triggered by the sound of someone coming up the stairs who absolutely should not have been coming up the stairs.

For a moment he found himself lost in a waking dream, facing his Uncle Dev, the older man pinching the bridge of his nose as he shook his head. "So let me get this straight, Rav," the waking dream's version of Dev was saying in the resigned tone of a man already regretting being in any way involved. "You not only teamed up with one of your patients, a vicar, and a rabbi, to break into a woman's house because you thought she was some sort of witch, but you dragged Mindy into it, too?"

Aware that now was not the time to freeze, Rav mentally punched his way out of the waking dream and back into reality. In the words of Ed Harris in Apollo 13, it was time to work the problem. He was standing in the house's main bedroom. Mindy, meanwhile, was downstairs in a front lounge that had been converted into an office, having the life coaching session they'd booked earlier that morning. Ponsonby must be with her, because had their target left the room for any reason, Mindy would have hit the panic button app they'd installed on her phone, which would have caused a buzzing sensation in Rav's nuts, given that he'd stuffed his muted phone into his front jeans pocket.

And right now, about the only thing not buzzing was his nuts.

So if it wasn't Ponsonby coming up the stairs, who the hell was it? The nanny and Moonbeam had left, and if they'd returned, Sam and Jackson — who were parked outside with Jess and the Professor — would have hit one of their panic button apps. Still the footsteps came. Thump, thump, thump. They were loud and thundering, possessing the rhythm and tone that in a patriarchal society generally indicates an alpha male raised to walk wherever he likes, however loudly he likes. Rav gave up working the problem and instead dived into one of the fitted wardrobes that lined the back wall of the room.

The interior of the wardrobe was pitch black, hot, and filled to the brim with items of clothing that felt expensive. Rav crouched down and squirmed his way in as best he could. Belatedly, his nuts began to buzz. He reached into his pocket, pulled his phone out, and hit the "Confirm" option the panic button app was displaying.

He was no longer sitting in darkness, thanks to the weak fingers of light emitted by his screen. It was a largely monochrome view, but good enough to reveal silky dresses, shoes, and a sex toy of such impressive length and girth that even at his current level of stress, he still managed to take a few moments to feel deeply inadequate. Pushing that thought aside, he quickly tapped out a message to Jackson.

Whats happening

The reply came back a few seconds later.

no idea not seen anything

Rav was about to reply when a second reply came in.

mindys coming out

That didn't make sense. The life coaching session had been booked for an hour, and she'd only been twenty minutes or so in. Rav was still trying to make sense of that when the bedroom door crashed open amid a chorus of giggles of two distinct pitches, followed a moment later by the sound of bodies hitting the bed.

"You are awful, Richard," said a female voice that he recognised as Ponsonby.

A male voice gave a Neanderthal grunt in reply.

"And I was actually with a client," Ponsonby continued. "It's one thing for you to let yourself in the back every time you fancy a shag, but you could check if it's convenient first."

A new message flashed onto Rav's screen.

mindys in the car says someone knocked on ponsonbys office door like some sort of code ponsonby said she had to finish session early there was no charge threw mindy out you okay

There was the sound of movement outside the wardrobe. Rav quickly blanked his screen just in time for the door across from him to open. A male hand reached in, feeling around and through the clothes, groping for something. The hand came within a couple of inches of Rav's left kneecap, reached past his foot, then fastened on the giant dildo, hauling it out before pushing the door closed and plunging Rav back into darkness.

A girlish squeal filtered through the wooden door.

Rav settled himself into his makeshift hide.

He had a horrible feeling he might be in for a long wait.

Hiding in the wardrobe was turning out to be the emotional equivalent of George Orwell's doublethink, the ability in this case to simultaneously hold two separate and largely contradictory emotions. On one hand, Rav was existing in a state of terror so heightened that he was in constant fear that at any moment, a muscled Neanderthal might throw the wardrobe's doors open, drag him out onto the bedroom's shag pile carpet, and then proceed to beat him to death with a ten-inch dildo.

But on the other hand, he was bored shitless.

And still the two of them shagged, to a soundtrack of the bed's squeaks, Ponsonby's moans, and a playlist of early nineties ambient house from the box on the far bedside unit. Rav had started their session suffering from feelings of inadequacy brought on by the sheer scale of Ponsonby's vibrator, but as time dragged on, it was the duration of the lovemaking her unseen lover was managing to sustain that was starting to depress him. (A former girlfriend had once joked that that he was quite capable of completing an entire shagging session during a typical ITV commercial break which, while not strictly true, wasn't sufficiently false enough for him to laugh it off

77

without said laugh being just a touch forced).

Still he waited. Every twenty minutes or so he sent a text to the guys outside, a single word, "ok", afraid that if he didn't, they might panic and do something stupid. It was after he'd sent the sixth or seventh such text that the dim illumination from his phone's screen tipped some sort of internal balance between terror and boredom in favour of the latter. He began, carefully, to move the phone around, illuminating the detritus scattered across the base of wardrobe. He checked out the cardboard box within which the Kong-job dildo had nestled, finding it filled with more sex toys, dirty mags, and bottles of lube. He flipped the lid of one of the bottles open, squeezed out a small quantity of lube onto a fingertip, and smelled it.

Strawberry.

Shortly after that, his phone's screen timed out and went black, removing its dim illumination and plunging the interior of the wardrobe into pitch darkness, at which point Rav discovered that besides smelling of strawberry, the lube was apparently fluorescent, if the fact that his fingertip was now glowing pink was anything to go by. Panicking, he rubbed the finger on his black jeans, which achieved the objective of stopping it from glowing by instead creating a glowing stripe across the denim covering his left thigh.

Bugger.

He gave it a further rub; the glow diminished slightly but not much.

For a moment, both the squeaking and the moans ceased. Rav held his breath. Was this the moment that the terror-boredom seesaw tipped back very much in favour of terror? Then after a muttered command, and what sounded like two people shifting position, both the squeaks and the moaning resumed, taking only a few beats to get back into the rhythm of the ambient house.

Rav let out his breath, made a concerted effort to get his collective mental shit back together, then returned the lube to the box before resuming his search. Standing on its side, sandwiched between the cardboard box and the wall, was one of those filing boxes that people typically buy during the four-to-six-week window between embarking on a project and abandoning it. Rav carefully eased it out, settled it onto his lap, then flipped the lid open. Inside were various books and pamphlets, hippy stuff mainly, spiritual self-help shit, with the crap covers and poor typography of self-published Amazon crap. He flipped through them, noting each one, but not lingering. With each uninspired cover he revealed, with each bullshit title and even more bullshit tag line, his belief that the box might contain something interesting faded. But then, at the bottom of the stack, he came across something different.

A tattered, creased, jiffy-type envelope, its once-stuck flap now torn and opened.

He pulled it out, and carefully eased it open. Inside were what looked like three small notebooks, each measuring perhaps a couple of inches square. He began to reach inside, moving very slowly for fear of making a noise.

And then Ponsonby and her mystery shagger began the process of simultaneously coming like a pair of British Rail, Class 47, diesel-electric locomotives. The first signal was the breaking of the synchronicity between their shagging and the ambient house soundtrack, as the rhythm of the squeaks and moans sped up, while the music did not. This was very quickly accompanied by vocal utterances from the mystery companion, who'd previously restricted himself to caveman grunts. Having now apparently evolved the power of speech, he began to scream, "Yes! Yes! Yes!" and then paused for a moment for Ponsonby to reply with "Come inside me! Fill me up with your hot creamy love!"

From somewhere in the midst of this insanity, Rav somehow found time to make the mental note that, at least in this, the two of them were broadly normal. (He'd once read an article in a social work magazine that said that modern teenagers were so influenced by Internet porn that they sincerely, genuinely thought that the standard, vanilla, romantic way to end a lovemaking session was for the man to withdraw and ejaculate on his partner's face).

Then whatever rhythm the pair might previously have possessed disintegrated as the bloke let out a cry that Johnny Weissmuller would have been proud of, Ponsonby emitted a scream that could have made champagne flutes shatter, the bed joined in with a creak that sounded like a tree being tortured, and then it all — mercifully — went silent.

Rav withdrew his hand from the envelope and sat very, very still.

There was the sound of tissues being tugged out of a tissue box, followed by the sound of wet flesh being wiped. All the while, Rav strained to hear, desperately trying to build up a mental map of what might be happening. What if she went to put the vibrator back? What if she opened the door to get a robe? What if, what if, what if?

Then came the sound of two sets of distinctly different footsteps leaving, followed by the sound of flushing toilets and running taps, and at least one person going downstairs. Rav gave it a couple of minutes, then carefully closed the box's lid and eased it back into its space. He kept the envelope containing the notebooks. (He had no reason to suspect they were anything significant, but having come this far, and having gone through this, he was damned if he was leaving empty-handed).

He eased the wardrobe door open a crack and peered through. The slice of the bedroom thus revealed was empty. He slowly pushed the door fully open, horribly, buttock-clenchingly aware that at any moment, the door's opening might reveal someone in the room, observing him.

But the room was empty. He carefully eased his way out of his crouch and out of the wardrobe, and onto the shag pile carpet, limping badly because his right foot had so thoroughly gone to sleep during the multiple hours of waiting that the only sensation he was getting from it was a thousand stabbing pins and needles. The bedroom door was ajar; from beyond came the sound of someone fussing in the bathroom.

He needed to get out.

A large double-glazed bay window looked out onto the road beyond and the houses opposite. It had no nets, and the curtains were open. The left pane of the window was swung partially open, allowing a cooling breeze to blow in. Rav realised he had no recollection of hearing the curtains being closed at the start of the encounter, nor of hearing them being opened after its conclusion. Had they been open the whole time? He looked through the windows, spotted a shadow in an upstairs window of the house across the road, focused hard on it, and realised that it was a naked man holding a pair of binoculars, through which he was observing Rav — having previously observed the shagging session, presumably.

Loud male footsteps started coming back up the stairs. In the absence of both a plan of action and the time in which to come up with such a plan, Rav settled for pushing the window fully open, and throwing himself through and out of the opening thus created, granting him a drone's eye view of the garden below. It was, he immediately realised, not so much a case of out of the frying pan and into the fire, as out of the severe beating, and into the twelve-foot drop to the ground.

It did then, belatedly, occur to him that perhaps he should have climbed back into the wardrobe instead of exiting via an upstairs window. But unless chronological reality included a rewind button he'd thus far failed to notice, that was no longer an option. He was still working through a highly compressed version of the Kübler-Ross model (Denial — "No way did I just jump out of a window"; Anger — "Why the hell did I just jump out of a window!"; Bargaining — "Look: how about if I land in something with a bit of give?"; Depression — "This is going to be really ba—") when he crashed into, and through, a bush; some bastard thing with thorns that might perhaps have absorbed his fall, but cut his flesh to buggery in return. Relieved, and slightly surprised to still be alive, he staggered, rolled, and fell out of the bush, cutting himself more in the process, then launched into a toppling, foot-pumping sprint that lasted only long enough for him to crash face-first onto the lawn.

A male voice shouted from above. "Oi! Who the fuck are you? India! There's some twat on your lawn!"

Rav hauled himself back to his feet, ran across a flowerbed, and vaulted over the wall onto the pavement beyond. Out of the corner of his eye, he sensed rather than saw the pervert opposite tracking him with the binoculars. Jackson's car was parked a few houses down, facing him, the engine already started. Rav sprinted down the pavement, ripped open the rear passenger door, and pushed in beside Mindy and the Professor, shoving a clearly disgruntled Jess onto Mindy's lap as he did so.

"Drive!"

Jackson didn't bother discussing it. Instead, he rammed the gear stick into first, popped the clutch, floored the accelerator and slithered out of the parking space, changed into second, then braked to a halt as a man dressed only in a pair of boxer shorts and built like a body-builder appeared in the middle of the road wielding some sort of golf club.

"Reverse?" suggested Sam, calmly, from the front passenger seat where he was sitting beside Jackson.

Again, Jackson didn't bother to discuss the proposal, but simply responded. Ramming the car into reverse he set off, twisted round in his seat to look backwards past the headrest, relying on Sam to give him a running commentary on the status of their pursuer.

"You might want to go a bit quicker. He's running bloody fast."

"Road's a bit tight," grunted Jackson. It was indeed so, lined on either side with cars that were scrolling past at quite a rate, considering they were travelling backwards.

Rav peered past the other side of Jackson's headrest at the bloke pursuing them. He was sprinting hard, not in an elegant, gazelle-like, Usain Bolt style, but in the classic 1988 Ben Johnson mould, powered by brute muscular force and a good ol' dose of 'roid-rage. It might not have been pretty, and given the bare feet, boxers, and swinging golf club, it certainly wasn't refined, but by God, it was efficient. As fast as Jackson was reversing, the guy was gaining.

"Erm, Rav?" asked Mindy, from her position wedged in between Rav and the Professor. "Who is that guy?"

"I think he's some bloke who came round to shag Ponsonby."

"So where were you when all that was happening?"

"Hiding in the wardrobe."

"Why were you hiding in the wardrobe?"

Rav pointed desperately past the driver's seat at the man who was now very, very close, close enough to see the anger on his face. "Do you have to ask?"

The car shot backwards across a junction, narrowly missing a Fiat Panda which, with brakes squealing and horn blaring, skidded ahead of them, its front-end colliding with their pursuer with enough force to send him sprawling onto its bonnet. He roared in anger, rolled off the car, and then started to hit the Panda's windscreen repeatedly with his golf club. Another car braked to a halt, two occupants tumbling out. Doors were opening. Shouts were being shouted. Phones were no doubt being phoned.

Their car, meanwhile, was stationary, its engine idling. Jess chose that moment to push herself into a sitting position and give Rav a long, hard look of canine protest. Sam reached over and touched Jackson on the arm. "Maybe we should leave?"

Jackson nodded. He pushed the gear stick back into first, and set off, gently weaving the car through the vehicular throng and down the adjoining road.

The Professor cleared his throat. "So, after all that, Ravinder, did you find anything?"

Rav realised he was still holding the jiffy envelope containing the three notebooks. "Don't know." He looked inside. "Maybe?"

Chapter Fifteen

Somewhere in Greater London.

Mortimer was asleep when the phone call came. It wasn't for him, of course. It never was. There was no phone in his cell, only a crude device with which he could communicate with his two captors. He approached the bars warily, but his captors were not watching him, their attention focused on the call, both listening to the astonishing object that they termed a phone.

He recognised the female voice coming from the phone's speaker. She'd called several times before, while he'd been eavesdropping, always speaking with the urgent, over-familiar drawl of someone who fancies themselves to be spiritual and artistic but is instead shallow and vulgar. She sounded different now. Shaken. Embarrassed.

Scared.

"I think it was him!"

"Who?" said the female captor. "What's happened, India?"

"The man you warned us about. The Asian one who was sniffing around the old warehouse where we did the last ritual. He was in my house!"

"Did he find anything?" asked the male captor.

"No, I don't think so. I was with someone. Not one of us. He chased him away."

"Okay. It's fine. Phoebe will come on over. Sit tight." Then he hit a button on the device's screen and dialled in a new number, apparently from memory.

"Yes?" said a man's voice.

"This is Arrow."

"This is Quiver."

"Contact the members. Tell them to go dark. Plan Stealth Shadow is now activated."

The other man answered, an edge of apprehension in his voice. "Problem?"

"A precaution." The male captor hung up.

The woman turned, and caught Mortimer looking at them. She approached the bars, the familiar, cruel smile upon her face. "Tsk, tsk, Mortimer," she said, shaking her head. "Listening in?"

Mortimer retreated to his bed. One day he would have his revenge. But this was not that day.

When they returned to Rav's flat, the Professor's first duty was to attend to Rav's welfare. He'd been visibly tired before the day's operation had begun, but now he appeared to be suffering from a deep exhaustion. Blank eyes stared out of sunken sockets, set within a face tight with tension. The Professor settled him down on the sofa then headed to the kitchen to make a round of hot, sweet tea, served with a biscuit assortment. Refreshments distributed, he sat down next to Mindy.

Jackson was wearing thin white gloves of the sort worn by detectives of the more cerebral, BBC4 subtitled kind. In front of him, laid carefully on the coffee table, was the jiffy envelope. "We thought we'd wait for you," the priest explained. He reached tentatively into the open package and pulled out a small notebook. It was square, perhaps two inches-by-two inches, and around half an inch thick. The paper was a mottled yellow and the cover looked to be made of thin grey card, its surface patterned by creases like the lines on a palm. He carefully turned the book over. The covers and the spine were blank, but for a single figure eight written upon the spine.

"Number eight," he mused. "Any thoughts?"

Rav spoke from behind the shield of the mug he clutched in both hands. "Be interesting to see what the other two have on them."

Jackson put the book down, and carefully drew the other two books from the envelope, examining them each in turn. "Number four, and number ten."

Sam, who was perched on the TV unit, let out a vaguely amused snort. "We could come up with a load of numerological theories, but it's probably something as basic as us possessing three books from a set of ten or more books."

"I concur," said the Professor. "I suspect that would be the conclusion William of Occam would have come to." He got a nod from Sam, and a set of questioning eyebrows from their three younger colleagues. Some exposition was clearly required. "He was a medieval philosopher and theologian who first described the problem-solving maxim that when there are competing hypotheses to explain some sort of occurrence or phenomena, in the absence of any other evidence, the one with the fewest assumptions should be taken to be correct."

"Oh, Occam's Razor," said Mindy, her look of satisfaction quickly turning to an angry scowl when she caught sight of the doubt all over Rav's face. "I did General Science GCSE, and unlike you, I actually listened!"

The Professor intervened, quickly. "Quite, my dear. But my interjection has delayed our investigation. Perhaps you should examine the books' interiors, Jackson?"

Rav chose that moment to interrupt, leaning forward out of his seat. "One question. Is the reason that we're taking this really slowly, step-by-step, because we don't want to risk disturbing any evidence, like fingerprints and stuff? Or is it because we think those books might be evil, tainted, magical things, and we want to reduce our exposure to them as much as possible?"

Jackson shrugged. "Bit of both." He held out the book. "You want to open it?"

Rav sat sharply back in his seat. "No, you're good."

The priest rested the spine of the book in his palm, then carefully pulled the cover open. Jackson turned over a page, and then another, and then another, and then finally jumped a whole section of pages before shaking his head. "They're all blank. Every page."

"What about the other two books?" asked Sam.

Jackson put the book down, and then repeated the process with the second book, and then the third. "Same. All blank."

"So they're just notebooks?" asked Mindy.

The priest shook his head. "No. When I pick them up, I feel, well, something. Like I really, really don't want to touch them, except at the same time, a dark part at the back of my soul craves their touch."

Sam shifted slightly. "You think they're magical, then?"

Jackson gave a grim nod. "Yeah." He carefully waved the third notebook in front of Jess. The dog, who'd been lying down, sniffed once, then bounced straight to her feet, snarling, the edges of her mouth curled up to reveal her fangs and the hairs on her back all standing on end.

"See what I mean?" the priest asked, withdrawing the notebook. Jess snarled again, let out a couple of confused and protesting whines, then settled back down onto the rug.

"Do people normally enchant blank notebooks?" asked Rav.

"No. And they don't normally keep them hidden in wardrobes, either. Were they with anything else, by the way?"

"A load of small press self-help books, a bunch of sex toys, a vibrator large enough to make a horse feel inadequate, and some fluorescent lube."

"Fluorescent lube?" asked Mindy, stifling a laugh.

"Don't ask."

Jackson, too, was pursing his mouth to prevent a snort emerging. "Okay, let's get back to the books. The point is, they're blank, see." He held the third book out and flicked through its pages, tilting the book so everybody could see it. "See, all blank."

"Hang on!" shouted Rav. "I thought I saw something."

"Really? Hang on."

The priest went back, page-by-page, but there was nothing there, every yellowed page blank save for the markings of age.

"I could swear I saw something, just for a moment."

A vague childhood memory began to stir within the Professor, a memory he suspected might be unique to him, given his position as the elder of the group. He cleared his throat. "Jackson? Might I perhaps examine the book? Perhaps after putting some gloves on, first."

Jackson gave him a smiling shrug. "Yeah, sure." He fished out a second set of thin latex gloves from his pocket, waited while the Professor carefully pulled them on, and then handed the book over.

The Professor rested the book in his hand and felt… something. More than an awareness, but not quite a sensation. The room suddenly felt colder, not literally so, but more in the way a space does when a known cad with a reptilian smile and a reputation for cruelty enters what had previously been a warm and welcoming conversation. Primitive feelings deep within him didn't want to hold this book; his conscious self was having to fight against a whole chorus of instincts screaming at him to hurl the infernal item into the farthest corner of the room. And yet at the same time, he was experiencing a dark, twisted, seductive call. He looked at Jackson. "I see what you mean about the sensation of holding it." He paused, struggling for words. "I can only describe it as not being emotionally inert in the manner one would expect, but I suspect a more superstitious man would describe it as cursed."

The young priest sniffed. "I think cursed is probably a fair description."

The Professor tried to put his emotions to one side. There was a reason he'd asked to examine the book, and it wasn't to determine for himself if it really was magical. It was because the sight of these books, their size, their shape, their thin card covers, had reminded him of similar books from his childhood, a childhood that had taken place when there were no computers or tablets, a television was an expensive box in the corner of the living room that your parents watched in the evening, and where, if you wanted to see moving pictures, your best bet was still the Saturday morning matinee at the local picture house. He pushed the book's spine into the fold of his palm, pushed hard enough with his thumb to cause the book to slightly arch and then — following his hunch — began to slide his thumb across the edge of the book, sending page after page flicking from right to left, several pages each second.

And now, the pages weren't blank. They had pictures on them, drawn in shades of grey as though created by pencil, but so lifelike and perfect that surely only a master portraitist could have drawn them. And as he flicked through the book, the pictures merged to produce a perfect moving image.

Of a man, talking.

And a voice was speaking.

Inside his head.

For several seconds, Rav watched the Professor flicking through the book, flip-book style. Then he watched for several seconds more as the older man sat still, saying nothing, before placing the book back onto the coffee table with slow, agonising caution, as though it were an unexploded bomb with a mercury tilt switch.

"What happened?" Rav asked, when the Professor showed no sign of elaborating.

"It had… pictures?" said Mindy, shaking her head. She'd been looking over the Professor's shoulder, Rav realised. "They made a moving image, of a man speaking."

"Really?" Rav looked at first the book, and then at Jackson. "You got another pair of gloves?"

Jackson nodded, and pulled a third pair from his pocket. Rav put them on, and then reached out for the book.

"I should warn you, Ravinder," said the Professor, speaking for the first time. "It's not merely a moving image. Not when one is holding the book. There's a soundtrack that plays within one's mind, in a manner that I found frankly unpleasant."

Rav took a moment to gather some of his dissipating resolve, then picked up the book. As the others had described, the book was radiating a seductive power, a power that spoke to his soul in a way that his brain told him was bad, but which a dark, lustful part of his heart yearned to embrace. He pushed those feelings as far aside as he could and began by examining the book one page at a time. The pages were, as Jackson had demonstrated, blank. That confirmed, he balanced the book on the palm of his hand, gripped the cover, and began to flip-play it.

The moving image of a man appeared, formed from a sequence of images somehow magically projected onto pages that would otherwise have been blank: a powerful looking man in late middle-age, dressed in suit, shirt and tie, his hair cropped into an old-fashioned short back-and-sides, a narrow moustache stretched across his upper lip. And as the Professor had said, the moving image was speaking, direct to Rav, into his brain, which might have been overwhelming had Rav not previously been so-contacted by a demon, and a furiously angry demon at that.

He'd missed what the man was saying. He took a deep breath and replayed the book, and this time, he listened.

"Make an error, large or small, and the forces you've conjured will devour your soul."

Rav looked up at the others and repeated the line.

"That's what the image is saying?" asked Sam.

"Yeah. It's a white bloke, late middle age, looks like something out of an old black-and-white movie. Not just because it looks like a pencil drawing, but it's his general, you know, appearance."

The Professor spoke again. "Is anyone else thinking that were we to find a picture of Sir Edward Mortimer it might prove to be of the same man?"

"You're reading my mind," Rav said.

Jackson was typing into a tablet he'd conjured from somewhere. "Okay, noting that line down. Which book was it?"

Rav checked the spine. "Number eight."

"You want to try the others?"

"Might as well." He put number eight down and picked up number four. "Okay, playing number four."

The same man appeared, and again he spoke.

"These books, that speak into your mind, are both taster and proof of what I am offering."

Rav repeated the line. Jackson again typed it in, before commenting. "Interesting. We've got books enchanted to contain a sort of magical movie in a flip-book, which works on two levels: as well as containing a message, their very existence proves that the capabilities he's talking about are real."

Sam smiled a reluctant smile. "That's actually quite clever, much as I hate to admit it, given that we're talking about evil people doing evil stuff for evil reasons."

Jackson nodded, equally reluctantly, and then chuckled. "Yeah. I should be disgusted and outraged by this, but I can't help but think that magical telepathic flip-books are really kind of cool." He tapped his foot. "Okay, anyhow, let's get back on topic. You want to play number ten, Rav?"

"Why not?" Again, Rav put down his current book and picked up the last, the not-yet played number ten. He took another deep breath, and then flipped it.

"From my long, cold wait in death's dark slumber, I await your spiritual call."

He repeated the line. There was a long silence before finally Jackson spoke. "I'm not sure that's good."

Chapter Sixteen

After the revelation of the flip-books, they'd taken a break by mutual consent to order pizza. While waiting for the food to arrive, they attempted to film the flip-book footage on their phones but found — as they'd half-expected — that the recordings showed only blank pages being flipped through. As with the false wall at the warehouse, this was clearly a hallucination played into the brain rather than an actual illusion of photons and light.

After a pause triggered by the arrival of the pizza bloke, the discussion resumed, tiredness now offset by an injection of fat, protein and carbohydrates. Rav took a bite of his Hawaiian, gave it a few chews, swallowed, and tried to get his head round the point he wanted to make.

"So what does this all mean?"

The Professor, who, as usual, was consuming his food in considerably smaller mouthfuls than Rav, and chewing them to a far greater degree, and who did, as a rule, refuse to talk with his mouth full, had, by happenstance, only just swallowed. He accepted the conversational can Rav had kicked. "As I see it, the flip-books do tell us a number of things, none of which are definitive by themselves, but all of which are significant, especially when combined with the fragments of information we already possess."

Jackson paused mid-bite of his Novaheat Chicken. (Having had that pizza in the past and lived — barely — to regret it, Rav had cautioned against it, describing it as a "toilet roll in the fridge job, mate", but Jackson had merely shrugged and said he liked his food spicy). "Go on," the priest said, interested.

The Professor began to count points off on his fingers. "Firstly, I think we can perhaps deduce the very rough outline of the scheme. Back in the nineteen-twenties and nineteen-thirties Sir Edward Mortimer followed various avenues of research in archaeology, Middle Eastern history, and what we might perhaps term the occult. It appears that he devised some sort of plan, of which the plot of the Hindustani is perhaps a distorted reflection, but was presumably unable to carry it out, for reasons that at this point it would probably be unwise to guess at. My conjecture is that he created the flip-books as some kind of time capsule message to people of a future era." He paused, adding emphasis to what he was about to say. "And I think the message was not simply a message, but an outline of a plan, and an invitation to the intended audience to carry out that plan."

Sam put down his Margherita. "Yes. I think I agree. In the fourth book, it says that the message is both a taster and a proof of what he's offering, which is the invitation. And in the eighth, he warns them of the penalties they face if they stray from the path he's outlining, which implies he's giving them a plan to follow."

Jackson laughed. "Spoken like a Talmudic scholar."

"Guilty as charged," said Sam, holding up his hands. "Which brings us onto book ten, which reads to me as though it were the last of the set."

"Quite. Let us review again what it says."

Jackson tapped a finger on his tablet to wake it up. "From my long, cold wait in death's dark slumber, I await your spiritual call."

The Professor let those words hang in the air for a moment, before resuming. "So, we have a man in the nineteen-thirties who devises a plan that will be executed far after his death, and leaves instructions for that plan to be carried out. That might normally beg the question of what, as our American friends might say, is in it for him? But I fear that book ten contains some sort of answer to that question."

Rav made an emergency swallow of his current mouthful. "Hang on a minute!" he choked. "Are you saying what I think you're saying?"

The Professor held up a placatory hand. "At this stage I'm merely pointing out implications and possibilities. I'm certainly not suggesting something along the lines of Mark 16, verse 6!"

Jackson and Sam nodded. Rav and Mindy didn't. "And for the benefit of us Hindus?" said Mindy, with a smile.

"Sorry," said Jackson. "It's one of the verses covering Jesus's resurrection. 'And he said to them, do not be alarmed. You seek Jesus of Nazareth, who was crucified. He has risen; he is not here. See the place where they laid him.'"

"Right." Rav took a moment to figuratively digest the quotation. "So what we're saying is that we don't think he was literally planning on coming back, but that he was planning on being involved in some way?"

Sam nodded. "Yeah. It pains me to say it, but that seems to be the implication. That he left the message behind as a kind of initial seed, that they would follow to contact him in the afterlife."

"It might be like when a computer boots up," said Mindy. "All that's built into the hardware itself is the knowledge of how to load an initial stub of the operating system from the hard drive. The hardware loads that initial stub and then the stub takes over." She noticed Rav's quizzical look and sighed in exasperation. "I did Computer Studies GCSE, too. Anyhow, maybe instead of leaving the full plan, he left just enough instructions to enable whoever received it to contact him in the afterlife, at which point he could take over and start guiding them."

The Professor jabbed a finger in agreement. "I suspect that is exactly it, my dear. I think we must assume that Sir Edward is in some way involved, in the here and now, and that the group we're investigating are following his plan, under his guidance. Which then brings us onto the question of the wider plan that's now being followed."

Rav put down his pizza. "We know some of that, right? They stole the tablet and used that as part of a ritual to capture the demon somehow, and bind it to the tattoos, with that demon then protecting anyone who's got the tattoo."

"Yeah," said Jackson. "And the fact that they've done this implies they're quite a few steps down the plan. They're up and running and doing things."

"True," agreed Sam. "But this spell, the tattoo, is presumably not the plan itself. Instead, it's a tool, a step, towards achieving their plan. By itself, it doesn't do anything. It merely provides protection they think they'll need when they do whatever it is they're going to do."

There was something bugging Rav, and suddenly it came to him. "If the tattoo's supposed to protect those wearing it, why's it screwing Ricky up?"

Mindy clicked her fingers. "Ponsonby was wearing a top with short sleeves. At one point, one rode up slightly and I could see a bit of what looked like the tattoo, on her upper arm."

"Yeah. And Killen told me he put it on the wizard's arm. So maybe the tattoo's designed to go there. Put it on your chest, above your heart, and it will, well, malfunction."

Sam nodded. "Seems like a reasonable hypothesis, but one that then takes us to a final question. If the tattoo's only a building block they need to carry out their plan, what's the actual plan? They must have one, right? No one goes to this much trouble for nothing."

"I don't think we can speculate as to what the plan might be," said the Professor. "But should we presume that it in some way involves the skull of St Horace, as the enigmatic Mister Fox believes?"

Rav gave a shrug in reply. "Who knows? Either way, what now? It's clear that Ponsonby's involved, but now she'll know we're onto her, right?"

"Yeah, I think we can say that," agreed Jackson. "Her boyfriend certainly got a good look at us. For now, we're probably best staying well clear of her. Which maybe brings us back to the skull, and this Russian."

"Except we're totally blocked on finding him."

Sam put his hands together. "Look, we're all exhausted. How about we call it a day for now and touch bases sometime tomorrow?"

He received in reply a round of slow, tired nods. Rav watched as Jackson fed the last of his Novaheat Chicken pizza into his mouth.

"You might want to have a bit of yoghurt before you go to bed."

Despite having spent half a lifetime working in the text-rich environment of academia, the Professor was still very much a two-fingered, hunt-and-peck typist, with his fruitlessly searching fingers typically spending far longer on the hunting than the pecking. But in yet one more demonstration of the principle that it's pure comedic irony that powers the universe, rather than any fate, destiny, or supreme being's plan, it was his frankly lamentable keyboard skills that played a key role in allowing him to track down the Russian.

Having resolved to resume his attempts to Google their quarry, and having then spent the morning running search after search on his care home's Internet terminal, he was about to give up and head off for a lunch when he tried one last search phrase. This wouldn't have been the first time his errant fingers managed to insert a random extra letter in a word. It wasn't the second, or even the third. But just as Darwinian evolution progresses due to one-in-a-thousand genetic mutations that by happenstance confer an advantage, so on this occasion the random extra letter produced not a malformed typo, but the correct answer.

Because this time rather than typing "Menshikov", he typed "Menschikov", and suddenly his screen was awash with promising results. Twenty minutes later he was phoning Rav.

"I think I have our Russian."

"Really? How? I couldn't find a sodding thing!"

"That's because, Ravinder, we were searching for Menshikov with an S-H, while our man is Menschikov with an S-C-H."

"Damn! Should have thought of that. Oh well," said Rav, in a tone of resigned amusement. "Guess you always were the brains of the outfit. Who is he, then? And how confident are you that he's our man?"

"I'm afraid that as is so often the case, this is still all circumstantial. But he fits the profile." The Professor picked up his notebook, which contained his scribbled notes. "His full name is Dimitri Alexei Menschikov. Born in Tallin, Estonia, of Russian parents in 1968. His father was in the KGB, his mother was a university lecturer. As a young entrepreneur, he managed to acquire a considerable fortune in the years immediately after the fall of the Soviet Union by means which no one appears able to fully understand."

"But where does the skull come in?"

"I confess I've found no direct link to that. But there are two very interesting facts about him. The first is that he apparently has deep interests in the occult, and in Russian, Slavic, and Christian Orthodox mysticism."

"So the mystical and possibly magical skull of an Orthodox saint might be right up his street?"

"Exactly. Which leads us nicely onto the second interesting fact, which is that he's a renowned collector, to the point of obsession, of artefacts connected to these interests, artefacts that he keeps in a personal museum located on his own private Airbus A380."

"Sorry, what? Rewind. He's got his own private plane, but it ain't a Learjet, it's a sodding super jumbo?"

"Yes. When I used the phrase, 'considerable fortune', I was not guilty of hyperbole. Mister Menschikov is in possession of a personal wealth estimated in tens of billions of dollars."

"Right." There was a long pause while Rav presumably considered the wisdom of going up against a man wealthy enough that had he been a sovereign nation, he'd have counted as comfortably mid-ranking, a consideration that the Professor would have to admit had briefly occurred to him, too. "Okay. Whatever. He sounds like our man. Any idea where he is?"

"That, Ravinder, is where we may be in luck. Because as fate would have it, he's flying into London the day after tomorrow to hold a party to celebrate something or other. And guess where he's holding the party?"

"You're seriously telling me he's holding his party on the Airbus?"

"He is indeed, Ravinder, which means that the task facing us appears clear and defined."

"Please tell me you're not going to suggest what I think you're about to suggest."

The Professor was very much aware that at some point in the very near future he would no doubt consider the enormity of what he was about to propose and, having done so, feel as aghast as his younger colleague now sounded. But right then, at that moment in time, he felt only an eager excitement at the adventure that was about to unfold. He took a moment to ensure his phone's handset was in the correct position, and then with a big smile on his face, delivered the line he'd been building up to. "I am indeed, Ravinder. We should set ourselves the task of gaining access to a party held at thirty-thousand feet by a billionaire in possession of security typically possessed only by mid-ranking heads of state, stealing one of his prized possessions from under his nose, and then escaping."

Chapter Seventeen

Rav had been keen to meet up with Jackson and Sam that evening, but it turned out that the earliest they could make a meeting was Monday morning, something that was apparently due to Jackson having found his Sunday filled by a variety of church-related activities, and Sam having to play catch up on all the stuff he'd skipped the previous day — a task that had apparently involved both a huge pulling in of favours and a considerable degree of nuanced theological argument. ("I spent the Sabbath breaking into someone's house, and I'm a rabbi. Do you have any idea what's involved in me doing stuff on Saturdays?")

Rav could have pointed out that in order to make a Monday morning meeting he'd have to pull an emergency sickie — something which would take him one tick box closer to a formal disciplinary meeting to discuss his future employment with the London Borough of Hounslow. But in the end, he decided that catching up on some much-needed sleep and taking a chance to dump some accumulated stress was probably the best option, and so Monday morning it was.

And if truth were to be told, he wasn't quite sure he really wanted to pursue this. A billionaire with enough money to buy the world's largest airliner and outfit it as his own mobile pleasure palace? And not only that, a billionaire who'd made his money in an environment so cut-throat and lawless that the dividing line between business entrepreneur and mafioso boss was sufficiently fluid and intangible that one could step across it merely by scuffing someone's shoes. Rav had a sudden waking vision of a Russian version of "The Apprentice", starring Menschikov, but differing from the format of the UK version in that fired candidates left the process not in a taxi but in a pair of concrete overboots, and with their destination being not the mainline railway station of their choice, but the bed of the River Moskva.

Back during his years at West Thames College, when he was en-route to gaining A-Level grades poor enough that whilst the world might still be his oyster, his careers advisers had made it clear that the only route by which he might get there would involve the sort of former Polytechnics who'd given former Polytechnics a bad name, Rav had spent a term studying the Russian revolution. That he'd since forgotten practically all of it did not qualify as any sort of "tears in the rain" tragedy, for while his name-now-forgotten history lecturer might have described the events of that time as though they were Roy Batty's attack ships on fire off the shoulders of Orion, most of it was incredibly boring, and those portions which fell short of boring were still rather forgettable. But one story, or to be precise one individual, having stuck in his memory then, returned now.

Rasputin. Or, as Boney M had called him, Ra-Ra Rasputin, lover of the Russian Queen.

Grigori Rasputin had been a big bear of a man, a wild-eyed, charismatic monk considered by some at the time, and frankly by Rav now, to have possessed mystical powers. Having gained a degree of influence over the Tsarina, and through her, the Tsar, by being able to supposedly heal her haemophiliac son and possibly also — if a manufactured nineteen-seventies German disco band were to be believed — by shagging her, he had, by the autumn of 1916 achieved a degree of power sufficient to concern anyone who wasn't happy to see their country's military and political strategy being driven by a man clearly a couple of sandwiches short of a picnic.

Eventually, in the absence of any sort of "will no one rid me of this turbulent priest" type suggestion from the cuckolded tsar, a group of young noblemen decided to do the ridding anyway, eventually managing to dispatch him only after getting him drunk, feeding him cakes laced with cyanide, shooting him several times in the body and once in the head, and then — when that still failed to despatch him — dumping him into the River Neva. He had, as a Deep South redneck might say, needed quite a bit of killing.

Having pushed that recollection aside and headed for bed a little after News at Ten, Rav eventually tossed and turned his way into a tangled series of dreams in which a bearskin-hatted Alan Sugar strapped him to a buzzsaw-equipped conveyor belt with the line, "No, Mister Shah, I expect you to die," while a frowning Karen Brady scribbled notes into a notepad.

Rav woke coughing to a room filled with black, choking smoke, harsh with the acrid tang of plastic carelessly thrown onto a campfire. It is, as Jane Austin might have said, had she exchanged letters with a teenaged Mary Shelley, a truth universally acknowledged that panic will always outrun logic. It was entirely in keeping with this principle that Rav's first panic-driven action upon waking was to take a deep breath, which merely tipped him into the sort of coughing fit one usually sees in seventy-something-year-old men sixty-something years into what will shortly turn out to be a terminal smoking habit.

He rolled off the bed onto the carpet, an act that could have been driven by an awareness that smoke rises, but which in reality probably came from the same hard-wired school of thought that causes dogs to hide under blankets when storms start firing thunderbolts. But whether driven by learned logic or instinctive panic, getting close to the floor did provide a slightly less smoke-filled environment. He took a couple of shallow breaths, spent a few seconds getting his respiratory system into working order, then tried to do the same with his misfiring brain.

This was a fire. His flat was on fire. Burning.

Smoke alarm. Why hadn't the smoke alarm gone off?

A memory surfaced, of a TV remote control that had stopped working, and which had been repaired not by a late-night trip to the shops to buy replacement batteries, but by a pragmatic solution in which replacement batteries had been acquired from the smoke alarm, with the honest intent of replacing them the next morning. An honest intent that, as is so often the case, had required only the passage of time and a dose of apathy to seamlessly transform into an effectively abandoned commitment.

And now it was going to kill him. This would be his epitaph. Here lies Ravinder Shah. He died that his TV remote might live. A death pointless enough that his funeral would be conducted under the shadow of the white elephant of his stupidity. A funeral in which the poor bastard giving his eulogy would be walking a narrow precipice bound on all sides by inadvertent black comedy. A death so stupid that it was almost a relief to have been raised in a religion that doesn't feature afterlives, so embarrassing might be the resulting conversations were he to find himself in one.

Focused, as he now was, on his apparently near-imminent death, Rav had time for a brief consideration of the effect on one's karma score of such a self-inflicted exit before the various waves of panic slopping around his brain managed to momentarily coalesce into a realisation that he really didn't want to die. Logic, its boots now firmly laced, took the opportunity to climb into the pilot's seat and strap itself in. He paused for an intentionally non-literal, metaphorical deep breath, then began to crawl towards the point where the door ought to be.

Unlike Rav, Jess had not spent the evening worrying about Russians of the mad, bad, and dangerous to know variety, with the result that when she'd followed Rav into his bedroom and flopped onto the dog blanket placed across from his bed, she'd fallen straight into a sleep that should have seen her through to the morning. But this night was not to be such a night. Because on this night, the half-open ear with which all dogs sleep sensed the sound of movement.

Like most Border Collies, Jess tended to the nervous and neurotic, and bitter experience had taught her that when in Rav's care, being nervous and neurotic constituted a sensible survival strategy. It was for this reason that rather than stagger to her feet and have a good stretch, as she might otherwise have done, she instead rolled off her blanket onto the carpet underneath Rav's bed, from where she commando-crawled to the bed's far side, following the direction of the noise.

The noise proved to be emanating from a figure apparently crawling across the carpet on his hands and knees, a figure that a couple of sniffs revealed to be Rav. But while the figure might have belonged to Rav, the way it was manoeuvring across the carpet wasn't — or at least it wasn't the figure of a half-asleep man stumbling towards the toilet for a wee, which was usually the reason for Rav to be up at this time of night.

Jess pushed her head forward and sniffed warily. There was an almost imperceptible scent in the air, a scent that was not so much a smell as a presence: of wrongness, of evil. It was something she'd smelled before, when Rav's new friend had waved the wrong-smelling thing before her. She pulled her head back.

Perhaps waiting was the best plan.

She crawled back toward her blanket.

The room was as black as black can be, the black of the dead of night on a moonless alien world, or the furthest cave of a prehistoric cavern complex forgotten for millennia until rediscovered by persons for whom squeezing through a space the size of a bread bin qualifies as a hobby rather than the theme of a recurring nightmare. But to state that the room was black was to understate to an epic degree the sensory disorientation Rav was now facing, for this was not an empty black, a black resulting from an absence of sensory input, but instead a toxic, blended mix of sensory confusion, containing as it did a corrosive cargo of choking smoke that tore at the throat and stung the eyes, followed by the probing fingers of oven-hot air.

The bed was only a few feet from the door, but now, on hands and knees in an environment turned utterly alien, those few feet felt like miles. With every shuffle, Rav's certainty as to his location diminished. With every pause, his confidence in his direction ebbed away. Slowly, painfully, he edged forward. Something appeared in his vision, a line of something that might almost have been grey penetrating the blackness. A light, he realised, seeping under the bedroom door. He crawled the last foot or so, reaching forward to feel the painted wood and chiselled shapes of the panelled door. He reached up, feeling for the door handle, only for his hand to recoil instinctively away from it when he sensed the heat emanating from the brass. Had he been wearing the pyjamas he'd worn as a boy he could have pulled a sleeve over his hand, but given that he was currently clad only in a pair of boxer shorts, that wasn't an option. Then he remembered the towel hanging from the hook mounted high on the door. He reached up further, found its tip, and pulled. It fell on him like a shroud, feeling chill in this world that was otherwise roasting. He wrapped it round his hand, then tugged the door open.

His lounge was on fire. He could see that, even through the thick, chemical smog that filled the room. The murky grey of his vision was assaulted by an army of dull glows — one for each sofa, each no doubt pouring forth carcinogens from their foam-filled interiors — and several more glows for what had been books, newspapers, and other assorted crap. The room seemed full of flames, with no way out. It was like the scene from The Towering Inferno, where Robert Wagner tells his secretary/lover that he'll be back in no time with the cavalry, and Rav remembered only too well how that had turned out.

He closed the door.

Then a guilty thought occurred to him.

Jess.

Chapter Eighteen

Rav crouched back down and began to crawl back towards Jess, his eyes clamped shut. The Border Collie stayed where she was, observing intently, her single-cylinder brain trying, and failing, to figure out what the hell was going on. Dim light filtered through the curtains, lending a faint but serviceable degree of illumination to the room's interior, a room that, as far as she could tell, was in a completely normal state, but for the faint scent of wrongness she'd previously detected, and the massive smell of stress and fear Rav was currently emitting.

Rav stopped a little way in front of her blanket. "Jess!" he hissed, following it up with a string of the many human sounds to which she could ascribe no meaning.

Still his eyes were closed.

"Jess!" he hissed again.

Human beings often behaved in ways that lay outside of Jess's limited comprehension, but this was something else entirely, and when combined with the fight-or-flight pheromones Rav was spraying around so heavily that they were masking the smell of the aftershave he slapped on each morning, it was starting to set her fur quite seriously on end. But he was calling her, and right now, for better or for worse, he was the pack leader and provider of food. She looked left, and then right, and then left again, and finally walked the few paces over to Rav. She gave him a quick nuzzle on the shoulder, and he responded by feeling his way to her collar and grabbing hold of it.

He muttered something else that was presumably supposed to be reassuring, but wasn't, then began to drag her across the room. Before she could quite figure out what was going on, he'd made it to the room's only window, shoved the curtains aside, pushed the window open, and then bent down to lift her up. Jess found herself looking out of the window at a ground that was a long way below, given that Rav's flat was on the upper floor of his block. She felt Rav pushing her forward, still muttering away.

It is a common misconception that dogs are stupid. Dogs are not stupid. Trees are stupid. A tree cannot learn or observe, cannot make decisions that predict future reality based on current observations combined with learned experience. A tree does not feel fear, or anticipation, or uncertainty, because it does not feel anything. To feel requires one to think, and a tree has no thoughts. A dog, by contrast, is born into the world in possession of a biological computer of such incredible sophistication that it is only when set against the even more sophisticated human brain that it begins to appear primitive.

Dogs are, in fact, highly intelligent when measured against any kind of scale not arranged logarithmically to divide the universe into mankind and everything else. They are, for example, astute judges of character. Jess was under no illusions when it came to Rav. He was not the most reliable of keepers. Mealtimes were often late, arriving only after intense twenty-minute staring sessions. Toilet breaks often required much scratching at both doors and legs. Walks were typically both too short and lacking in variety. But while his behaviour towards Jess could often have been described as borderline neglectful, he'd never actually tried to kill her before.

Which is what he now appeared to be doing.

Jess's brain was in possession of some one-hundred-and-sixty million neurons, and right now those one-hundred-and-sixty million neurons were all operating according to a unanimous conclusion that letting Rav throw her out of the window would be a very bad move. Jess might not have been familiar with the works of Sir Isaac Newton, but she had a very deep, intuitive understanding that when it comes to falls of more than a few feet, Mister Gravity is no longer your friend.

She put her front paws out to catch hold of the frame either side of the now-opened window and braced herself hard. She wasn't heading out of this window; if Rav had a problem with that, tough.

Once, many years ago, Rav had watched the Ron Howard film *Backdraft*, which features a scene in which a grizzled Kurt Russell introduces a young Billy Baldwin to the mystical ways in which a raging fire behaves. Unfortunately, as is so often the case in life, Rav had so forgotten the contents of that scene that all he had left was the knowledge that there were things you could do with fires that were inadvisable to a degree that would kill you, but no actual recollection of what those things were. Opening the window had, as a result, been a highly stressful affair. But when the action of opening failed to trigger any kind of fireball exploding through his bedroom door, he was able to relax slightly, and get on with the job of getting Jess out.

The thick toxic smoke was now streaming past him, drawn by the coldness of the early morning air, but he could just make out the skip full of cardboard that had been abandoned by persons unknown right underneath his bedroom window some five weeks earlier. (At this point, Rav could only mutter a silent prayer of thanks to fate, destiny, Vishnu, and local authority incompetence so ingrained that the three separate bollocking phone calls he'd made to the council's environmental services department demanding its removal had been blatantly ignored).

There was just one problem.

Jess didn't appear to want to be rescued anytime soon. The dog had braced her front paws against the window frame either side of the opening and was pushing back hard against Rav's every attempt to shove her through. He shifted his grip and tried pushing at a slightly different angle, but after a frantic bout of claw-scrabbling, she managed to block that as well. Meanwhile, Rav could feel the heat burning at his back, his skin beginning to tighten. The smoke was, if anything, thicker. He was taking in only the briefest of shallow breaths but even so, his lungs felt as though they were on fire. That it's usually the smoke that kills you was a cliché that Rav was now realising to be true. And clawing at every thought was the dull roar of the adjacent inferno consuming his living room in an orgy of fire-borne fury. A fury that at any moment might blast through the door that was currently the only thing standing between Rav and the inferno.

Some months earlier, Rav had attended a mandatory fire safety training course. The course had featured an informational film typical of the health and safety genre, with bad acting, limited budget, and a committee-written script combining to produce something that oscillated between dire tedium and unintentional comedy, often wildly so. Rav had spent most of the course trying, and failing, to score with one of the female attendees with the result that the actual content of the lesson had largely passed him by. But apart from the knowledge that fire extinguishers are colour coded and if you use the wrong type on the wrong fire, you'll die, the only thing that stayed with him was the image of a man in a security guard's uniform staggering around an office on fire, like a reanimated and subsequently Molotov-cocktailed mummy in the climactic scene of a nineteen-fifties horror film.

Rav really, really didn't want to die.

He pulled Jess back for a moment, flipped her around, then threw her away from him. He had a brief glimpse of a snapping jaw and terrified staring eyes and then she was falling from view. Rav didn't pause. The heat was so strong now, so stinging, so burning, that he still would have climbed up onto the windowsill had this been the thirtieth floor, rather than the first. He knew now what had driven those poor souls to jump from the World Trade Centre on the eleventh of September 2001. Some things are worse than death, and burning alive is one of them. He climbed up onto the windowsill and let his momentum carry him forward.

He was free.

And falling.

Rav smashed down hard into the compacted cardboard with enough impact to knock free what little air remained in his lungs. He groaned, then breathed in.

The air was pure, clean, and cold, mercifully so. He took a series of deep, shuddering breaths that only served to reinforce how great an oxygen debt he'd been building up.

He was alive.

He rolled sideways and encountered something warm, furry, and apparently angry, if the snarling growl was anything to go by.

He opened his eyes.

He was lying in a skip beneath an early morning sky of grey clouds shot through with the scarlet rays of a rising sun. From behind him, a soon-to-be extinguished streetlight cast its ghostly glow across the scene. And above him, his open window gaped, its curtains flapping in a gentle breeze. No smoke poured from its maw. Not even a wisp. He realised that his skin, which only moments ago had seemed to be somewhere between cured leather and twice-fried bacon, now felt chilled, cold, even. He was shivering. And his lungs, which had felt scarred and tortured by the toxic smoke, had now recovered with an impossible rapidity.

It wasn't real.

None of it was.

There was no fire.

A cold realisation began to dawn upon him, a realisation that things had not been as they had seemed. The conspirator cultists had got inside his head, and to do that, they must surely have got into his home, physically. He had to believe that, because scary as them knowing where he lived was, the alternative, that they could remotely get inside his head, from anywhere, as though they were a teenaged cyberpunk from Vladivostok hacking into your laptop, was scarier. A new wave of panic began to bubble up inside him. They'd got into his head, and they'd damned near killed him.

Jess.

He took a panicky look around and spotted the dog crouching a couple of feet away on a slab-shaped section of cardboard, her eyes wild and terror-filled, her muzzle curled to expose warning teeth, her claws slightly splayed, her tense frame coiled like a spring ready to explode into action. She was okay, albeit unhappy, which — at least — was something.

Rav climbed carefully out of the rusting skip, dropping down to the tarmac below, then reached back to help Jess out. She made a reasonably serious attempt to bite off his hand, followed that up with several seconds of very hard staring, then made her own way out of the skip, landing with a thump and then looking back up at Rav with an expression that appeared to suggest that they would be talking about this again, later.

The chilling revelation of the truth was beginning to be accompanied now by a sensation of actual, non-metaphorical cold. It might have been July, but this was an early morning July on a day that hadn't been forecast to be particularly warm, and Rav was clad only in a pair of boxer shorts. He took stock of his situation. He was standing beside the skip, on the patch of grass that divided the side of his apartment block from the residents' car park. In front of him was the road, and round the corner would be the block's front door. He walked quickly to the entrance, starting to shiver now, before remembering that he had no key.

Entry-phone.

Eight buttons stared back at him, for eight flats. It was at times like this, when he was considering which of his neighbours to wake up at do-you-know-what-time-it-is o'clock, that he wished he'd got to know them better. A cautiously sauntering Jess paused a few feet away to take the piss that Rav would have taken, were he keen to not add indecent exposure to straight exposure.

He was still considering which button to take a stab at when he heard a car easing to a halt behind him.

"Excuse me, sir... Rav?"

Chapter Nineteen

The voice belonged to Paul, a copper from Hounslow police station, with whom Rav had a working relationship from those times Paul had found a confused bloke wandering around in his boxer shorts, and Rav had been the duty social worker he'd ended up calling. It was frankly disconcerting to both of them to have Rav now occupying the other role in the scenario, but after accepting his explanation of a highly unfortunate bout of sleepwalking, Paul managed to find a ladder from somewhere, allowing Rav to re-enter his flat via the window from which he had but recently exited.

The flat clearly being unsafe, Rav didn't linger. Filling a sports bag with a few days' worth of essential supplies, he headed over to Mindy's parents' place, figuring that while the resulting conversation with his Uncle Tony might be awkward, it would beat having that conversation with his mother. And at least this way, he had Mindy — who, notionally good girl that she was, still lived at home — to fight his corner.

That, and his mother had some kind of sixth sense superpower when it came to spotting his lies.

So, after deploying the cover story he'd pre-arranged with Mindy in a phone call on the way over — "Some kind of problem with the building's sewage... unfit for human habitation... can't say when, water board, unions, you know, tsk!... don't want to worry my mum, you know how she worries... I can stay a few days? Great! You know I've got a dog, right? Brilliant! Come on, Jess!" — he'd settled himself, his sports bag, his laptop, Jess's dog blanket, and finally Jess, into his cousin Amrit's room, Amrit conveniently being away for a few weeks on what his parents believed was a business trip to Johannesburg. (Amrit, a geologist working for a mining corporation, had genuinely flown into Johannesburg, but had then taken a further two flights to an exploration camp in Angola, where he was now living some kind of boys' own adventure story where, as he'd put it to Rav in an email: "It's great. I get to have my own AK47. But don't tell my mum.")

Now, several cups of tea and a spot of driving later, Rav and the Professor were navigating their way through a multi-storey car park off the North Circular where they'd agreed to meet up with Jackson and Sam, for no other reason than it being located at a geographical halfway point. When they nosed up the final ramp onto the car park's top deck, they found the two other men already there, stood beside Jackson's parked car. Other than their two cars, the entire upper deck was empty. Rav let Jess out and left her to have a sniff while the rest of them got down to business, with the first item on the agenda being for him to describe the events of the previous night.

"Shit," said Jackson, when he'd finished. "That's pretty horrifying. Have you got any clue on how they found your place, and how they managed to cast the spell?"

Rav did. He reached through the open driver's side window of his car and pulled out a clear plastic document wallet, inside of which was a single sheet of laser printed paper and handed it over to Jackson. The priest looked at it intently.

"This is the printout of the whois result for your website's domain."

"Yeah. I found it posted through the letterbox."

"Sorry, what's a whois result?" asked Sam.

Jackson hand-waved an apology. "Sorry. Any computer domain, like bbc dot co dot uk, or in this case west ken pda dot com, is registered with the worldwide domain name system. That registration has the name and address of the person who owns it and is freely searchable via the whois system."

"Isn't that a bit questionable from a privacy point of view?"

The priest looked over at Rav, a half-smile on his face. "Yeah. Which is why private individuals usually pay extra to register via an intermediary company that hides their details from public view."

Rav felt his cheeks starting to burn. "I thought I had, but I guess it lapsed. Probably deleted the reminder thinking it was spam or something."

Jackson shrugged sympathetically. "Happens. The point is this: they figured out where you live, and they wanted you to know that. If they weren't trying to kill you, they sure as hell wanted to send you a very, very strong message. You got any idea how they cast the spell?"

Rav reached into the car and pulled out a second package, this one a clear sandwich bag, inside of which was a mixed-up mass of broken eggshell, egg white, raw runny yolk, and amid all that, the tangled form of a dead chicken foetus. "I found this by the front door, in the corner of my lounge. They must have got into the flats somehow, and then pushed it through the letterbox. When I went back in, Jess sniffed at it, and then went ape shit barking at it."

Sam reached over to take the bag, holding it gingerly between thumb and finger as though it contained poison, and examined it carefully. "Clever. Very clever. You've seen that it was fertilised?"

"Yeah."

The rabbi spent a few further moments examining it, before looking back up. "Eggs are powerful things, in both the magical and spiritual sense. The egg has long been considered a symbol of fertility, and of life itself, with roots so deep in pagan mythology that it persists to this day in the eggs we exchange at Easter."

"We?" asked Jackson, raising a quizzical eyebrow.

"What? I can't enjoy a long weekend with chocolate? Anyhow, considering it further, the idea of an egg as a symbol of life is literal as well as metaphorical, especially when fertilised, as this poor thing was. A fertilised egg contains not merely the seed of life, but the fuel needed to create that life. It's a potent container of spiritual energy and biological potential."

"Almost like it was custom-made as a delivery mechanism for a spell," said Rav, his tone as grim as his mood.

"Yeah. The spell would have been cast in some sort of ritual where the egg was the focus. Then, when the egg shattered, and the foetus died, that would have acted as a spiritual trigger to the spell, releasing the hallucination created by the ritual."

His sentence lapsed into a silence that no one felt compelled to break. Finally, it was Jackson who spoke. "Look, what's done is done. You're alive, Jess is alive. Yesterday, before all of this, you said you'd found some stuff about the Russian. How about you tell us what you found?"

Jackson was right, Rav realised. The bastards might have sent him a message, but they couldn't make him listen to it. He'd have plenty of time when this was over to beat himself up over the fiasco of letting his domain protection lapse. He'd spent too much of the last twenty-four hours doubting his resolve. Now was the time to push those doubts aside and go all in with whatever reserves of determination and stubbornness he had left.

He took a deep breath and began to speak.

Rav began his explanation by outlining what the Professor had discovered, and his own subsequent research, although that research didn't really amount to much more than some newspaper puff pieces he'd downloaded from the Internet about the sort of layout Airbus could offer, were someone to purchase a custom A380 from them, 'custom', of course, being the clue as to how useful the attached floor plans might prove. Already, he could feel his newly gathered resolve dribbling away. Nonetheless, he read off a few of the statistics, if for no other reason than it delayed the point where he was forced to stop talking and the undeniable stupidity of what he was proposing would inevitably enter the conversation.

"Okay," he said, pacing up and down in front of the two cars. "A standard A380 has a wingspan of seventy-nine metres, a length of seventy-two metres, a cabin width of seven metres, and a range of eight-thousand miles. There are three decks: the bottom one for cargo and the upper two for passengers. This is a completely custom aircraft, so it could have any sort of interior layout. We'll know where the cockpit is, but that's about the extent of our knowledge. We can surmise that it will be divided into a number of separate rooms, and we believe there's a private museum somewhere on board, but we currently have no idea where that is."

He took a breath.

"As for dates, times and places, the plane will be landing at Heathrow tomorrow afternoon, and then taking off in the early evening, having taken the party guests on board. It will make a leisurely circumnavigation of the British Isles before returning to Heathrow in the early hours of Wednesday morning, to depart later that day. And between its initial arrival and its final departure, we need to acquire the skull from the on-board museum." He put his laptop down on the bonnet of his car and tried to channel every single stiff-upper-lipped commanding officer he'd ever seen in old-time war movies. "Thoughts, gentlemen?"

To his amazement, they didn't laugh. Or point. Or cry. Or even get back into their car and leave, which is probably what Rav would have been doing had he not been the one who'd called the meeting. Instead, Jackson and Sam said nothing, thinking hard, an activity shared by the Professor (but not Jess, who, having run out of things to sniff at, had found a stretch of sun-warmed tarmac to snooze on).

On the six-lane North Circular below, cars strung out like beads on a multi-braided necklace hummed around a gentle bend, their engine noises blending into a pure, clear hum. In the cloudless sky above, a jet climbing out of Heathrow left a pair of fluffy white contrails behind it. Finally, Jackson — who was sat on the bonnet of his car, feet on the bumper — spoke. "It's a mad idea, and if it goes wrong, I suspect I'll find myself envying Sam for being a follower of a religion that doesn't have much in the way of religious hierarchies."

Rav wasn't following him. "Sorry?"

"He doesn't have a bishop to give him a bollocking."

Sam laughed. "No. I've only got a wife, a mother, a teenaged daughter who already thinks I'm an idiot, and a synagogue's worth of little old ladies for whom this would be the best gossip this century. Plus there's the Metropolitan Police." He thought for a moment. "But if you were leading up to saying that mad as it is, we should probably go for it, I'm inclined to agree with you. We're facing a conspiracy of people who've demonstrated a worrying degree of knowledge, who appear to have a considerable head start on us, and who now appear to have the backing of an extremely wealthy and powerful man. I don't quite know why, but I can't help but feel that this skull is likely to be a key component in their plans. It's entirely possible that it isn't on the plane, especially if it's been earmarked for a specific purpose by the conspiracy. But if he's the only lead we have, and right now it seems he is, then either way, we should probably follow it up, regardless of the risks such a course of action might entail."

When he stopped speaking, there was silence for several seconds before Jackson spoke. "Last night I had a vision. I guess the more scientifically minded might say it was a dream, and I suppose strictly speaking, it was. But in my dream, I felt a voice speaking to me, a voice that spoke of the tragedies that would unfold if we were to do nothing. These people are evil, and they have evil intent. Like Sam said, there's no guarantee the skull is even on the plane, or that it will be transferred to the conspiracy during the visit. But we have one shot at this. If we allow this guy to fly in, and then fly out, and do nothing, we might later realise that that was our chance, and we didn't take it. So I say we go for it."

Rav was nodding before he'd finished the sentence. Jackson and Sam might be seeing the bigger picture Evil in all of this, and that was good. But for him this was about what it always had been. Ricky and Scarlet. He'd made a promise, and some promises must be kept no matter what the potential cost, and this was one of them. He didn't know how any of this fitted together. He didn't know how the skull connected to Ricky, or even that it did. But he knew that Ricky's madness was connected to the conspirators and right now, it seemed that the only thing that might save Ricky was to smash his way into the heart of conspiracy and destroy it.

And that was what he intended to do.

Jackson continued. "From now on, given what happened to Rav last night, I think we have to assume they're onto us. Our usual locations aren't safe. Sam? Of the four of us, you're the only one with immediate family. Are there things you can do?"

The rabbi nodded. "There are. How can I put this? I'm a member of a people who've historically never known absolute safety. Taking precautions and making plans for danger is written into our cultural DNA. There are networks I can contact. I'll call my wife. She and the kids can stay in a safe house until this blows over."

Jackson nodded. "Then I'd say we're good to go. Rav? What's the plan?"

Rav took a deep breath, and then resumed channelling his fictional Second World War general. "Okay. We're going to do what everyone'll say can't be done. We've got a long way to go, and a short time to get there." He realised to his horror that his channelling had somehow switched from a generic nineteen-sixties war film to a very nineteen-seventies Smokey and the Bandit, but it was too late to do a full handbrake turn now.

He considered channelling a bit of James T Kirk instead, but realised that any attempt to go "full Shatner" was almost guaranteed to overshoot the original series and crash-land instead on Galaxy Quest's Jason Nesmith. Only Shatner could ever carry off the full Shatner, and even that was debatable. He realised his three colleagues were still staring at him, waiting for him to stop mentally dicking around over the manner of his delivery and actually say something. He took a deep breath and snapped himself back to the moment. "Let's divvy up the tasks and start planning, yeah?"

Chapter Twenty

Rav was a social worker, not a conman, but he'd binged a shitload of episodes of Hustle and seen every single Oceans whatever movie (and the nineteen-sixty Rat Pack original, come to that), and had developed what he figured was a pretty good understanding of how to pull off a caper like this. And as Monday morning turned into Monday afternoon on its way towards Monday evening, he could feel the bones of a plan starting to come together.

He knew that firstly, the grifter needs to understand the mark. Who he is and what he wants, and what you can use against him. That had been Sam's job, and his phone call came in a little after three. "Okay, I talked to a Russian journalist I know on the Jewish Chronicle."

"And what did he say?"

"She! Anyhow, not much is known about Menschikov, but the general picture is of a man with an outlook on life unpleasant to the point where it probably qualifies as a personality disorder. He's got no real friends, except for his wife, and given that she's not only his fourth wife, but three years into what has historically proved a four-year position, it's debatable whether even she qualifies as a friend. He likes to think of himself as a master manipulator, who collects the powerful and famous like he collects the exhibits in his museum, but he ends up surrounding himself with the sort of non-entities you get on celebrity reality shows. I found the guest list of a party he held at the Metropolitan Museum in New York and I recognised about four names out of four hundred."

Secondly, the grifter must understand the environment he'll be working in. Rav had sent Jackson and the Professor to scout out the airport, and they reported back to his temporary office in Hounslow High Street's Costa Coffee a little after Sam's call. "We got talking to a bunch of plane spotters out by Hatton Cross tube station," Jackson said, in between bites of a panini that was serving as a late lunch. "Turns out they already knew it was coming. Some jungle grapevine they have. They've got stuff on their laptops that shows a flight map of everything in the air. I've arranged for them to give us a ring when it's on its way."

"Did they know where it will end up after it lands?"

The Professor answered that question. "They're of the opinion that it will not head for any of the main terminals but will instead taxi to a secluded area out on the apron reserved for governmental and diplomatic aircraft and so on. The party guests will then go to a separate VIP terminal typically used by the rich and famous, from where they can be driven directly to the aircraft, either via a fleet of limousines or a bus."

"Any chance of getting access to the plane?"

Jackson shook his head. "Pretty much none, I reckon. We had a drive around the perimeter. There's nothing obvious, but if you look carefully, you'll see that there's security cameras everywhere, in addition to a bloody big fence. I'd say the whole area's locked down so tight that if you attempt to get into it, you'll pretty soon find yourself staring down the wrong end of a gun barrel."

Thirdly, any Mickey Bricks wannabes must understand the circumstances within which they'll be operating. And that was Rav's job. "Ms Hill? Can I call you Evangeline? Evie? Great! My name's Sebastian Singh, and I'm a reporter with Buzzfeed London. I'm doing a piece on celebrity party planners, the people you go to when you figure you're the best, you want your party to be the best, and so you need to hire the best. And the people I've talked to say that you're the best in London. I was wondering if I could have a little chat with you. Do you have any parties coming up? You do?"

Fourth piece of Hustle lore? Establish your lines of entry, the channels you can use to access the mark and carry out the heist, and if growing up just a few miles from your heist's location has given you a few useful contacts, then leverage them, and leverage them hard. "Dave, mate, it's Rav! I know, long time, no see. Look, I need a favour."

"Favour?"

"Hey, you owe me. Remember that time in Year Eight you had dysentery and shat yourself behind the bike sheds? Who was it who smuggled you into the bogs and then got some emergency trousers from the school nurse?"

"Yeah, yeah, fair point. What is it you need?"

"I heard you work in personnel for one of the firms that do the catering for the airlines at Heathrow?"

"Yeah, why?"

"There's an A380 coming in tomorrow night. Some Russian billionaire's private jet. He's having a party. I heard you guys were doing the catering?"

"Might be. Why are you asking?"

"I need a couple of friends added to the staff you're sending on board. I figure it's all going to be casual workers, zero hours contract stuff, right, so can you swap a couple of names in?"

"No way!"

"Dave, it's not dodgy, honestly. They're plane spotters. Mad for it. Want to see the inside of this plane. Worst thing they might do is take a few discreet pictures with their phones. That's it."

There was a long pause. "You swear on your mother's life they're not sodding ISIS."

"They're not ISIS."

Another number, retrieved from an old email. "Saj, hi. How you doing? Been ages! You still working for the passport office? You are? Wow, that's great! And how did your parents react when you told them you were gay? Oh. So, you haven't told them yet?"

A few more hours and several further phone calls later, and with his bank account now whacked deeply into overdraft territory and his credit card hiding in the back of his wallet in a foetal position, he had a plan. A real, honest-to-god plan. The sort of plan that would do a Hollywood blockbuster justice. The sort of plan that he could present to the rest of the guys without having to channel fictional characters. It was a good plan.

Except for one slight gaping hole of a flaw that he had no idea how to patch. Every single person that would go on board that plane — and every single thing they carried — would be going through security, the people through a metal detector and the items through an X-ray scanner. And if there's one thing guaranteed to make a bored, half-asleep security scanner operator wake up with a start and hit the reverse button on his conveyor belt controls, one thing short of an actual box full of wires, batteries and a lump of Semtex that is, it's a human skull. Try to go through security with a skull in your hand luggage and your trip will be over before it's begun.

See, the problem wasn't getting the skull of St Horace off the plane.

It was getting the duplicate skull (which he'd arranged to borrow off a mate who worked as a junior doctor at a Central London teaching hospital) onto the plane in the first place. The duplicate skull that was the key to Menschikov and his people not realising that the original skull had been stolen.

And bypassing security was turning out to be as hard as you'd expect, which, under any other circumstances would have been reassuring, but in this case was a bloody nuisance. No matter how hard Rav sucked on his pencil, no matter how many searches he conducted or how many phone calls he made, it seemed an insurmountable problem. He had a pretty big network of old friends and extended family, but it was looking as if that network had hit its limit. And then it occurred to him that perhaps his pride had caused him to overlook the person who perhaps should have been the first contact he tapped up. He shoved that pride back into the box he should have been keeping it in all along, grabbed his phone, looked up a number in its history, and hit dial.

"Mister Shah?" Fox sounded as annoyingly chirpy as he had done back in Istanbul.

"Yeah, it's me."

"Good, good. So have you had any luck in our mutual endeavour? Any progress to report?"

From where Rav was sitting, it didn't seem like there was much in the way of mutuality about the situation. Fox had set Rav and the Professor off on a dance. Perhaps now was the time for him to enter the dance floor himself. "We think we might have found the item. We're working on acquiring it. But there's one problem."

"And that is?"

"We need to get an item past security at Heathrow, tomorrow evening. A duplicate skull. We've got everything else worked out, but this one we're stuck on. So maybe it's time for Her Majesty's government, or at least a certain representative of Her Majesty's government, to get his fingers a little bit dirty."

There was a pause, followed by what sounded like a chuckle. "Would you be asking for my help, Mister Shah?"

"Yeah."

"You know what, Mister Shah? Sometimes it's a tad boring playing M. Sometimes you just want to get out in the field and be double-oh-seven again, pension be damned, if you know what I mean." He paused again, and when he resumed speaking it was in a voice stripped of its previous jocularity. "I think we both know what we're facing here, Mister Shah. You've got my help. I'll get your duplicate skull past security."

Chapter Twenty-One

Evie Hill's initial plan for the party had been for the entertainment to be performed by the year's newest and brightest YouTube singing sensation, Jess Richards, but due to a set of unfortunate circumstances, Richards had abruptly cancelled shortly after Evie had outlined her plan to the lovely Sebastian Singh. This had left Evie with something of a hole to plug, but fortuitously, when she mentioned her newly acquired predicament to Singh, he was able to put her on to an up-and-coming West London DJ of his acquaintance, one DJ Dev D, who by happenstance was available that evening.

Thus it was that by eight o'clock on Tuesday evening, having cleared security at the private terminal, Rav found himself ensconced in a makeshift DJ's booth at the far end of the A380's ballroom, hidden behind a borrowed Gemini GMX digital mixing deck, pumping out a series of easy listening classics to those early arrivals who'd thus far turned up.

At the far end of the ballroom, in the doorway that led to the aircraft's main entrance lobby, a worried looking Evie Hill appeared. She caught sight of Rav and gave him a wave and a smile, her face returning a moment later to its previously fraught expression as she advanced into the ballroom and launched into an intensive bollocking involving a table laden with filled champagne flutes and a waiter who didn't appear to give much of a damn.

Rav reached for the slim laptop that was linked to the deck, cancelled the pending track that he'd cued up — Paul McCartney's perennial classic, Yesterday — and replaced it with Pink's "Get the Party Started", which, in the private code he and the guys had worked out, indicated that Evie Hill had arrived on the scene. As the previous track came to its conclusion, he smoothly threaded Pink in, the music booming out through the top-of-the-range sound system mounted around the room.

So far, so good.

From his DJ-ing vantage point beside the room's pop-up cocktail bar, Rav was able to watch the stream of Z-list celebrities and corrupt, money-drawn politicians arrive, all of whom greeted the situation with the carefully masked unease of people who know, deep down, that in their case the impostor syndrome they suffer from is both genuine and deserved.

It wasn't until a good twenty minutes in that he spotted anybody he recognised, they being Jenson Peters, "the Archaeology Guy", and his glamorous girlfriend, Jasmine. The Archaeology Guy was a charismatic and entertaining vlogger who'd shot to online fame via his eponymous YouTube channel, in which he popularised archaeology through walks and examinations, often accompanied by Jasmine and their mongrel, Muttley. At least that was who he'd been by mid-afternoon that very day, when Evie Hill — acting on Sebastian Singh's recommendation — had checked out his YouTube channel. There, she would have found a dozen or so videos (shot that morning by a wedding videographer of Rav's acquaintance, and exclusively featuring locations around Hounslow and "artefacts" stolen from Rav's mum's collection of ornaments and knick-knacks) and several tens of thousands of "followers", all of whom had been conjured from the ether by a hacker acquaintance of Rav's called Charlie, who'd helped him out on previous occasions.

He gave Jackson and Mindy a vague nod, and faded his deck across to The Buggles' electro-classic, "Video Killed the Radio Star", which in their private code both announced their safe arrival and confirmed that everything was going according to plan. And so far, it was. True, Jackson's persona wouldn't survive close scrutiny, given that a typical video on his channel would be the one in which he talked random bullshit about Ancient Greece whilst pointing to a five-euro souvenir Rav's mum had brought back from a holiday in Crete. But it had fooled Evie, and had got him and Mindy here, and for now, that was pretty good.

Rav finished fading The Buggles in, then looked back up to check that the third member of Jackson and Mindy's entourage had made it on board. She had.

But she didn't look very happy.

Jess was not having a good day. First had come a visit to a place of noise and strange smells, where someone with the touch and command of a human who bossed dogs around on a daily basis had lifted her bodily onto a raised table. For a moment, Jess had worried that this might be a visit to the vets, that place of cruel sadists who poked at her and jabbed her with needles, and then attempted to buy her forgiveness with treats of insultingly small proportions. But the vets didn't smell like this, or sound like this.

Instead, she'd found her fur being shorn by a buzzing, itching, scratching damnation of a thing, followed by the thing's wielder rubbing a foul-smelling liquid over every patch of her body. While this was happening, Jess had kept her thoughts to herself. She didn't bark. She didn't growl. She didn't even curl her lips to reveal her canines. Instead, she'd watched, and waited, warily — and had continued to do so through the several hours and several journeys that had followed, until she found herself in a strange room whose furnishings failed to mask the coldness of its structure. Then, after some minutes, a human voice, loud and harsh, echoed around the room. All the humans, including Mindy, who Jess liked, and Rav's new friend Jackson, who she was still considering, retired to the chairs that lined each side of the room and strapped themselves in.

Jess's built-in paranoia meter — which was always dialled pretty high but was now well into the red zone after the events of today — moved up another notch. A faint whine penetrated through the walls from somewhere outside, and then she felt a movement, a sensation that built and built until she could feel it pulling at her.

And then the room tipped abruptly up, and her stomach dropped away.

She let out a little whine of fear.

The Professor had attended university in a gentler era, in which the children of middle-class parents could attend university for free, supported by the taxes of working-class people who had, by contrast, left school at sixteen and walked straight into paid employment. He'd even been granted a small maintenance grant, which had covered his modest outgoings of rent, food, academic supplies, and the occasional trip to the student union bar.

He had, however, supplanted his funds by working as a waiter in one of London's better hotels through the summer months, something which, besides giving him the opportunity to prove that his prejudices about American tourists were correct, had given him a pretty comprehensive education in the principles and practices of food service.

Compared to that job, what he had to do now was relatively simple, even if he was having to do it using a body that was some forty-something years older and unaccustomed to physical labour. Shortly after his arrival on the A380, a Pole, apparently monosyllabic by nature rather than by linguistic origin (given the perfect command of the English language he'd displayed on the rare occasions he had spoken) had begun feeding a stream of pre-cooked hors d'oeuvres through the lower-deck galley's range of ovens. The Professor's task was to transport silver trays stacked with the warm hors d'oeuvres from the galley to the ballroom, via the ornate spiral staircase that connected the aircraft's three levels, and then distribute the food to the largely uncouth detritus of humanity who were gradually filling that space.

Returning from his second such trip, he took the chance to exchange a quick nod with Sam, who, lacking his experience, had been press-ganged into the job of chief washer-upper, grabbed the latest tray, and headed back upstairs, just as the kitchen's built-in speakers segued from an unfamiliar track to the now — as of this afternoon — familiar "Video Killed the Radio Star".

Three more members of the team safely arrived. The Professor was a cautious man by nature, but right now he was hiding an inward smile as he hit the spiral staircase with something of a spring in his step, daring to think a thought that had seemed unthinkable only forty-eight hours earlier.

They might actually pull this off.

Fox had been vague about his exact plans for getting on board the A380, and as time marched on without him making an appearance, the cocktail of stress, irritation and anxiety forming in Rav's stomach continued to ferment, its metaphorical alcoholic proof level peaking at the point where the plane had clawed its way into the sky. It wasn't until some five minutes after the seatbelt lights had clicked off and Rav had resumed manual control of his decks, relieving the long-play mix CD he'd left auto piloting them, that the spook had appeared beside him, grinning like a well-groomed Cheshire Cat.

"All going well, Mister Shah?" he asked, out of the corner of his mouth.

Rav gave a pointedly grumpy grunt in reply, devoting his time instead to fading out the current track and feeding in Ylvis's 2013 novelty hit, "The Fox (What Does the Fox Say?)".

Fox considered the song for a few moments, then broke into a smile as he realised its meaning. "Oh, well played, Mister Shah. Well played." He paused for a moment, then leaned close, in a manner that couldn't have looked more conspiratorial if he'd tried. "The package is loaded and awaiting pick up when required. Until then, I think I might circulate." He gave Rav a brief fingertip salute. "Toodle-pip!"

Rav watched as Fox threaded his way across the dance floor with the annoying nonchalance and panache of a man born into affluence and raised into entitlement. The team had successfully boarded. Now all they had to do was figure out where the museum was located, and if the skull of Horace was anywhere in it.

Chapter Twenty-Two

The Professor's first task beyond his cover role of delivering refreshments to the party guests, was to reconnoitre the A380's interior, its private and customised layout being a mystery their research had proved unable to penetrate. This he was able to do with some success, through a mixture of volunteering for extra duties, and asking the occasional question in what he hoped was a casual and curious tone that avoided straying into inappropriate inquisitiveness.

An hour or so in, after conversations with some of the permanent staff — carefully timed to avoid the watching gaze of Menschikov's near-omnipresent Head of Security, a giant Armenian by the name of Saroyan —he'd managed to assemble what was hopefully a reasonably accurate mental map of the vehicle.

Passengers entered the aircraft through a main entrance hatch located on the middle level towards the nose of the plane, arriving into a sumptuously decorated lobby. In the centre of the lobby stood a spiral staircase wrapped around a cylindrical lift shaft, with the staircase connecting all three floors, and the lift additionally being able to drop down to the ground below the aircraft, for occasions when air-stairs were unavailable. Going forward, a corridor led between two rows of unisex toilets, beyond which was a sleeping cabin for the crew, complete with bunks, and then the cockpit itself.

On the lower level, which in the regular passenger variant held luggage and cargo, the area ahead of the spiral staircase was occupied by the kitchen. Going aft, a corridor ran along the port side of the aircraft, past a small but apparently well-equipped gym and a small and not particularly well-equipped toilet for the staff, before ending in a door that led to a luggage compartment. Beyond that, further progress was — as the Professor's source had cheerfully informed him — impossible, given that the space was occupied by the A380's impressively large landing gear and its twenty separate wheels.

Beyond the landing gear, the same source had told him in a tone that had changed down from cheerful to conspiratorially breathless, was a parking garage containing Menschikov's gold-plated Rolls Royce Phantom, complete with a ramp that could drop down and extend to allow the vehicle to be driven off the plane.

Back in the lobby, going aft, an impressive set of double doors — constructed from what was either genuine mahogany, or the most impressive carbon composite material the Professor had yet encountered — led into the large ballroom within which Rav was pumping out his tunes, Jackson and Mindy were circulating, and the annoyingly charismatic Fox was holding court to a cluster of middle-aged women in designer dresses while their husbands attempted to assassinate him with death-ray stares.

A second set of double doors in the ballroom's far wall led to a smaller cabin, lined with standard airliner type seats, to which those passengers who'd not found seats in the ballroom had been required to retire to during the take-off (the staff having to make do with cabin-crew style fold-downs in their work areas). A small cylindrical space beyond held a second lift, which apparently ran from the parking garage, through the cabin, to the upper floor. And behind that was supposedly a small, but well-equipped private cinema, in which Menschikov was said to enjoy watching a somewhat quixotic mix of programming varying from Soviet-era classics to the latest action movie slaughter-fests.

That left the craft's upper level. A single sandwich delivering expedition up the staircase had revealed a small leather-lined bar and lounge area. Further access to the upper level aft was barred by a key card and numeric pad-controlled door, but from the descriptions the Professor had managed to elicit, a port-side corridor ran past a set of four guest suites to a board room whose long heavy table could double as a formal dining table. From there, the port-side corridor continued past Menschikov's private suite (which, in addition to the expected en-suite bathroom contained a separate lounge) to the room they'd been seeking.

The museum.

It wasn't until the final snatched exchange in the series of apparently casual conversations the Professor had so carefully invoked that the final piece of the puzzle was slotted into place, when Menschikov's half-giggling, half-horrified cleaning supervisor had whispered her distaste at having to dust her employer's latest prized exhibit: an actual human skull sitting totally exposed on a velvet-clad spike.

If the Professor had been both forty years younger and not the product of an emotionally stunted English public-school education, her whispered revelation might have produced something of a fist pump. As it was, he felt a rush of excitement easily the equal of anything he might have felt in his younger days, whether that be winning a debate against his school's hated rivals, coming top of the class at Latin, or blowing up the headmaster's personal toilet block using plastic explosive stolen from the school's combined cadet force.

Now he just had to get this information to Rav.

The floor might have regained its equilibrium, but Jess's mental state had failed to follow suit. The surface upon which she stood was now level and relatively stable, but there was still a faint vibration coming up through her paws, and a persistent whine that was setting her teeth on edge, and she was still surrounded by people who smelt of deception and insincerity. Her nose could sniff out a bullshitting bastard a mile off, and this place was full of them.

Border Collies have pessimism hard-coded into their genes; optimism is for Labradors, not for dogs bred to keep track of two-hundred sheep too stupid to understand the things that might hurt them. Behind the worried eyes and hesitatingly wagging tail lies an over-thinking brain that fully understands that however bad things might be, they can always get worse. But even so, Jess still managed to feel a stab of disappointment as another smell managed to slither its way into the surrounding stench.

A smell with the taint of evil.

For a moment, the thought that it might be feline crossed Jess's mind. The scent did indeed share the cat's evil taint, that smell that told a story of ancestral conflict stretching back ten thousand years to the beginnings of agriculture in Mesopotamia — when the first generations of farmers found their stores of hard-grown grain falling prey to rodent infestation, and the happily monogamous relationship of hunter-gathering man and his dog that had endured for tens of thousands of years found itself being forced into an uneasy, polygamous triangle of man-dog-cat doomed to eternal conflict.

But no, this was not the smell of a cat. It was finer, more nuanced. More evil.

She'd smelt this before, first faintly at the place beside the water, and then more strongly in Rav's flat, in the small objects he and his friends had been examining. She looked first at Rav, and then at Mindy and Jackson, but they all seemed occupied, their collective body languages reeking of stress and tension. The room was full of people and things, mingled into tangled patterns. Any one of them could be the source of this evil. It occurred to Jess that she could venture forth into the room, and try to sniff out the evil's precise location, but it equally occurred to her that she could not, and having weighed up the options, she decided that *not* was probably the more prudent choice. Rav, Mindy, and Jackson might be fellow members of her pack, but if they wanted her help, they could ask for it, and besides, she still hadn't quite forgiven Rav for throwing her out of a window.

She retreated to a convenient table from the underneath of which she could observe proceedings, snout cradled on front paws, eyes warily searching.

Watching.

The party wasn't really happening, at least not in the way that parties are supposed to happen. It was partly Rav's fault. Contrary to what some overly hyped and narcissistic members of the profession might believe, a DJ is an entertainer, not a musician; their job is to create the atmosphere within which emotions may be heightened and inhibitions released, and then let the tunes do the work. Music is an important tool in a DJ's toolbox, the most crucial arrow in his or her creative quiver, but as with violins and penises, it's not the tool itself that counts, but the manner in which one uses it. This was always going to be a challenging gig, comprising, as it did, a bunch of has-beens, non-entities, wannabes, and never-weres, and being hosted by a toxic individual whose lack of charisma was so legendary that he could never have been the life and soul of the party had he even bothered to turn up, which thus far he hadn't.

But a better man than Rav, one with greater drive, better resolve, and a stronger willingness to put his enthusiasm on the line, could perhaps have made something of the party, could have pushed it over the crest of the mountain top by sheer force of will, could have taken this disparate bunch of losers and forged them into something better, creating a moment, a bubble in time within which the collective party goers could have become greater than the sum of their parts. It could have been more than a party, more than a gathering. It could have been a reminder of what humanity can be, a reminder of that spark of brotherhood stretching back to the Nile Rift Valley hundreds of thousands of years ago when semi-intelligent apes began a journey that would take them to every corner of the Earth, and beyond.

Rav, interloper that he was, had failed the party.

Luckily, he didn't give a damn.

He feathered in a new track, keeping one eye on Jackson and Mindy and the other, warier eye, on Fox, then noticed the Professor entering with another tray of nibbles and reaching up with his free hand to rub his ear lobe, making sure to catch Rav's eye as he did so.

In their private code, this was the signal for "I have information, we need to meet".

In a move that didn't so much ignore the principles of good DJ-ing as pre-emptively punch them in the face, Rav faded out the track he'd only just faded in, cut in with an abrupt blast of the Black Eyed Peas "Meet Me Halfway" dropped straight into the chorus, let that play long enough for Fox, Jackson and Mindy to each indicate through a variety of non-verbal cues that the message had been received, then, like a lunatic driver cutting across three lanes of motorway to make an exit that from a purely legal perspective he'd already missed, segued into the second of the many long-playing mix tracks programmed into his decks.

Leaving that playing he headed across the dance floor past the clearly worried Evie Hill, telling her he was "off to take a piss", pitching his voice loud enough for it to carry through the beat to the listening Jackson, Mindy, Fox, and the Professor, who were actually the intended recipients of the message.

He strode quickly across the lobby, trusting that his companions would be following in his wake, timing their departures so as not to look too suspicious. Four of the six toilets were occupied, which was not surprising given that for a gathering such as this they would be doing triple duty: not simply a place to relieve oneself, but also a place to consume leisure pharmaceuticals or join the mile-high club. Luckily, the far right-hand toilet was vacant. Rav went in, pushing the inward opening door almost — but not quite — shut.

Within a few moments the Professor arrived, followed a little later by Jackson and Mindy, and then some seconds later by Fox. While Rav checked outside to see if Sam was coming before giving up and then bolting the door, the four newcomers arranged themselves in the toilet's interior which, while spacious when compared with standard airline toilets, had clearly not been designed to host meetings. Rav began. "I figure Sam probably didn't hear the signal, but the Prof can tell him anything we need him to know."

"Which is?" Mindy asked, from her perch on an expensive-looking vanity unit, Fox having taken the toilet and its mahogany seat.

Rav nodded at the Professor. "Prof? What you got?"

Chapter Twenty-Three

Considering that it wasn't much more than ninety minutes since they'd boarded the plane, Rav was deeply impressed by the knowledge the Professor had managed to accumulate, especially given that all he'd managed to achieve during the same period was to kill a party. The Professor had delivered a crisp and concise presentation that combined detail with insight. At the end, he smiled tightly with the satisfaction of a man who'd been given a task and had performed it well, then ceded the floor.

"Okay," said Rav. "So that's some of the details filled in. The good news is that the skull's in the museum, and we now know where the museum is. So that's one part of the plan we can activate." He looked across at Jackson.

The priest nodded, confirming his point. "Yeah, I've already primed Evie with talk about the whole archaeology thing. So now I can go to her and say that I've heard about this fabulous museum on the plane and ask if I can see it." He shrugged. "Course, we don't know that she'll go for it, and even if she does, either Menschikov or his people might say no…" He let his voice trail off.

He was correct, Rav couldn't deny that. A plan such as this is always built on assumptions and possibilities, and he'd seen enough third-act plot twists to know that. "Get in early and ask her. Part of our problem here is that we don't know how Menschikov fits into the conspiracy, but if he's come to hand the skull over to our bad guys, he might be removing it at any time, so the sooner we can do the switch, the better. You know the signals to give me, to let me know her answer. If she says yes, get her to arrange it, but then stall until I give you the signal."

Mindy broke in. "I can do the stalling. Jackson can say he can't go until I'm ready, and I can be having some conversation that I absolutely have to finish first."

"Great, sounds good," Rav said. "Okay, so if you two get in there for a viewing, that means they'll have to turn most of the security system off. But you'll be being watched, so there won't be any easy way for you to switch skulls, and besides, there's no way you'll be able to walk in there with a holdall." He looked across at Fox. "Actually, where is the replacement skull?"

He'd thought Fox might answer in his usual elliptical manner, but his reply was refreshingly direct. "It's in the parking garage, in a holdall, hidden in a consignment of Rolls Royce spares that were delivered shortly after landing. The balaclavas and gloves are there too. Which brings us to the question of how we get into the garage, which itself leads us to the question of how we get into the secure area."

"Yeah." Rav turned his attention back to the Professor. "Okay, so you said there's a secure door that controls access to the rest of the upper level, which requires both an access card and a numeric key entry to get in?"

"Yes."

"Okay. I went out back into the seating cabin and saw the same type of door leading to the rear lift shaft. Are there any other doors beyond those?"

"According to the cleaning supervisor, there are additional security doors at the entrances of each private guest suite, to Menschikov's private quarters, and to the museum. The cleaning staff have cards that can get them into the guest suites, but whenever anyone goes into either Menschikov's quarters or the museum to clean, they must be accompanied by either Saroyan or one of his team, with those locations being beyond the reach of standard cards. But not the garage. My cleaning contact described having to go down in the lift to clean the Rolls and made no mention of any additional security."

"I hate to say it," said Jackson, "but there's a slight hole in our plan."

"Which is that we need to get our hands on one of those cards?"

"Yeah."

Rav decided now was the time to deploy one of the discussion techniques he'd recently learned on a conflict resolution course. "Well, let's assume for now we can get a card. I think then we have a plan." He began to count the elements off on his fingers. "Mister Fox, the Professor and I use the card to gain access to the lift at the rear of the seating cabin. We travel down to the garage, retrieve the duplicate skull, then head back to the upper level where we find somewhere to hide. Meanwhile, Jackson and Mindy head to the museum for their private viewing. At some point they cause a distraction."

"What kind of distraction?" asked Jackson.

"Something that both distracts whoever is with you and sets off whatever alarms are still on."

"Like picking something up that you're not supposed to pick up?"

"Yeah. Do it the other side of the room so they're facing away from the skull. And then while that's all going on, Fox and I dash in, switch the skulls, and dash out."

"Just like that?" asked Jackson with a smile.

"That's the plan."

"What if they've got magic shit deployed?" asked Mindy. "For all we know, we might be walking around an empty room looking at things that don't exist, like the kid in Knightmare with the bucket on his head."

Rav nodded. "Yeah, which is why we're going to take Jess with us. Where is she, by the way?"

"Still sulking under that table. I tried to drag her out, but she wasn't having any of it and I didn't want to make a scene."

"No, you did right. Anyhow, when me, the Prof, and James here head off to the rear lift shaft, we'll take her with us. Hopefully, she'll alert us if there's anything weird. When we get to the museum, we'll let her be part of the distraction, as though she found her own way up there looking for you. We'll leave her there when we get out, and you can take her back down."

The Professor cleared his throat. "Which leaves only the issue of the access card. Do you have any thoughts, Ravinder?"

Rav didn't. But Mindy was looking at him with an expression of impish mischief that immediately set his spidey sense tingling.

"What?"

"You know the blonde girl in the turquoise dress, who went up to chat with you about ten minutes ago?"

Rav wasn't quite sure where she was going with this. He certainly remembered the girl — a stunning blonde squeezed into a dress whose price tag was probably inversely proportional to its surface area, with a vodka-over-honey accent normally associated with one of James Bond's conquests.

For a moment, he found himself transported to a waking dream in which a tanned Sean Connery poured out something alcoholic from a crystal decanter, examined the blonde lying before him on the bed with a stare that was almost surgical in its intensity, before uttering in the drawl beloved of a million amateur impersonators the immortal line—

"Are you even listening?"

"Sorry." He returned his attention to Mindy. "What about her? She came up because she wanted to request a track ."

Mindy gave him an exasperated sigh. "God, you really are dense, aren't you? It's like back when we were in secondary school and my mate Shanzi was desperate to shag you."

"Shanzi was desperate to shag me?"

"Massively!"

"So why are you telling me now? Why didn't you tell me then?"

A burst of laughter broke in: Fox, who was clearly trying to stop his shoulders from heaving. "Priceless as this is," he said, wiping away a tear, "and reluctant as I am to bring the comedy to a premature halt, perhaps, Mindy, you could tell us where exactly you're going with this? Are you suggesting that Rav should use his seduction skills to part this apparently romantically inclined girl from any access card she might possess?"

"Yeah," Mindy said. "I heard her tell someone that she's staying on the plane. Niece of someone, apparently. So she'll presumably have a card. I get the feeling that back home, maybe her horizons are kept a bit limited, and now's she out and about, well, you know…" She looked at Rav, smiling. "You're the DJ, the man with the tunes and all that, and some exotic looks—" the smile was now accompanied by air quotes "—that might qualify as some sort of rebellion against her family."

"A lot of leading Russian businessmen are on the fringes of the various Russian neo-Nazi movements," said Sam in a manner Rav frankly found unhelpful, considering the plan of action Mindy appeared to be suggesting.

"Yeah," Mindy continued. "So normally while she'd be way out of your league, what with her being like Premier League, and you being—" She halted, fingers clicking as she searched for the next word.

"Championship?" Rav suggested.

"I was actually going for Conference, but anyhow, the point is, for whatever reason, I'm telling you, that girl wants to shag you."

For a moment, Rav lost track of the reality of the situation. "Really?" he asked, his libido beginning to stir from its habitually cowed position. What Mindy had said was bang on: this girl was so far out of his league it wasn't true. Could he really be in with a chance? Then grim reality and gibbering terror crashed back in like a couple of hungry post-pub-crawl orangutans smashing their way into a locked and shuttered greengrocers'. Were they really going to hang the entire success of this operation on his ability to sweet-talk and seduce a pampered Russian princess? The very thought of it was enough to send his penis into such a retreat that it would probably have made it all the way to the safety of his ribcage were it not firmly attached to his groin.

Fox sniffed. "Good. So it's decided, then. Rav, talk to the girl, go up to her room, do whatever, get the card. Any other questions?"

No one else appeared to have any, and Rav was still trying to get his brain the right way up, rendering him temporarily speechless.

"Excellent!" Fox declared, pausing for a moment to illuminate the toilet's interior with his perfect smile before reaching over to unlock the door and peer carefully out. "I can't see any sign of Mr Saroyan, so I think we perhaps should be getting back to our positions before someone wonders where we all are." He looked across at Rav. "Good luck, old bean."

This was madness. He was eight miles high in a vehicle weighing more than five-hundred tonnes, with only the laws of physics supplemented by four engines with a combined power equal to more than a hundred Formula One cars keeping it there, and he was about to approach a girl who was so far beyond him that even giving her a smile would practically qualify as unwanted sexual attention. Attempting to punch above his weight was one thing, but this was like bringing a toothpick to a gunfight.

And there she was, surrounded by a trio of men, each of whom looked like someone, even if Rav couldn't place exactly which someone they were. The men were talking, as men do, and she was listening, as women are forced to do, leaning back slightly, and biting her lip in a way that couldn't have been sexier if she'd been backlit and photoshopped to buggery by one of those sleazy photographers who mix two parts genuine talent with three parts scumbag sexism.

If he'd been anywhere but here, and in any situation other than this, and if people's lives weren't depending on it, and if this hadn't been about defeating a bunch of evil bastards who'd made a pretty serious attempt to top him, he'd have run right back to the toilets and switched the lock to engaged. But then he caught Mindy's stare, and her mouthed, "Go on!"

He gave his borrowed leather jacket a tug, sniffed a rogue bit of snot into the back of his throat, cleared said throat, then vectored in towards his target on a curved approach necessitated by the fact that one of his legs appeared to be better able to walk than the other. He stuck his head into the conversational cluster and smiled.

"Hi!" he said.

The three male heads swivelled to focus on him, each stare a promise of a certain degree of violence, all three united by an anger that the previously fragile truce within which they'd each been attempting to pull the girl had been so totally disrupted. It took quite some degree of resolve and willpower for Rav to keep himself in position, given the weight of psychic fire he was taking from the combined stares.

And then the girl smiled back. "Hey!"

Chapter Twenty-Four

Ivana's room was small, but it had a full-sized double bed and a small combined wardrobe and dressing table unit, and an en-suite toilet with shower, which put it a long way ahead of the cramped seat in which Rav had once spent twenty-two hours flying to Australia. It could have been any hotel room anywhere were it not for one thing, that being the four evenly-spaced windows offering a view of scattered clouds below.

Rav already had Ivana's PIN number, 2323, having looked over her shoulder as she'd let the two of them, giggling, through the door at the back of the upper level lounge. Now he needed the card itself, and that was in her small clutch bag, a dainty thing of turquoise and gold accessorised to match the clinging dress and the gold band around her neck. The trouble was that the bag was with Ivana, and she was in the en-suite — whose door was almost, but not quite closed — doing God knows what.

If this had been a movie in which he was the suave, smooth-talking protagonist, it was easy to see the way in which this would go: he would give the girl the shagging of her life, a shagging so incredible that following it she would settle into a sleep so deep and satisfied that to retrieve the card from her clutch bag and slip quietly away would be simplicity itself.

But that wasn't how it was ever going to go down here.

It wasn't that Rav didn't want to sleep with her. He did. Hell, he would have sold his left bollock and mortgaged the right, just for one night with her. But when he tried to "visualise" himself shooting, and scoring, it wouldn't, couldn't come. He was never going to be able to make it with this girl. She hadn't even come out of the en-suite yet and already his genitals were trying to find some sort of hitherto undiscovered retraction method, his heart was thumping, his palms were clammy, and he was starting to feel light-headed.

Rav's favourite comic character, the Authority's Midnighter, was fond of telling opponents that he'd already fought the fight against them in his head a million different ways, and thus already knew the moves he could make to defeat them. Right now, Rav felt like he'd shagged this girl in his head a million times, and every single one of those times had ended in disaster, most of them involving either premature ejaculation, erectile failure, or both. He needed the million-and-first path, the one where it somehow ended okay. There's a fine line between superstitious believer and paranoid agnostic, and right now Rav was straddling that line, with pleas to fate and destiny running through his brain that weren't quite prayers to any deities in particular, but sure as hell weren't any kind of logical, "working the problem", either.

There was a knock at the door. Rav gulped, worked his way through a million more scenarios, most of which involved him being beaten up by improbably huge Armenians, and decided that all things considered, there was no way in hell he was going to answer that door. Then Ivana's husky Slavic tones emerged from the around the en-suite's not-quite-closed door. "Hey babe, can you get that?"

That husky, throwaway use of the word "babe" caused Rav's penis to momentarily stir, before it remembered where it was and returned to its now permanent state of panic. Rav gulped, gave himself a moment to indulge in some uninhibited terror, then staggered over to the door on legs that felt like they belonged to someone else.

A stiffly uniformed and impeccably groomed man stood before him, holding a silver tray upon which lay four lines of cocaine. Four crisp five-hundred Euro notes lay in a perfect fan to the left of the lines; a slightly optimistic spread of four foil-wrapped condoms lay on the right. The man advanced past Rav and into the room to be met by Ivana, who'd emerged from the en-suite in a state of naked perfection, the turquoise dress gone now to leave only the gold band and a body that could have launched a thousand pimped-out Cadillacs.

The man slid the tray onto the room's marble coffee table, then turned to face Ivana. "Will there be anything else, ma'am?" he asked in a voice that had the faintest of Eastern European overtones. Somehow, he was looking at the absolute perfection of her body without showing the slightest sign of reaction; either he was one hundred percent homosexual from the nucleotides of his DNA to the tips of his fingers, or Menschikov had had the guy carved out of granite.

Ivana shook her head curtly. The man glided backwards out of the room and closed the door, leaving Rav alone with a naked Eastern European goddess, four lines of finest Columbian marching powder, three condoms more than he could possibly ever require, and a scenario that could never have supplied the plot of a porn film if for no other reason than it would have blown the budget several times over. Which was a shame, because right now Rav could have used a broken washing machine that he could pretend he was there to mend as some kind, any kind, of distraction, while he figured out what the hell he was going to do.

Behind him, bent over in a pose that his panic-induced chivalry was ensuring that he was not taking an eyeful of, Ivana was snorting lines. Any moment now she would turn back around and in the flat, blurred awareness of his peripheral vision say something like—

"So, lover boy, you going to show me the moves behind the looks?"

The Professor held his breath as Rav shoved the card into the slot and tapped in a four-digit number, resuming his breathing only when the door slid open to reveal the lift beyond. Rav had been tight-lipped when he'd returned to the ballroom, communicating nothing beyond the rubbing of his left earlobe— the signal for a successful acquisition of the Russian girl's key card.

If pressed, the Professor would have to admit to some curiosity as to precisely what events had transpired between Rav leaving the ballroom with the girl on his arm and returning alone, in possession of her key card, but as he followed Rav and Jess into the lift, with James Fox bringing up their rear, he realised that this was one of those subjects best left as a mystery between men.

From the way Fox's left eyebrow was twitching he was similarly intrigued, and unlike the Professor he had apparently no compunction in raising the subject, because as soon as the lift doors slid closed, he raised it.

"Come on then Mister Shah. Spill the beans. What happened?"

It is a little-known fact that the human anus contains not one, but two sphincters, an external one under the conscious control of its owner, and an internal one, which runs autonomously. Most days, Rav's internal anal sphincter had a relatively easy life, staying tight until Rav's bowels had filled, and then relaxing, allowing pressure to then build on its external partner, with that pressure informing its owner that it was time to grab his phone and head for the loo.

When Ivana had casually suggested that it was time for him to show her his moves, it had swiftly become apparent to Rav's internal anal sphincter that this was not going to be one of those routine days. Because right then, the network of nerves that formed Rav's autonomic nervous system, the network by which his various autonomous organs were managed, was in the process of initiating a complete, system-wide flight-or-fight reflex.

Like a panicking Commander Will Riker shouting "Red Alert" at the first sight of anything vaguely scary on the view screen, Rav's body began preparing for action. Arteries that carried blood to muscles were dilating, while those carrying blood to areas deemed unnecessary to the imminent conflict were contracting. Nutrients needed for muscular action were being released. Yet more adrenaline was being pushed out, causing Rav's already racing heart to push into its red zone. And those autonomous muscular systems whose regular ongoing mission was to stay tightly constricted were now being told, in the words of a certain Disney snow queen, to "Let it go".

Rav's internal anal sphincter had initiated the process of letting it go.

Like passengers at an overcrowded train station being waved through permanently opened barriers, the contents of Rav's bowels began to press down upon his external sphincter which had no option but to pass on the message that the bomber was apparently approaching Berlin to Rav's already overloaded brain, with an addendum that the bomb bay doors appeared to be opening.

Which all amounted to one thing. Just at the point when Rav was approaching maximum stress, having worked through the million different ways in which the resulting encounter could go wrong, the desired million-and-first option did now appear, only to be revealed as something that managed, somehow, to be even worse.

Having spent the previous five minutes figuratively shitting himself, he was about to move from figuratively to literally.

As they say, shit was about to get real.

Even more adrenaline surged through him, as fight-or-flight morphed into something that was more akin to primeval panic.

Do something.

Anything!

Rav looked Fox hard in the eye, and with a finality that the Professor wasn't quite sure was genuine, growled, "You don't want to know." He held the stare for a few seconds, then punched at the "1" button on the panel beside him. With a barely audible whine, the lift began to descend.

The passage of conscious time in Ivana's airborne apartment had now slowed to a frame-by-frame, slow-motion crawl. As Rav's desperate mental command of "Anything!" bounced around his various systems, it was his stomach that chose to step up to the plate, initiating a serious of initially dry heaves that quickly segued into a full on upchuck that sprayed the entire contents of his stomach onto the thick, shag pile carpet.

Rav broke through Ivana's stunned, horrified silence by pointing at the bathroom. "Do you mind if I, erm, visit…"

The Professor thought it best to change tack. "So how long do you think we've got before she notices that her card has gone?"

Rav shrugged. "I left her micromanaging a maid on a cleaning job. I figure if I can get back there within twenty minutes, they'll still be at it and I can put the card back in her handbag, and she won't ever know."

Fox's left eyebrow resumed its dance. "Cleaning job?"

"Like I said, you don't want to know."

The lift eased to a halt, with the smooth elegance one would expect from an item custom created by Airbus's Corporate Jets division, and opened its doors to reveal a gleaming, gold Rolls Royce Phantom, parked inside a bright, aluminium garage lined with an array of high-tech lockers.

Beside the Professor, Rav let out an awed sigh, followed by a muttered, "Shit…"

The Professor was no particular fan of things automotive, so much so that he'd once mistaken Nigel Mansell for a photocopier repairman. But even he had to admit that this was a magnificent piece of machinery, if also a tad vulgar, and unsafe to boot, given that its gold bodywork was so reflective that if driven on a sunny day it surely risked burning out the retinas of oncoming drivers. Rav crouched down and breathed on a section of door, which proceeded to fog up, as gold does.

After a few seconds, Fox interrupted the silence, breaking the spell the car had cast over them all, Jess excepted. "Right! To work!" He looked down at Jess, who looked warily back at him, then looked back to Rav and the Professor. "Does that dog always look like she's suspicious about something?"

Rav shrugged. "Pretty much. If there was magic around here, she'd be a lot more unhappy, so I think we're good. Where's the skull?"

Fox grinned one of his trademark Cheshire Cat grins, then reached out to open the locker beside which he was standing. Inside was a plain brown canvas tool bag, which he carefully lowered to the floor. He reached inside, his hand emerging holding a skull, poor-Yorick style. "Mister Shah. Professor Richardson. Never let it be said that Her Majesty's officers do not keep their promises."

Chapter Twenty-Five

Rav's woollen balaclava was scratchy upon his face. He checked his watch. Three minutes since the last time he'd checked it. The four of them were crouched down in a linen cupboard a few feet down from the museum, with no option left on the table than to wait for the alarm to go off. This was it. No plan B. At his feet, Jess was still letting out the low growl she'd begun to emit as soon as they'd exited the lift onto the upper corridor. Rav was hoping that a low growl rather than complete freak-out implied that while there were magical items in the museum, there was no full-on magical security system.

He hoped.

Not for the first time, it occurred to him that things would have been so much easier had Jess been the sort of dog beloved of those old time Saturday morning movie matinees. "What's that, girl? There's a magical beam, scanning across the room at a height of a metre?"

He checked his watch again.

Four minutes.

Then the shrill staccato beeps of an angry alarm cut through the silence.

Rav pushed himself to his feet. "Okay, let's go!"

The room was full of evil, so much so that when Rav hurled her through the doorway Jess didn't know whether to fight, run, or hide, and if she were to fight, what to fight, and if she were to hide, what to hide from. So she darted and barked, and barked and darted, her heart racing so fast it felt like it would burst in her chest. Amid the evil, a pulsing noise was thudding around the room, pitched so high her teeth were hurting. Rav and Fox were somewhere behind her, and Mindy and Jackson were there too, in the heart of the danger, with two other women, shouting women, women who, unlike the things around her, weren't actually evil but were very, very angry—

And then the noise was stopping, and Mindy was grabbing her, and talking, leading her out of the room of evil.

Somewhere in Jess's limited but still capable brain, a set of learning subroutines added yet another entry to the long list of occasions when Rav had led her right into deep shit. In as much as a dog is capable of making resolutions, Jess made one.

There'd better be a good-sized treat at the end of this.

Rav could hardly believe it. It had all worked like clockwork. Better than that, even. It couldn't have run smoother if it were hand-made Swiss clockwork lubricated by a good spray of WD40. While Jess, Mindy and Jackson had distracted Evie and Menschikov's PA, Rav and Fox had made their way along the opposite side of the museum in low crouches, swapped the skulls, and snuck back out. Five seconds later they were piling into the lift, which the Professor had called as soon as the three of them had exited the cupboard, and Rav was punching at the "1" button.

The lift began to descend.

The Professor nodded at the skull cradled against Rav's chest. "Is that Saint Horace?"

Rav nodded, feeling a grin starting to emerge. They'd done it. They'd actually done it.

The lift glided to a halt, the doors opening to reveal the gold-plated plutocrat-wagon. Fox was already striding along the garage between car and wall, towards the locker where the holdall was stored. "Gentlemen!" he barked. "Balaclavas and gloves off. We'll shove them all back in the holdall with the skull for Rav to take out with his DJ-ing equipment."

For a moment Rav let his head tip forward into his hands as he began to transition from adrenaline high to adrenaline crash. He felt Fox lifting the skull away from him, gave himself a moment to take a deep breath, then pulled the balaclava off his head — to see Fox stepping away from him, holding the skull in one hand and pulling some sort of backpack out of the opened locker.

Fox strapped the strange looking backpack on, flipping the skull from one hand to the other as he did so, then hit a stud at the far end of the garage, located above the car's long nose. A low growl emerged from somewhere around them, and the floor began to tilt.

In hindsight, jumping Fox right at that moment — in the couple of seconds or so the leisurely working of the ramp had granted them — would have been a good move. But stunned as he was, Rav merely watched as the floor's tilt continued to increase, the far end dropping to reveal a blue sky set above a carpet of white, fluffy cloud. Meanwhile, a hurricane of air was rushing past Rav; the pressurised air, he realised, pouring out into the rarefied atmosphere outside, so hard that he was having to brace himself against the car. Fox lifted some sort of mask to his face and then, holding the skull against his chest with one hand and cheerily waving with the other, stepped backwards off what was now a ramp and disappeared from view.

A second later, the holdall followed him through the open maw.

For an uncomprehending moment, Rav thought Fox had killed himself, until two realisations crashed in, the first being that the backpack had been a parachute and the second being that the bastard had double-crossed them. Then a third realisation arrived: that the rush of air was ceasing, accompanied by a light-headed sensation in his head and a burning in his lungs. The elevator doors must have formed a pressurised seal, meaning that while the rest of the plane might be safe from depressurisation, he and the Professor were not. He took a worried look sideways; the Professor was similarly wedged in front of the car but was near to fainting.

He had to get the ramp closed now, or the two of them would die here.

When the floor had dropped away, with the car attached to it by a set of four clamps, a narrow ledge had remained along the length of the garage, flanking the lockers. Rav edged along it, trying not to look down at the fluffy clouds showing through the gap, a gap that looked ever bigger as he worked his way along. Finally, he made it to the far end, the thumping in his head telling him that he had only seconds of consciousness thought remaining. There were a bunch of buttons there. But which button to close the ramp? Which button?

He pressed one.

Four simultaneous cracks sounded, dull in the thin air, as four clamps abruptly released. Slowly, fighting against its parking brake, the Roller slid down the ramp and dropped lazily into the blue sky, holding steady for a moment before tumbling end-over-end. From somewhere a dim thought oozed through what was currently passing for Rav's brain.

They really should have put the hand brake on.

He hit the button beside the one that had turned out to be the wrong button, operating now not so much on instinct as panic, and a deep inner reluctance to give up and die. The ramp began to come back up. Slowly, so slowly. It clicked into place, and after several seconds, Rav heard a hiss of incoming air and realised that his lungs were no longer coming up empty. He staggered back over to the Professor, who, thankfully, had not followed the car into the void. "We need to get out of here. They'll have had about a thousand alarms go off on the flight deck."

The Professor nodded, straightened up, then blinked. "What happened to the car?"

Chapter Twenty-Six

A thousand alarms had indeed gone off on the flight deck, and that had been their salvation, necessitating a precautionary emergency landing at Glasgow's Prestwick airport, accompanied by all the usual accoutrements — siren-blaring fire engines, ambulances, passengers exiting via the inflatable slides, and a total absence of any kind of Dunkirk spirit (said oft-quoted spirit having proven to be, as is so often the case, good at talking the nationalistic talk but an utter failure when trying to walk the cold-reality walk).

Having said that, it probably didn't help that the plane's occupants consisted in the main of braying toffs with an entitlement complex, Z-list celebrities with self-beliefs that far exceeded any actual talent, and a bunch of minimum wage Eastern European workers who — quite understandably — had zero desire to suffer any personal risk in order to protect the previous two groups. Add in firefighters and maintenance workers trying to do their jobs, airport PR and liaison teams trying to make some sense of the situation, a hundred or so people trying to call for an Uber, the sleeting Glasgow night, and any number of drunken and/or drugged up idiots who, having enjoyed the rides down the slides, were now trying to climb back up them, events swiftly went from bad, but manageable, to worse.

To call the resulting situation "chaos" would be an understatement so huge that it was almost an insult to the word itself. But for lack of any better phrase in the thesaurus, that "chaos" had allowed Rav, the Professor, Jackson, Sam, Mindy, and Jess to slip away. Now, an hour or so later, holed up in a Premier Inn a little way outside the airport perimeter, they could finally turn their attention to what in the name of hell had happened. Rav and the Professor had already given their colleagues the summary on the way over, that summary being "that bastard Fox shafted us", but now they retold the story, from the start, minus the expletives.

But all the way along, one thought was going through Rav's brain.

I've screwed up.

Epically.

Finally, Rav stuttered to a halt, as one does when retelling a story that has no satisfying ending. "So, erm, yeah. That's it." He looked around the tiny twin-bed room, at the ten pairs of eyes staring back at him — God, even the dog looked disappointed. "Sorry guys. I don't know what to say. This is such a screw-up I'm not even quite sure how, or where, we screwed up."

Sam walked over to him and patted him on the back. "Don't worry about it. Like it says in James chapter three, verse two, we all stumble in many ways."

"That's the New Testament," Jackson pointed out, a faintly protesting smile appearing on what had been a pretty downcast face.

"It's a good book!" Sam replied, chuckling. "Look, you people can't go around leaving copies of it in every hotel room from Almaty to Anchorage and then complain when people read it! Anyhow, look. Something's happened. We need to figure out what it is."

"Fox clearly ain't who he said he was," said Jackson.

"And he wanted the skull," said Mindy. "Like, he set this whole thing up so we could help him steal it, right?"

The Professor nodded. "It would appear that way."

"So Menschikov's got nothing to do with conspiracy? He's just some collector that got to something the conspirators wanted before they did?"

"Again, that would appear to be the case."

"Hang on. Doesn't that mean that we weren't on Menschikov's shit list before, but we are now, on account of stealing his skull, ruining his birthday party, and making his plane do an emergency landing?"

"And dumping his gold-plated Rolls Royce into the sky thirty-five thousand feet up," added Jackson.

"That too."

Rav dragged his depressed brain back into the conversation. "I'm thinking he won't know it was us. I managed to catch up with Ivana on the way out and slide the card back into her handbag. And we swapped the skulls, so hopefully he won't spot that. Why should he suspect the DJ, a waiter, and a couple of the guests? I mean you guys, Jackson and Mindy, yeah you were in the museum when the Roller got dropped and the alarms went off, but that's actually like an alibi, right?" He trailed off. "Not that I'm not trying to say it wasn't still a massive screwup."

Sam was pacing the room now, counting points off on his fingers. "Okay, so we can conclude that Menschikov had nothing to do with the conspiracy. He was just some guy who bought a skull. Hopefully, he won't connect us to this evening's debacle, so let's forget that for now. I think it's safe to assume that Fox wanted the skull for some reason, didn't feel inclined to go after it himself, so he set up this situation so we'd get hold of it for him. But that would then imply that this was his plan right from the start—" His voice trailed off. "Where was this police station?"

Rav shrugged. "Dunno. Somewhere across the big river thing from the Old City."

"Across the Bosphorus? In Asia?"

"No, across the little river thing, then."

"The Golden Horn?"

"Yeah, that's the one. The police picked us up from a museum in the Old City and drove us across a bridge, but then we went into a maze of streets. To be honest, I wasn't really following where we were going."

The Professor shrugged helplessly. "If I were there, I think I could retrace my steps. But without being there, I am somewhat at a loss."

For the first time in the conversation, Jackson allowed a full smile to emerge. "Rav! You grabbed your laptop on the way out of the plane, right?"

Rav had indeed managed to grab his laptop. He reached down now and pulled it out of his backpack. "Yeah, why?"

Jackson spread his hands wide. "Street View, man. Street View."

Not for the first time, the Professor was forced to admit that, crude and uncouth as it often was, this new world of the twenty-first century was not without its wonders. Google's Street View was a marvel, a tool of wonder that allowed Jackson to drop a little figure of a man on a map of the Galata Bridge, to produce the view one would see were one to be standing, right now, at that location. Then slowly, hesitantly, they had "walked" across the bridge, and into the maze of streets beyond. There were a few false starts where they'd had to backtrack, and several occasions where it had taken several minutes of spinning the view for the Professor to spot some detail that hooked into his fragmented and fogged memories of that strange evening's drive of some weeks ago. But eventually, they "emerged" into a long narrow square that even the still-morose Rav admitted was definitely the place they'd been taken to. There was just one problem.

The police station that had stood at the centre of the square's western edge did not exist. Instead, in the spot that both Rav and the

Professor swore it would be, wedged in between a convenience store and a chemist's, was a narrow, three-storey building that appeared to house some sort of nondescript office.

"That's it!" said Rav, bafflement breaking into his voice. "I recognise those double doors. It looked exactly like that, but it had a police sign above it."

Jackson clicked his fingers. "Hang on. I read about something like this once. It's a scam where some people set up a fake police station. They'd go out, and arrest—" he made air quotes around the word arrest "—some tourists and take them back to the fake police station. Like they'd shove up a police sign thirty seconds before the tourists arrived, and then take it down thirty seconds after they got them through the door. Then all they had to do was spend an hour shouting at them, and then give them an on-the-spot fine." The air quotes came out again around the word fine. "The tourists would be so scared that they'd happily hand over a pretty big sum of money, just so they could get out."

"But they didn't fine us," Rav protested.

"No, but..."

Sam turned and jabbed the air. "Let's work this through. Let's say the police station isn't real. It's part of a pop-up scam run by some local grifters who generally use it to scam tourists. But Fox, he knows them, yeah? Is able to rent them and their scam to use as part of *his*."

"His scam being to trick Rav and the Prof into stealing the skull for him?" suggested Mindy.

"Exactly."

"But how exactly would he set this up?" asked the Professor. "How would he have determined that he could use us as pawns? How would he have arranged to have his associates perform our fake arrest at the museum, and how would he have known when we were there?"

"Osman." That one word was spoken by Rav, in a tone hard enough to punch through the conversation and cause five heads to swivel towards him, waiting for further elaboration. "Mehmet Osman," he resumed. "The curator at the museum. He's in on the whole thing."

"Go on," said Jackson.

"He must be the one who stole the tablet for the conspirators. If it was an inside job, that would explain a load of things, right? Fox must have been the one who got him to steal it, so as soon as the

Professor's friend, Lord Dene, called Osman to let him know we were coming to ask him questions about the tablet, he'd have been on the phone to Fox."

"Makes sense," said Sam.

"Fox could have then figured out that we were the people who'd bumped into his mate at the warehouse."

"How?" asked Mindy. "What would the connection have been?"

"Dene gave Osman our names, right? And he probably said the Professor was an old friend of his and that I was his younger colleague. Fox could figure out from the names that the Prof's white and I'm Asian, and if the description he had from his wizard mate was an old white guy and a young Asian guy, it ain't that hard to put two-and-two together.

"Knowing who we likely were," he continued, "he'd have known he had to do something to get us off the trail. And maybe at the same time, now he'd got the tablet, he'd been working on a second artefact the conspiracy needed, which was the skull of St Horace."

"Except he'd screwed up on that one," said Jackson. "He got there too late. Menschikov beat him to it."

"Yeah. Exactly. Knowing him, he probably tried to set up something overly clever and elaborate, something other than simply paying the damn price, and maybe while he was doing that, Menschikov came in and bought it. Who knows? But whatever, when we came along, he figured he could kill two birds with one stone and rectify a screwup. All he had to do was call in a favour from his grifter mates, then come out with a line of bullshit about being MI6 and send us off after the Russian in search of the skull. That way, he diverted us away from the trail, and it gave him a second chance of getting his hands on the skull without him having to get his hands dirty."

"Which turned out to be a half-decent plan," sighed Sam. "Given that he now has the skull." He sat up, a thought occurring to him. "And that ties everything together, right? The skull's connected to Fox. Fox is connected to the theft of the tablet. The tablet's connected to the tattoos because its text is part of the design. And the tattoos are connected to the conspiracy because India Ponsonby has one, and because it was the voice of the tattoo that—"

"Asag," Jackson said, interrupting.

"Sorry?"

"The voice of the tattoo," repeated Jackson. "It's called Asag.

From what Rav and the Professor have told us, it seems there's a demon called Asag that they've somehow captured and bound to the tattoos. That's the voice of the tattoo."

Sam nodded, in recognition of a point well made. "Sorry, yes. It was Asag who gave Rav the vision of the warehouse where he and the Professor found the ankh on the first night, and bumped into the wizard bloke on the second, which links him in."

The Professor cleared his throat. "But if Fox wasn't a member of MI6," he mused, "but is instead a member of the conspiracy, who on earth is he?"

A fleeting thought came to Rav, although it was not so much a tangible thought as a flash of intuition, something in his subconscious nagging at a not-quite-fully-recalled fragment. He reached down to his backpack and pulled out the card folder in which he'd been shoving any and all kinds of printed material relevant to the case.

"You remembered something?" asked Jackson.

"Don't know."

He flipped through the folder until he came to the item that his intuition was musing on: the torn-off fragment of shipping label upon which the bazaar smallholder's son had miswritten Menschikov's name. He held it for a moment, focusing on the writing, then flipped it over. His intuition was trying to tell him something. It had parked the clue train at the station, and now it was waiting for him to climb aboard. What was it?

"Dayjack Import Export Ltd," read the label.

Dayjack.

A thought came to him. A young, smiling, cravat-wearing Edward Fox, driving a sports car through nineteen-sixties France. The Day of the Jackal. Sixties movie classic. Day Jack. Fox. Posh smiling Englishman, charming but ruthless. Blond hair. Fox. Men who attempt to self-grant themselves laudatory nicknames. Men whose vanity influences the aliases they create. Men who name their endeavours to reflect their ego.

He grabbed the laptop from the coffee table and typed "Dayjack Import Export" into Google. A few seconds and a click later, and he was looking at Dayjack's home page. At the far end of the top menu strip was an "About" button. Rav clicked on it and found himself looking at a picture of the man he knew as "James Fox". He swivelled the laptop around so the others could see it.

"James Henderson," Jackson read. "Managing Director. Sorry, how? What?"

Rav handed over the shipping label. "This was the shipping label the boy at the bazaar wrote Menschikov's name on. He ripped it off one of the boxes his dad was throwing away. Looks like our man Fox is actually some sort of import-export guy, who ships stuff through Istanbul. He must have done some business with the guy who was selling the skull, perhaps part of some scheme to get hold of it. It's our dumb luck that this was the label the boy used."

Jackson was still holding the shipping label. "Maybe. Then again, it was his dumb stupidity to be using his day job business to deal with someone that he was trying to use for his conspiracy. Hang on—" He put the shipping label down and picked up the laptop. "There's an address here. Somewhere in Berkshire. Business park. Warehouse, maybe?"

For the first time since Fox had lowered the ramp, Rav felt a glimmer of something that might perhaps have been hope. "So that's our lead, right?"

Sam slapped him on the back. "I think it is, my friend. Guess we've got ourselves somewhere to stake out."

Chapter Twenty-Seven

It was a measure of how urgent their situation was that on the drive down from Glasgow in a hired car, Rav's suggestion that they take the M6 Toll road rather than the regular M6 was met with no opposition, something that was — in his previous experience — unprecedented. (His uncles Manan and Pranav had once had such a falling-out over this question, that to this day, they still had to be seated separately at family occasions). Stopping only to refuel, relieve bladders, purchase food, and make whatever phone calls needed to be made to justify their absences — something that in Rav's case involved a not terribly veiled suggestion from his boss Fen that he would be facing disciplinary action if and when he eventually managed to make it into work — they finally arrived in the vicinity of central Berkshire sometime in the early afternoon.

They'd not spent the journey entirely in silence. Large parts of it had been spent in animated discussion of what courses of action might be available to them. But when they arrived on the outskirts of Newbury, the town in which the warehouse was located, they'd still not managed to come to any consensus as to how they should proceed. It was while they were waiting to make the right turn into the business park that their ongoing discussions were interrupted by the arrival in the opposite direction of a white van whose driver Rav immediately recognised.

It was the frock-coated, dandy-haired wizard who'd cast the paralysis spell on him at the Grand Union canal.

"That's him!" Rav muttered.

"Who?" asked Jackson.

Two oncoming cars later, a break appeared in the traffic flow opposite. Rav gunned the accelerator and spun the car across the road and through the business park's open gates. The van was a little way ahead.

"That white van up there. The bloke driving it. He's the wizard who cast the spell on me."

"Two guesses where he's going," said Sam from behind them.

The white van did indeed pull up in front of a slightly tired looking warehouse with "Dayjack Import Export" written across it in peeling paint. Rav continued past, consciously avoiding any glances at the van and its occupant, and parked up a little way round the bend.

Handbrake on, he twisted round to address his four human — and one canine — companions.

"Now what?"

"Our wizard friend's appearance can hardly be a coincidence," said the Professor.

"No way," Mindy agreed. "He'll be here to pick up that skull, right?"

"We could wait for him to do whatever he's come here to do, and then try to trail the van?" Jackson suggested, the lack of enthusiasm in his tone betraying the doubts he felt over such a course.

"Be hard," Sam mused. "Trailing him all the way from here to West London, without either losing him or being clocked."

A course of action was already building its case within Rav's perpetually warring subconscious, but he resisted voicing that urge. He'd led his companions into enough trouble already, screwed up enough times. This time, this once, he'd rather let them (metaphorically) drive.

"And if we were to wait here," pointed out the Professor, "we would learn nothing of what might be being done, or said, during this meeting. It might be that our wizard friend has driven fifty miles down the M4 merely to pick up a parcel, but it might not. We have an opportunity to observe what might be the inner workings of this conspiracy, and risky as that might be, I can't help but feel that it's a risk we ought to take."

"You suggesting we sneak in?" asked Jackson.

"I believe I am."

Rav took the chance now to give a questioning glance to each one of his companions in turn, receiving from each some kind of nod, or wag, of acceptance (although to be fair to the dog, she probably thought she was merely signing up for a walk).

He turned back and pulled the ignition key out of the barrel.

"Okay. Let's do it."

It was once said of the Carthaginian general Hannibal that he knew how to gain a victory, but not how to use it. As they embarked on their attempt to break into the warehouse's locked rear entrance, the Professor couldn't help but feel that in their case, the situation was somewhat reversed, in that while they knew what to do once they penetrated the building, they were currently struggling to open its door. Rav was fumbling at the rusted handle, tugging and pulling at it as though if manipulated with sufficient firmness the lock might spontaneously open. Sam and Mindy were with the car, parked up out of sight, leaving only Jackson, the Professor, and Jess to huddle around Rav as he made his fruitless attempt at entry. Then a quote from Hannibal himself appeared in the Professor's thoughts.

I will either find a way, or make one.

He handed Jess's lead to the waiting Jackson, picked up a dirty piece of cloth that was in the process of being blown across the dusty rear yard, wrapped it round his fist, then punched hard at the dirty glass of the window situated next to the door. The glass held the first punch but cracked along its length at the impact of a second. He gave it a third, cautious punch, then reached in with his other hand to gently pull a shard of glass free, revealing an opening large enough for him to extend an arm through and open the door from the inside.

Rav gave him a look that mixed horror and admiration in equal measure then advanced through the door. The Professor waved Jackson and Jess through, took a last glance around the near enclosed yard, then followed.

The breakthrough had been made.

Now the victory needed to be seized.

The interior of the warehouse was dark enough that it took Rav's eyes a few seconds to adjust. They appeared to be in a dirty and cluttered kitchen area. A half-eaten pot noodle, a fork still extending from its open top, sat on a table whose monochrome Formica top had been rendered multi-coloured by an assortment of stubborn-looking food stains. At one end of the room, a battered fridge emitted an unpleasant sound pitched somewhere between a whine and a buzz. At the other, a grease-encrusted stovetop stood mercifully silent. Clearly, one would have needed a strong stomach to have the courage to eat anything prepared here, and a stronger stomach still to survive the experience without feeling the need to pebbledash the toilet.

From somewhere, a smell wafted on the air, a smell bad enough that Rav didn't need Jess's three-hundred million olfactory receptors to detect its existence and note that it was horrifically bad. Making sure to breathe though his mouth, he advanced past the fridge and peered through the open doorway that led to the warehouse's interior.

Frankly, he was almost disappointed in Fox. Annoyed to buggery and back as he had been by the man's betrayal, Fox had, by his appearance and demeanour, fed Rav's inner need to feel that his was a life of cinematic quality. The post-betrayal Fox had been the rogue MI6 agent from a Bond film, or the Eton-educated Russian from a Mission Impossible or Bourne flick. Posh, smooth-talking, slick, and charismatic — if a man can measure himself by the quality of his antagonist, then it had seemed to Rav that he must indeed be someone.

But then he'd found himself here, in this paint-peeling, crap-smelling, shit-heap of a warehouse — in sodding Newbury.

Newbury.

He pushed his annoyance to one side and concentrated instead on what he was now seeing. Beyond the door was an open space broken by the high vertical barriers of metal shelving units, each several metres in height and loaded with a variety of shrink-wrapped goods sitting on wooden pallets, through which filtered a number of muffled voices. Rav took a last look around, turned back to motion to the Professor and Jackson to follow him, then dashed across to the shelving, edging to the side to peer around the shrink-wrapped package he was hiding behind.

Up ahead, through the narrow gap between this package and the next, he could see Fox, the van, and a bunch of other blokes, but no wizard. Then he heard a low growling from Jess, who'd appeared beside him. He turned his head and saw the wizard standing at the end of the aisle, arms already raised, mouth moving, and felt—

A wave of evil flooded over Jess, making the hairs across her back stand on end and setting her whiskers twitching. Ahead of her, at the far end of the room, stood a man she recognised, the man she and Rav had chased beside the water some days ago. The bad man, whose badness was in some way linked to Rav falling into the canal.

She looked across at Rav, seeking his instruction, but he was still, not alert still, or careful still, but still like a tree, still like something not living. She looked back to the Professor and Jackson, but they too stood frozen, unmoving in a way she simply couldn't process. Not for the first time, Jess found herself unable to comprehend events (said incomprehension being a common circumstance when your brain's been forced to share the interior of a tennis ball-sized skull with a set of powerful jaw muscles and the jaw muscles got there first). Had her walnut-sized brain been more sophisticated, then she too might have been similarly enslaved by the spell, but she of course did not know that. She knew only one thing.

The bad man had done something to her pack.

She took a step back, and then another, whining in fear even though she knew there was no pack around her to receive the warning. Jess was not the bravest of dogs. Border Collies often aren't. Dumb, unthinking bravery is for Alsatians and Dobermans, not a creature bred through generations to solve problems and think creatively. And Jess was scared now, deeply scared, scared to her very core. Every instinct was telling her to bolt for the door through which they'd entered, and run, and not stop running.

But something told her no. Terrible pack member as he might be, perpetual disappointment as he was, Rav was still the man who fed her food, and somewhere deep in an instinctive loyalty bred over several tens of thousands of years, she knew that had to count for something.

A decision queued up inside her released, and with her paws scrabbling on the dirty concrete she set off straight at the bad man. He waved his arms and shouted angry words and she felt more evil washing over her, but the spirt of the wolf was within her now. She leapt, her jaws twisting to get at his throat, smashing into him and bowling him over.

—something.

Rav blinked. Jess had been right next to him, but now she wasn't. She was instead at the far end of the aisle on top of the now falling wizard, tearing at the man's face like a beast possessed. Rav wasn't quite sure what the hell had happened, and from the confused expressions bouncing across Jackson's face like the balls on a pinball table after the multi-ball option's been activated, the priest wasn't quite sure either.

And somewhere deep inside Rav's consciousness, his usually quiescent body clock was screaming a muted protest.

Then a bunch of blokes appeared from around the corner of the shelving stack, wielding Stanley-type knives and looking like they were quite keen to use them. Rav grabbed hold of a box and hauled hard on its corner, causing a stack of boxes to tumble onto the floor in between him and the guys with the knives, then hauled again to send a second stack tumbling after the first. A scrabble of claws told him that Jess had decided that she'd done her bit for now, and had beat a hasty retreat back to them. The boxes were being lifted, amid shouts and the scuffling of work boots on concrete. There were too many of them, and accompanying them was the wizard, who sooner or later was going to get over being savaged by a Border Collie and was going to get back up.

They weren't all going to get out of here. He grabbed hold of the Professor and shoved him towards the door, then grabbed hold of Jackson's arm. "Get him and Jess out of here!"

The priest made as though to argue, but then began moving as the reality of their situation presumably crashed in upon him. Rav grabbed hold of a strut on the shelving, pulled himself up, then kicked hard at a box to push it off the edge, hearing a satisfying cry as it crashed to the floor. Someone was grabbing at his foot, and he lashed out, feeling his trainer collide with someone's face. He twisted round, and saw Jess giving him a final guilty look as she paused at the door before turning to follow the departing backs of Jackson and the Professor.

More hands grabbed at him, and he fell, hard, to the floor.

And then the wizard was standing over him, angry, snarling, blood weeping from the cuts on his face even as his mouth shaped harsh and alien syllables and his hand reached out to point.

Rav made a last attempt to shake himself loose from his grapplers, but—

The universe froze.

Chapter Twenty-Eight

After making it into the car barely ahead of the pursuing pack of warehouse workers, the four of them — five, if you counted Jess — had headed south-east on the A339, not wanting to risk the M4, eventually joining the M3 at Basingstoke and following that into London, finally holing up in a budget hotel somewhere off the Hammersmith flyover.

Running out on Rav like that had felt like cowardice to the Professor; but how could they fight against people who were able to freeze their souls by the mere speaking of words, and who now were forewarned of their presence? To have broken into the warehouse without planning had, in hindsight, been reckless. To attempt a second entry would have been suicidal, and by the time they managed it, Rav and his captors would no doubt have been long gone.

Now, sitting in Jackson and Sam's hotel room, in one of its two functional chairs, he glanced around at his companions, seeing that they looked as defeated as he: Jackson, lost in thought; Mindy blinking through the tears she was clearly determined not to cry; Jess, head cradled upon paws; and Sam on the phone to his family, using a cheap pay-as-you-go they'd picked up at a roadside stop, his tone grim. They'd discussed their situation during the two-hours-plus drive; they'd made no progress then, and little since.

On the wall, the television had spent the last half hour silently displaying the ten o'clock news. Jackson reached for the remote and dialled the volume up, his body language that of a man killing time. The newsreader finished an item, paused, smiled, and then launched into what was clearly pitched as an interesting diversion to end the broadcast.

"And finally, Police Scotland are baffled by a rather unusual crash deep in the heart of the Cairngorm mountains."

The view shifted to a shot of gorse-covered peaks, before which stood a wind-worn old man and a smartly anoraked newsman, microphone in hand.

"I were taking the dogs for a walk," the old man said, in the tone of a man who's already told the story enough times that his memory of the telling of the story is in danger of overtaking his memory of the actual event. "When I saw it."

"And what was that?" the newsman asked.

"Well now, at first I thought it must have been a plane crash, what with it being this far up the mountain, and the way it was just fragments of metal scattered across four, maybe five acres. But the metal fragments were gold, and I never did hear of a gold aeroplane. And then I found a steering wheel—"

The TV clicked off.

"I had a thought," Jackson said. "My predecessors at the Deliverance Ministry have been keeping records for centuries. All right, not quite as many as me, perhaps. But there are records. Maybe there's something in there that might help us."

"What would you look for?" asked Sam. "We haven't really got anything to go on, have we?"

"Dunno."

A thought occurred to the Professor. "Mortimer. Sir Edward. Given that his novel was published in 1937, we can reasonably assume that he was active in the mid-nineteen thirties. Perhaps he did something to come up on the radar of your predecessors of that era?"

Jackson managed something that wasn't quite a smile but had a suggestion of a nod. "Seems worth a try," he said, hauling himself to his feet. "I'm not in the mood to sleep. You want to come with me, Prof? Sam, you and Mindy maybe stay here, try and get some rest?"

The Universe resumed. Rav was sitting in a chair, in a room he had never been in before. For perhaps the first time in his life, he felt absolutely at peace. He had no doubts now, no confusion, no desire other than to do everything he could to please the man sitting in front of him. The man leaned forward and spoke.

"Do you know who you are?"

"Yes."

"Who are you?"

"Ravinder Shah."

"Good. Now I'm going to ask you some questions, and you're going to answer them."

The Church of England Record Centre, to which Jackson had taken the Professor, turned out to be located in an anonymous office building in Southwark, in a leafy street whose central London location was betrayed only by the huge viaduct that ran some way behind it, carrying the mainline Southern railway into the heart of

London. This late at night, the building was occupied only by a lone security guard, but Jackson apparently had some kind of metaphorical all-hours pass, because a few brief words had the guard ushering both of them in. Jackson led the Professor past the various public rooms until they found themselves down in the basement, before a locked door.

Jackson took a card out from his wallet and shoved it into a slot beside the door. "This is where we keep the sensitive records," he said. After a second's pause, a light lit green and something within the door clicked. The priest pushed it open to reveal a darkened room. He reached around to flick a switch, triggering an array of neon lights, which flickered on one-by-one, gradually revealing a large space covered with metal shelving units full of cardboard boxes. Jackson shrugged. "It's not particularly well indexed. At least, my stuff isn't. Come on. I'll show you where it is, and we can take it a box at a time."

Jackson had not been joking when he'd referred to the lack of filing systems. The Deliverance Ministry's archives were simply a bunch of shelved boxes in the far corner, one box per year, with that year's contents shoved in randomly. For want of any better strategy, they divvied the task up with Jackson taking the even numbers and the Professor taking the odd, starting with the box for 1938 and working backwards.

It was slow going, made all the more exhausting by the lateness of the hour and the harshness of the cold, neon-lit environment. Much of it was mundane; reports of what would now be recognised as mental illness interspersed with the administrative detritus that had infested damn near all human activity since the first tax-related scratchings on ancient Mesopotamian clay tablets.

Admittedly, there was the occasional interesting nugget, such as a fascinating account of a vicar who'd managed to disappear without trace from within a locked room. But of Sir Edward Mortimer, or tattoos, or strange cults in West London, there was no mention. And then, while the Professor was almost midway through the 1933 box, Jackson let out a hopeful sounding, "Ah-ha!"

The Professor laid the stack of paper he was currently searching through onto the large reading table he'd commandeered, and stepped over to the table where his colleague had been working on the 1934 box. "Do you have something?"

"Might do," Jackson grunted, his eyes flicking from left to right as he read through the typed document he was holding. He finished reading, paused for a moment, then handed it to the Professor. "It's a letter sent out by the vicar of a church in Richmond to one of my predecessors, stating his concerns that a couple at his church had got into some sort of secret society that he feared was having a corrosive impact on their spiritual health. But the bit that caught my eye was this." He reached over and stabbed his finger on a section of the letter around two-thirds down.

"I have been assured," the Professor read aloud, "by another of my parishioners, Sir Edward Mortimer, who is also a member of this secretive society, this Hidden Mysteries Society, that it is a harmless gathering devoted to the pursuit of Oriental archaeological knowledge."

"That's pretty much it," said Jackson.

The Professor quickly scanned through the letter. Other than that one tantalising detail, the letter dealt merely with the spiritual health of the unnamed couple, and a request for general advice about how such matters might be handled. The Professor put the letter down, then pointed at the box. "Perhaps there might be a follow up report in there?"

Jackson smiled. "Good point. Let's check."

They went through the rest of the box, and then rechecked the contents Jackson had already examined, but found nothing. Whatever the true story might have been of this unnamed nineteen-thirties couple, it was a story that had only briefly spluttered into life before going cold — or at least, if there had been more to the story, it was a truth that had failed to find its way into the archives.

The two of them sat down, deflated. Failure would have been one thing, but this was much harder to bear. Nearly a century ago, the truth had been out there waiting to be grasped, but those who'd been tasked with grasping it had spurned the chance, and now any information that had been left behind was virtually useless. There were no witnesses they could interview, since all concerned would now have returned to the soil whence they came. Then the Professor realised that Jackson was not in a similar state of deflation as he but was instead tapping upon his teeth in a manner that the Professor had learned indicated that the younger man was lost in thought. After a few seconds he spoke. "That society."

"The Hidden Mysteries Society?"

"Yeah. I've heard that somewhere before. I just can't place it."

This not being something the Professor could help him with, he could only sit silently alongside Jackson as he settled into a near trance. Then, what must have been a good several minutes in, Jackson stiffened so sharply it was as though a switch had been thrown. "Got it!" he announced. "I was doing some background research for a case I'd been working on. A woman who'd had a troubled upbringing on account of a mother with a history of mental illness. I found out that the mother had herself come into contact with us back in the seventies, back when people were still inclined to see such things as demonic possession, and I wanted to look at the case notes. There was something in the year I was searching through about a Hidden Mysteries Society. It wasn't connected to her case, so I didn't look at it in any detail."

"And which year would this be?"

"1973," said Jackson after a moment's thought. "Glam rock and all that."

The Professor allowed himself the luxury of a minor smile. "Perhaps we should search through 1973's box?"

The nineteen-seventies were on an adjacent shelf. Jackson located the box and lifted it onto a table. The Professor watched silently as the younger man efficiently worked through the cluttered contents. Then finally, when he was nearly at the bottom, Jackson draw out a card folder, upon which was printed in neat, hand-lettered block capitals, the words "Hidden Mysteries Society". He rested the folder's spine upon his hand and then carefully opened it, to reveal a sheaf of neatly fastened documents, some typed, some handwritten.

He looked up at the Professor, smiling. "Bingo!"

Chapter Twenty-Nine

It was breakfast the next morning before they were able to report back with their findings, Mindy and Sam having both been asleep when they'd finally returned to the hotel, and the Professor and Jackson feeling dead on their feet. Three hours of sleep later, the Professor wasn't feeling significantly more human, so he let Jackson do the talking.

"Okay," the priest was saying. "So first we found a reference from 1934 to a society that Mortimer was apparently a member of, called the Hidden Mysteries Society, which he claimed was a harmless organisation dedicated to the study of archaeological knowledge."

"Harmless?" queried Sam.

"Apparently not, because the reference was in a letter from a vicar concerned about the effects that membership of this society was having on the spiritual health of a couple attending his church."

"That sounds exactly like what we're looking for, right?" said Mindy.

"Yeah, except there's basically no detail at all in the letter except for the mention of Mortimer."

The priest let that hang in the air for the moment, but it was obvious from the smile edging onto his face that he had more information to deliver. Eventually, Sam gave up waiting. "Go on then!" he said, smiling. "Spit it out."

"Then I remembered that somewhere I'd seen a reference to a Hidden Mysteries Society in a box from the nineteen-seventies that I'd searched through a while back looking for something completely different. And this—" he paused to pull the card folder out of the Tesco bag-for-life within which it had been resting, "—is it. A rather comprehensive account of the nineteen-seventies incarnation of the Hidden Mysteries Society."

"Sorry," said Mindy. "The nineteen-seventies incarnation? You're saying this thing's been going on since the seventies?"

Jackson shook his head. "No. What seems to have happened is this. The society existed in the thirties. We don't know much about this, but we're guessing that at some point it fizzled out. Then in the late sixties, a new incarnation of the society apparently started, one which ended up appearing on the radar of one of my predecessors when they were discovered performing some sort of ritual on the altar of a church in Twickenham."

"Some sort of… ritual?"

"Yeah. Exactly. That sort of ritual. Anyhow, the gist of it is that initially my predecessor was worried they were dabbling in some quite serious magic, but it seems like eventually they all got side-tracked by the whole sex-magic thing and it basically just degenerated into some kind of wife-swapping circle."

Sam was clearly having to work hard to keep a straight face. "Okay, so we have a first incarnation of the society back in the thirties. And they maybe had some sort of plan, but for whatever reasons, couldn't carry it out. So Mortimer prepared a sort of occult time capsule which he intended for a later generation who would re-found the society, bring him back in some way, and then presumably carry out his plan. And that started to happen in the sixties, but the people concerned didn't quite manage to get their act together."

"Either that, or they found the wife-swapping more interesting," said Mindy, who was also trying to keep a straight face.

"Exactly. But it seems that the time capsule — the flip-books and whatever else — was still around, and got found a second time, by people who then created a third incarnation of the society. And this time they're not getting distracted by the possibility of some easy sex." The rabbi thought for a moment. "But how does the knowledge of the middle group help us, if it's the third group we're looking for?"

Jackson pointed down at the card folder. "Because there's a lot more detail in here. The ringleaders of the group were a bloke called Peter Bishop, and his wife, Cynthia. Meetings used to take place at their house in Richmond, something my predecessor found particularly concerning as they had a young son, Jason, who would now be in his early fifties."

Sam pursed his lips. "Anyone else thinking we ought to try checking out one Jason Bishop?"

The plan had been for Jackson and the Professor to perform a drive-by reconnaissance of a house in Mortlake registered to a Jason Bishop, with a potential follow-up investigation on foot. However, as one-time Prussian Chief of Staff Helmuth von Moltke the Elder had once sagely remarked, no battle plan survives contract with the enemy, for when a plan meets the real world, the real world invariably wins. And thus far, it did indeed appear that reality was currently well ahead of them on points.

On this occasion, as Jackson drove the hire car slowly past the target location, it quickly become apparent that once again, events were going to seize control of the narrative. A hired Volkswagen van was parked outside of the house, the knowledge that it was hired acquired not though any Sherlockian levels of deduction but through simple observation of the slogan "Easy Hire Vans" emblazoned in red upon its side. A dazed-looking Rav was being guided towards the van's open rear doors by the frock-coated wizard. The man looked up and gazed straight at them as they glided past at a stately speed that now seemed absurdly pedestrian, even if it was in compliance with the newly installed twenty miles-per-hour speed limit.

Jackson was viewing events through the rear-view mirror. "They're doing a runner."

He immediately swung the car sharply to the right. Had they been American, this might have been the start of a tyre-screeching handbrake turn. However, given the narrower width of UK roads, the aforementioned speed limit, and basic civic decency, it was instead merely the prelude to a hurried, kerb clipping, three-point turn of the sort that would have a British driving examiner shaking their head and marking a small cross on their clipboard.

As they completed the manoeuvre, the van was already setting off back down the way they'd just come, a cloud of dirty smoke pouring from its rear exhaust pipe. It reached the end of the street and took a sharp right, the resulting chorus of horns indicating the degree to which this operation had failed to comply with the Highway Code.

Jackson braked to a halt beside the give way sign, cursing under his breath. Lines of slowly moving traffic moved up and down a high street that could have been any one of a thousand across the urban sprawl that was Greater London. Jackson edged the car forward into a break in the traffic that could just about be called a gap, waited a moment, then spun the car into a squealing right turn in front of an oncoming camper van. "Can you see them?" he asked.

The Professor leaned to his left, trying to see round the cars in front, and was rewarded with intermittent glimpses of the Volkswagen's flank a little way ahead. "Yes. They're four cars further on. And apparently weaving."

"They're trying to overtake. No, wait. They've cocked it up."

Ahead of them, the van had moved out into the oncoming lane in an attempt to overtake, only to find itself halted nose-to-nose with a bus that had chosen that moment to pull out of its stop, and whose driver was now angrily gesticulating at the van's driver. After a few seconds, the van pulled back into its own lane, but only after Jackson and the Professor had managed to draw to within one car of it.

The convoy of traffic glided down the street at second-gear pace before being halted by a red light at the junction that lay at the end of the street.

"Should I perhaps get out?" the Professor asked.

"And do what?"

"I could try opening the rear door."

Ahead of them, the van was creeping, slowly eating up the inches that lay between it and whatever vehicle was in front.

"Worth a try, I guess."

The Professor got out of the car and walked past the silver Nissan Micra that separated the two vehicles, horribly aware that he would be easily visible in the van's large passenger-side wing mirror, but not sure quite what he could do about it. But after what turned out to be an anti-climactic few seconds, he reached the van's rear door unscathed and reached out to tug on the door handle.

It was locked.

The lights chose that moment to change, followed an instant later by a fresh billow of smoke as the van pulled away. The Professor stepped out of the path of the Micra (whose elderly driver appeared to be in no mood to yield to any pedestrians), and quickly bundled himself in beside Jackson as the priest momentarily braked to a halt beside him. Then they followed the van through the left turn into a new set of traffic, this one even more choked than the previous iteration.

They were now right behind the van. Waiting. Unmoving.

"This is the South Circular at lunchtime," Jackson remarked. "It's going to be the shittiest car chase ever."

The pause gave the Professor time to consider the sight of an almost soulless Rav being ushered into the van that now stood before them, a soulless Rav who was now mere feet away from them, but imprisoned both physically and mentally. "I fear Ravinder will not be able to aid us in his rescue."

"No."

The traffic moved forward several feet, then stopped again.

"Problem is," mused Jackson, " I don't really want to encounter that evil sod Bishop. Not when he can bind a man to evil with thoughts alone."

"Should not your faith, if forewarned, protect you against his magic?"

Jackson gave the Professor an exasperated look. "Theoretically, yeah." He looked up at the car's cream padded ceiling, spent several seconds engaged in what looked to be some sort of inner struggle, then smiled a rueful smile. "Fuck it." He flicked the car door open and climbed out, unzipping his leather jacket and reaching inside to grasp the wooden crucifix that hung round his neck. He raised it towards whatever washed out sunshine was making it through the overcast sky.

"Our Father in heaven," he screamed, as he walked towards the van, the crucifix held out before him. "Hallowed be your Name."

After a moment's pause, the Professor opened his own door and eased himself out with as much haste as he could muster.

"Your Kingdom come," Jackson cried. "Your will be done on earth as in heaven."

The priest appeared to be causing something of a stir, this degree of uninhibited religious activity not being something to which British people are accustomed. Hands were being pointed; pictures were being taken on camera phones; sandwich and pasty eaters were pausing mid-bite. As the Professor continued forward on the other side of the van, he lost sight of Jackson but could still hear his impassioned, shouted prayer.

"Give us today our daily bread."

The Professor reached the passenger side door and peered in; the wizard, Bishop, was sitting in the driver's seat, looking away from the Professor at the almost unnatural, not-of-this-Earth features of the priest screaming at him through the opposite window.

"Forgive us our sins," Jackson shouted. "As we forgive those who sin against us."

Bishop opened his door, and got out, Jackson dropping back before him as though repelled, but still shouting, still holding the crucifix outstretched. "Lead us not into temptation. But deliver us from evil."

The Professor tugged at the passenger side door handle; it opened. He leaned in, only to discover that behind the two seats lay a solid wall of rough chipboard that completely separated him from the van's cargo compartment, and Rav.

"For the kingdom, the power…"

The wizard paused before Jackson, his long frock coat falling over his immaculately pressed denim jeans, his hair flowing over his shoulders, he and the priest, utterly incongruous in the South London street.

"…and the glory, are yours."

Bishop raised his hands and began to chant, but his actions were hesitant, his words choked, the supercilious sneer that had marked his features when he'd previously cast, gone now.

"Now… and forever!"

The wizard's chant stuttered. He paused and took a step back. Then he spun round, breaking into a sprint that took him away down the street, weaving between the paused pasty eaters and the phone-wielding picture takers.

Jackson took a step forward on shaky legs, breathed deeply, then looked to the sky.

"Amen."

For a few seconds the two of them watched Bishop running into the distance. Then Jackson reached in to grab the van keys, which were still in the ignition.

"Come on," he said. "Let's get Rav out." A thought flickered across his face. "You know what? Maybe we should take the van as well. Might be something useful in it."

Chapter Thirty

Getting Rav back to the hotel had been something of a logistical challenge. They'd considered it prudent to stop halfway and dump the van in case it had some sort of tracking device installed, and when it turned out to be loaded with various boxes, figured they should take those as well. But having eventually got Rav, and the contents of the van, back to the hotel, a more serious problem became apparent. Rav was still deep in the grip of whatever magic had been cast upon him. He was completely unresponsive, so much so that when Mindy ran an upturned finger back and forth before his face, his eyes stayed rigidly locked ahead. Shouts, shaking, and even a not-so-mild slap made no change to his condition. He simply sat on the sofa to which they'd guided him, staring sightlessly at the wall opposite.

Eventually, they gave up trying to break the spell, and while Mindy spoon-fed him a mashed-up lunch and squirted bottled water down his throat, they turned their attention to the rather large pile of boxes that a sweating Jackson had now carried up from the hotel's basement car park. Opening them one by one, they began to take inventory.

Clothes.

More clothes.

Crockery, mixed in with cutlery.

Pots, pans, and casserole dishes.

Magazines: horse riding, mountaineering, pornography, new age self-help, more pornography, word searches, cookery, classical music, and yet more pornography.

"I guess you could call that eclectic," remarked Sam.

Ornaments and fridge magnets.

Random pieces of electrical crap.

Finally, there was only one box left. Jackson sliced open the parcel tape, opened up the cardboard flaps, and peered in.

"What the hell?"

"What is it?" asked Mindy.

Jackson lifted out a small wire cage, holding it by the folding handle affixed to its top. Inside was a small blue house, apparently full of straw, and a brown rat that currently stood on its hind legs, gripping the bars with its front paws and staring hard at Jackson. The priest pointed at it. "It's a rat."

"Who the hell puts a rat in cardboard box?" mused Mindy.

Jackson shrugged, then pointed at the holes punched through the side of the box. "Guess that's what the holes are for. But yeah, these people do strike me as a bit sociopathic."

"Anything else?" asked the Professor.

Jackson put the cage down beside him, and turned his attention back to the box, rifling through its contents. "Some straw, food, and a…" He pulled out a red, bulbous, rubber figure of a man. "Dog chew toy?"

"And that's it?" Sam queried.

Jackson took a final look through the box. "Yep?"

The Professor sat back on his char. "So what now, gentlemen and lady?"

Jess was bored to doggy tears. She'd been in this room for what seemed like an eternity, while the Professor, Jackson, Sam, and Mindy talked. And talked. And talked. They were upset, she knew that; they'd been emitting stress and spraying the scent of fear for days. And now their voices were raised and full of confusion. She didn't particularly care; whatever problem they had was for them to worry about. She wanted to get out, have a walk, sniff some smells.

She'd tried the usual repertoire she deployed on such occasions: the whine; the paw on the arm; the meaningful stare at the door. She'd even tried scratching at the door. But whatever it was the others were talking about, it was clearly more important to them than her. And Rav was no help at all. He sat looking straight ahead, lifeless, in a way she found deeply disturbing, enough so that she made no attempt to request his aid in her pursuit of a walk.

Eventually, accepting that a walk simply wasn't going to happen anytime soon, she retreated to the far corner of the room where she found that some sort of chew toy had appeared. This, at least, was something positive. She settled down, gripped it between her two front paws, and began to chew.

Rav screamed.

It took the Professor a moment to process events, so disconnect[ed] had Rav been from the almost heated conversation that had b[een] going on for the last half hour. He quickly stepped over[, and] crouched beside him. "Ravinder?"

Rav didn't respond. Though there was pain in his eyes, he still appeared unaware of his surroundings. Jess appeared beside the Professor and started sniffing at Rav's legs in concern.

Mindy was the other side of Rav. "Rav! What's up? Can you hear me?"

Nothing.

For long seconds they stared at him, willing his spirit to return. But eventually, when it became apparent that the scream had been some sort of transient event that would not be repeating itself, they returned to their places — the Professor on the chair, Sam on the bed, Jackson leaning against the en-suite door frame, and Jess in the corner with the chew toy.

Sam shook his head. "Anyone got any—"

Rav screamed again. Five heads swivelled back towards him. The Professor observed him for several seconds, then turned his attention back to Jess, who was lying down with the chew toy gripped between her two front paws, her snout now pointed at Rav. "I think Ravinder's episodes of pain might be occurring when Jess chews that toy."

Jackson shoulder-shoved himself away from the doorframe, walked over to Jess, and then in one fluid movement reached down to deftly tug the chew toy from between the dog's paws. Ignoring the furious glare that Jess sent his way in retaliation, he held the man-shaped toy up in front of him, then gave one of the man's arms an experimental bend.

Across the room, Rav flinched.

Jackson glanced across at Sam. "Are you thinking what I'm thinking?"

"That they've bound the toy to him to use as an interface to the spell?"

"Yeah. Something like that."

"Hang on," said Mindy, waving her hands in confusion. "Are you ⸱g that's like some sort of voodoo doll?"

⸱ave her a pained grimace. "Yeah, sort of. In both cases, the ⸱ically linked to a person, such that an action on the item ⸱rson. But it's not like in the films where you start ⸱he doll. The theory, as I understand it, is that once ⸱p, you can cast spells on the person by casting

"

Jackson took over. "Say you need to cast a really heavy-duty spell against someone, and it's a spell that you need to touch them to cast, but you can't because they're fifty miles away in a concrete bunker, lined with barbed wire, and guarded by Rottweilers and mercenaries. But luckily, you earlier cast a spell to magically link them to a separate object."

Mindy nodded. "Oh, I see. If you've got the item, you can cast the spell on the item, touching that, and it will then affect the poor bastard who's fifty miles away in the concrete bunker."

"Yeah. Supposedly."

"And if we had Rav now, like we do, but they still had the toy, they could start casting spells on him to make him attack us, or try to escape, or whatever." She shuddered. "Good job we've got the toy, then."

The Professor cleared his throat. "The question then would seem to be, given that we do have the toy, can we use it to remove the spell that appears to be currently cast upon poor Ravinder?"

A worryingly long silence greeted his suggestion. Finally, Sam spoke.

"We could try destroying it."

"And would that break the spell?"

"Don't know. I'm thinking that it might break something, somehow." The rabbi looked up at Jackson. "What do you reckon?"

The priest waggled the chew toy as he thought, then stopped when it became apparent that it was having a bad effect on Rav. "I don't know. I really don't. This is so far out of my area of expertise it isn't true. You have to understand that when all's said and done, I'm basically a mental health social worker like Rav, except with a dog collar. Exorcisms are about as exotic as it's supposed to get, according to the job description. And yeah, I know that now and again, Sam and I get into something a bit weirder than that, but this is as weird as it's ever got for us — and then some."

"I'll say," agreed Sam.

"I've heard tales of this sort of stuff, sure, but we're talking third-hand accounts of crap that went down in places like Haiti, not the Home Counties. Now, if you're looking for actual knowledge, there' a library in my office. Old books, passed down from way back. Wei almanacs. Grimoires. Memoirs of madmen. Hand-inked o goatskin, that kind of thing. But if you try and read this stuff. stumble into an insanity inducing mix of half-truths and lies. ⅂

169

to sift through in pursuit of some sort of coherent understanding…" He spread his hands and shrugged.

"So basically," said Mindy, a note of frustration in her voice, "you don't know. It might break the spell, or it might just break the means of contacting the spell, leaving the spell still running inside him. Or it might just kill him."

"That's about it. Sorry."

Silence resumed. Eventually, the Professor felt compelled to speak. Of the four of them, he was the oldest, the one who'd been granted the most years in which to supposedly gain wisdom. And besides, Rav was his friend and colleague. Perhaps it fell to him to take the decision, rather than burden others with it. "I think we must face facts, my friends, and perhaps make a hard choice. Right now, Ravinder is as good as dead. We have no way of knowing if he will ever recover, should we do nothing. I suspect that if we take him to the authorities, we ensure only that he will remain this way, for as long as the spell lasts."

Mindy nodded. "Yeah, it ain't like they're going to call in some kind of NHS sorcery department."

"Quite. And added to that, we have the urgency of the case. I know Ravinder feels very strongly about the promise he made to young Scarlet Fletcher. I think if he were here, he would want us to take any actions that we felt had a reasonable chance of restoring him to consciousness, no matter the possible risk."

Sam looked across at Mindy. "This isn't about Jackson and me. You're his cousin. Do you agree?"

With tears pricking at the corners of her eye but a determined set to her jaw, she nodded.

"Okay," said Sam. "We're going to destroy the toy. Question is, how?"

The Universe resumed.

v was burning, his skin curling, tearing away from his flesh. He throat opening into one long scream that seemed to stretch it of his stomach to the sky above. He took a staggering

ain was gone, like a light whose off-switch has been d to his knees, then felt hands upon him, — the Professor's.

as?"

From somewhere, he found the physical strength to lift his head and the mental strength to open his eyes and found himself looking at the Professor's concerned features, with the equally concerned features of Jackson and Sam to either side. "Yeah, erm, what? Where the hell am I?" He looked around and found that they appeared to be in some sort of derelict site, an apron of pock-marked concrete lined with crumbling garages, and marked only by their parked hire car and an old oil drum, within which a raging fire was burning. A dim memory returned, of a room, and a man he recognised as the spell-caster, questioning him, and he answering, wanting nothing more than to answer. "I was in a room, and then nothing, until this?"

"You had a spell cast on you," Jackson explained. "It was bound to a rubber doll. We had to destroy the doll to break the spell."

Rav found his gaze drawn to the flame-filled oil drum. "And that was by burning, was it?"

Jackson squirmed. "Sorry, mate. But flame's often said to have mystical and magical properties. We figured this gave the best chance of destroying the item in a way that would break the magic. Did it hurt?"

Rav was too exhausted to manage sarcasm. "Yeah. Like buggery. Still, I'm back. Where are we with the case?"

The Professor gave him a fatherly smile. "The case can wait. Let's get you back to our hotel, and get you fed."

Rav was, he realised, ravenously hungry. "Sounds good, I could murder a kebab."

Jackson slapped him on the back. "Kebabs it is then. It's good to have you back, mate."

Rav managed a faint smile in return. "It's good to be back."

Chapter Thirty-One

Back at the hotel, over kebabs, chips, and drinks, the team filled Rav in on the details of what had happened during his capture, and he in turn attempted to describe his experiences, although in his case this was limited to only fragmentary recollections. When he'd finished, he took a swig of his Diet Coke, then shrugged an apology. "So I don't really know what I told him, guys, but I guess we have to assume it was everything. Sorry."

"No apologies needed, mate," Jackson said. "You were enslaved by evil people using evil powers. I might have a strong belief that they'll see a punishment in the afterlife, but right now they scare the living shit out of me, because I know that if they got hold of me, I'd have no chance."

Rav smiled at him. "I don't know, mate. From what the Professor said, it sounded like you was pretty awesome when you rescued me. Advancing on him chanting the Lord's Prayer and all that."

"It was most impressive," the Professor said.

Jackson held up his hands, protesting. "Much as I'd like to claim my iron faith—" he made a set of air quotes, "—was behind all that, I think it might have had more to do with him being scared to do magic in front of dozens of witnesses and being distracted by a mad vicar shouting at him."

"Perhaps," said the Professor, smiling. "But you still did it."

Rav held his Diet Coke out. "Anyhow, cheers." He waited until Jackson had clinked his can against Rav's, then settled back. It was at that moment that he spotted a cage on one side of the room; a cage he'd somehow previously missed. A rat sat in the cage, staring straight at him. "Why have we got a rat?"

"It was in the van," Mindy said. "With a bunch of other stuff. It seemed like they were moving out. Maybe they're scared that we're onto them, so they're going into hiding or something?"

"Why's it staring at us?"

"It's a rat. Does it matter?"

The four of them watched the rat. The rodent held their collective gaze for a few seconds, then reached out a front leg to point off to one side.

It was the Professor who spoke first. "Is it me, or is that rat pointing at something?"

"It's pointing at something," said Sam.

"It can't be pointing," protested Mindy. "It's a rat."

Jackson walked over to the pile of boxes they'd taken from the van. He gestured at one. "This one?"

The rat shook its head.

"Jesus Christ!" screamed Mindy, expressing a degree of shock similar to that which Rav was currently experiencing, although in his case, he'd managed to restrict his external reaction to merely a flinch sufficient to spill a splash of his drink.

Jackson pointed at a second box. Again, the rat shook its head.

"Are we really saying that this rat understands us?" asked Sam.

"It's a rat," said Mindy, more to herself than anything else. Then she abruptly stood, picking up two coasters, one blue, one red, from the coffee table. She crouched down in front of the cage, holding the red coaster in one hand and the blue in the other. "Which one of these is red?"

For a long moment the rat stared at her with an expression that several seconds ago Rav would have assumed simply to be the dumb incomprehension you'd expect a rat to display in such a circumstance, but which he now had a horrible fear might actually be frustrated annoyance. Then the rat reached out a paw to point at the red coaster.

"Bloody hell," said Mindy, dropping both coasters.

Then the rat banged the bars with as much fury as it could muster, given that it was only about six inches long, before pointing furiously in the direction of Jackson and the pile of boxes.

"I think it wants us to focus," said Sam.

"It's a rat," said Rav, finally managing to enter the conversation, albeit with a completely redundant point. (In his defence, he was coming into things off the back of a very stressful period and was still trying to catch up).

Mindy backed slowly away and sat down on the sofa. "This is screwed up."

"It's a rat," Rav repeated. He made a mental note to stop talking until he could think of something else to say other than an observation about the rat being a rat.

Jackson pointed at a third box. "This one?"

This time, the rat nodded enthusiastically.

Jackson opened the box, and started to retrieve the various items — chargers, extension leads, old radios — that had been secreted within it, pausing on each to allow the rat to shake its head. Then, as he retrieved an item that looked like a big multi-coloured keypad with an attached LCD screen, the rat began to nod frantically.

Rav had seen one of these before: it was a simplified keyboard that allowed people with certain physical disabilities to communicate. Still not quite able to speak, he grabbed it off Jackson, turned it on, then knelt in front of the cage, opening the door to put the keypad inside the cage, and arranging the screen on its stand outside.

"What is your name?" he asked the rat.

His thought in doing all of this had been that the rat would be able to use the device to communicate, and yet the idea that it might actually do so was so comically insane that he nonetheless felt a deep sense of dislocation when the rat started to push away on the keypad's four arrow buttons.

Tap, tap, tap went the rat. Rav knew from personal experience that such communication was painfully slow, given the inefficiencies inherent in the interface. Finally, the rodent sat up on its haunches, examined the screen, then reached forward to click the "speak" button.

"Mortimer," said the built-in speaker.

The negotiations with Mortimer had been protracted and painful, partly due to the inefficiencies of the interface through which he was required to communicate, but mainly because it was clear that his death and subsequent reincarnation had done little to alter the fact that as people went, he was very much one of the scrapings from the bottom of humanity's bucket. Within minutes it had become apparent that as well as being racist, he was anti-Semitic too, harboured a deep hated of clergy, and felt no particular compunction to keep any of this to himself.

Having agreed, reluctantly, to his demand that the Professor be the only person to address him, negotiations proceeded onto the terms required for Mortimer to tell all. Tangents and rambling, ranting monologues aside, this eventually boiled down to three things: a little single-malt whisky in his water bottle each night, guaranteed internet access, and his own Wikipedia entry (Wikipedia being something he'd managed to learn about by listening in on other people's conversations).

Demands finally identified, Sam settled back in his chair. "That shouldn't be too hard, should it?"

Rav shook his head. "A Wikipedia entry's tricky. You can't just create one for anyone, on account of it's supposed to be an encyclopaedia, not a social media network. All that will happen is that you'll create it, and then five minutes later some self-appointed delete-Nazi will delete it saying you're non-notable. And then you're pretty much blocked."

"How would you know?" asked Mindy, grinning impishly. "Any personal anecdotes you'd like to tell us about?"

"Look, I'm only passing on general knowledge, right?" Rav said, trying, but failing, to keep his voice at the correct octave. "I'll put Charlie onto it. He can make sure it links to enough stuff to look kosher." He turned his attention back to the rat. "So that's everything, right?"

Mortimer nodded, managing somehow to pack several layers of contempt into the gesture.

A few hours, a couple of phone calls, and one trip to PC World later, it was all set up. Placed in front of Mortimer's cage was an LCD monitor connected to a laptop on the shelf below, with his in-cage keypad synched into the laptop as an alternative interface. They waited for several minutes while the rat slowly read, whiskers twitching and paw occasionally tapping on the down arrow, through the newly created Wikipedia entry for Sir Edward Mortimer, Author and Orientalist, 1877 to 1941, until finally it looked back up, pushed the switch that turned the keypad back to the communicator, and began typing.

"That is adequate."

Rav squatted down in front of him. "So you'll talk?"

Somewhere in Greater London.
The Hindustani remained squatting before Mortimer's prison, awaiting his reply. Anger and resentment seethed through Mortimer at the fate to which destiny had delivered him. This was not how it was supposed to be. But ultimately, he knew that this man, inferior though he was, was not his enemy. Bishop was his enemy. Fey, supercilious, treacherous Bishop, and his equally vain wife. Traitors to their race, to the cause, to history. Bishop's grandfather had been a flawed man in many ways, but he would have rolled in his grave had he known of the disappointment his grandson had become.

He, Mortimer, had offered the Bishops a share of glory, and in their greed and stupidity they'd decided to take not only their share, but his too, reincarnating him not in the body of the single, socially-isolated young man his instructions had specified, but in this drastically inferior rodent form. A rat, as Phoebe Bishop had gleefully informed him, that they'd bought from a pet shop for the price of a sandwich.

The Bishops had to pay for their betrayal, and if this man, this Hindustani, was the man to do it, then so be it. Mortimer took a deep breath, reached across for the nozzle of his upturned water bottle to take a sip of whisky and water, then began to type.

Chapter Thirty-Two

Silbury Hill, Wiltshire, 1936.

Night. To the south lies the long snaking ribbon of the newly christened A4 highway, along whose high-speed tarmacked surface the members of the Hidden Mysteries Society have arrived via an assortment of motorcars. Mortimer allows himself a moment to appreciate the majesty of what they are about to do, then walks across to where John Rhys Netherford is busy assembling items on a makeshift altar set at the centre of the flattened summit.

"Are you ready, John?" he asks.

The younger man nods. Mortimer feels no surprise. He knows his colleague is prepared; his question is aimed more at quelling any nerves Rhys Netherford might be feeling. Mortimer himself has no doubts. Besides his meticulous, thorough, and dedicated nature, Rhys Netherford possesses a streak of intellectual brilliance. Perhaps the most gifted mathematician of his generation, only through his talents may this scheme hope to succeed.

Mortimer is well aware of his personal faults, but he's no fool. It is true that the conception of this undertaking was his, and his alone. It was he who devised its outline, he who envisioned the possibility, and he who deduced how it might be done. But knowing that its implementation required a greater mind than his, he had first sought and then recruited the younger man, in order that his vision might be made real.

Satisfied, he leaves Rhys Netherford to his final preparations, and walks over to where Stanley Bishop stands looking out over the darkened plain beyond, his hands wrapped around a mug of tea dispensed from the flask that stands on the bonnet of his motorcar. They exchange nods.

"Are all the devices in place?" Mortimer asks.

"They are, Edward," Bishop replies. "I myself planted the devices at St Michael's Mount and the Hurlers. Sylvia and Peter took Cadbury Castle, Glastonbury Tor, and Avebury. Jonathan handled Sinodun Camp. And Patrick and James laid the devices at Royston, Bury St Edmunds, and Hopton. Do you think they will be adequate? Is the placing correct?"

Mortimer dismisses his friend's concerns. "They will be fine. Nine devices will be more than sufficient for this test." He has no fears over this, nor the placement of the devices. He and Rhys Netherford have chosen ancient sites for one reason only, that being the certainty of location they offered; in truth, the devices could have been placed at any reasonably spread locations along the ley line. It has been a long day, one that has followed a long night, and he realises that of them all, Bishop has done the most driving, along pitifully inadequate roads. Oh, for the autobahns being built in Germany!

A few minutes later he is shaken from his thoughts by the approaching figure of Rhys Netherford. "Are the preparations complete?" he asks him.

Rhys Netherford nods. "I think so."

They gather the various members of the assembled Society from their motorcars and lead them to the altar, where the ritual will be conducted. The awareness of what they are about to attempt weighs heavily upon Mortimer, a weight made even greater by the knowledge that the limited magical charges enchanted into the devices will soon run out; the ritual must succeed and succeed now, or the entire experiment will have to be repeated.

He glances at each solemn face in turn, then begins to chant.

"Ancient gods! Ancient beings…"

It took several hours, including a break for pizza, for Mortimer's paws to finish typing out his story. Finally, by which time it was well into the early hours of the morning, Rav and his companions were able to settle back and consider their new knowledge.

It was not a consideration that rested easily upon their shoulders. At least, it certainly didn't sit easily upon Rav's, and from the looks on his companions' faces, they seemed just as troubled. This was big. In terms of scale of vision, this plot they were chasing had now elevated itself from low-budget, one-off BBC2 drama to franchise-launching, Hollywood blockbuster.

"Perhaps I should summarise," said Sam, apparently volunteering to break the horrified silence. "Mortimer, you came up with an idea for a device that would generate enormous quantities of magical energy, energy that could be used to cast spells of a greater magnitude than anything yet seen on this Earth. You would do this by casting a ritual into a ley line that would open a channel of communication into the ley itself, a channel into which you could pass spell castings held within mathematically encoded messages. Devices spread along the ley line would receive and recast those messages, turning the entire ley into one, single, magical conduit."

The rat tipped its head in confirmation.

"The upshot is that if located in the vicinity on the ley, you could cast a magical ritual into the ley and the ley itself would repeatedly recast it along its length, massively boosting both the effect and the reach of your ritual."

From somewhere, Rav's misfiring brain delivered him an insight, which he in turn delivered to the group. "It's like turning a ley line into a magical Internet network. It's like the cloud, but for magic."

"Hang on," said Mindy. "That was the bit that confused me when he said it. For the benefit of those of us who don't generally make it further than ITV2 on the TV remote's up button, what the hell's a ley line?"

Sam steepled his fingers before replying. "According to our new age friends, it's a line of mystical energy stretching across the surface of the earth in a straight line."

"And what is it actually?"

It was Jackson who answered now. "I think maybe it is actually a line of mystical energy stretching across the surface of the earth. Look!" He reached out for his laptop, which he'd been tapping away at while Sam was speaking, and spun it around to face them. "That date Mortimer gave us? For the test? I Googled it."

Richmond-upon-Thames, Surrey, 1936. Two days later.

Rhys Netherford slaps a thick stack of newspapers down upon Mortimer's desk, rousing the older man from the near trance that an afternoon spent studying an arcane and ancient manuscript has bought upon him.

"It worked, Sir Edward!" he exclaims. "The test was successful."

Mortimer puts the manuscript aside and turns his attention to the stack of newspapers. Rhys Netherford must have let himself in, using the key Mortimer had entrusted to him several months previously. He goes to pick up the topmost newspaper, but Rhys Netherford — clearly too excited to contain his enthusiasm — beats him to it.

"Penzance," he says, flicking the topmost newspaper off the stack. "Bodmin. Taunton. Devizes. Luton. Bury St Edmunds. Great Yarmouth. Every single one of those newspapers contains reports of strange events on the night before last, at just around the time that we conducted the ritual. Animals behaving hysterically. Motorcar engines mysteriously dying. Violent hailstorms on a clement night.

And look, this one." He rifles through the scattered newspapers, withdrawing one that bears the title of Somerset County Gazette. "Here it is," he tells Mortimer. "Page five. A vicar stripped naked in a public house and tried to strangle the landlord's German Shepherd!"

Mortimer takes the proffered newspaper, and skims through the article, finding its prose limp and its language weak. In truth, he is not particularly interested in any specific effects that the ritual may have caused. Their experiment sought merely to test the methodology of using Rhys Netherford's mathematically communicating— no wait, what is the term the younger man uses? Network, that's it. Since they were seeking merely to test the... network, the choice of which specific ritual to cast was rendered largely irrelevant. Knowing this, they'd chosen a simple, general purpose curse, with the reasoning that such a ritual's effects would be visibly apparent.

And they have been. Clearly.

Mortimer allows himself the luxury of several moments of self-satisfaction but ceases when he becomes aware his colleague is not sharing his joy. "You should allow yourself a short while to savour our accomplishment, John," he gently chides. "There will be time enough for us to plan our next steps."

Rhys Netherford sits down on the chaise-longue that lies opposite Mortimer's desk, his head dropping to his hands for several seconds until he raises it back up, his wide eyes shot through with despair. "But to come this close, knowing we can go no further! To create the network, but only partially, only for mere seconds. The things we could do if we were able to create the full circle, allow the network to deliver its full power! Even if we manage to extend the life of the device's initial charge from one day to several..."

His speech trails off, a nervous tic fighting at the corner of his mouth. Mortimer is worried about him. The work they are performing is important, vital even. But he fears that, like Marie Curie, Rhys Netherford might be destined to be killed by the forces to which his research exposes him. And in truth, so might he. The forces they are conjuring are dark and terrible ones, and Mortimer is under no illusions of the damage being done to their collective sanities. He pushes that thought aside and gives what he hopes is a genial smile. "Yes, John. We can go no further, not yet. But the world is changing. Be patient."

"You're talking about the Hindenburg?"

"Yes, John. I'm taking about the Hindenburg, and its successors.

Our day will come, sooner than you think."

Chapter Thirty-Three

"Okay," said Sam, casting a glance across at Mortimer. "So you'd created a proof of concept using the section of the St Michael's ley line running from Penzance to the East Anglian coast, with a network that came up for just a few seconds before the inherent instability created by its partial nature caused the devices to be destroyed?"

The rat nodded.

"Because that stretch across Great Britain is merely a small fragment of what's actually a line that encircles the earth along a great circle path, and to unlock the true power of the network, you would have had to place devices along the entire circumference of the globe."

Once again Jackson spun his laptop around. "I found a map someone knocked up."

Rav leaned forward. The map showed a curving line that arced through Europe and across Asia, then down and across Australia and New Zealand, before heading back over South America to cross the Atlantic to Penzance.

"It's a curved line," he observed. "Isn't a ley line supposed to be straight?"

"That's a flat map, Ravinder," said the Professor, "which is representing a round world. If we were to trace that line across a globe, it would be straight."

"Right."

Sam continued summarising the story Mortimer had just told them. "If placed along that path, the magical devices would be able to bring the network up fully, with energies circling the globe such that the network would become stable, persisting until the initial charge cast into the devices expired, allowing the casting of complex rituals."

"But the initial ritual to enchant the devices must be performed on them all as one single action," broke in Jackson. "And they've got a limited charge that will run out in a matter of days at best."

"Meaning," added the Professor, "that for the endeavour to work, it is necessary to have available global travel of sufficient haste that devices can be transported from Britain to South America and the Antipodes in days rather than weeks. And after the destruction of the Hindenburg, you realised that it would likely be decades before that become possible."

Sam fixed his attention back on the rat. "Which is when you came up with a new plan."

Sunbury-upon-Thames, Middlesex, 1941.

Mortimer rocks sideways in his chair, only its deep wings preventing him from tumbling to the floor. He is not certain of his location; this house is not his house, and the people in it are not his friends. Nor are any of them his servants, for though they serve him, they do so with none of the deference due from servant to master. A thought emerges somewhere in that part of his mind that is still comparatively lucid. Bolshevism. That's where the rot started. That, and an England so scared of the Bolshevik threat that it granted the vote to not only the so-called working men but, worse, to their women folk.

At the end of the lounge within which he now sits, a set of French doors lead to a manicured lawn that dips down to a gently meandering river. He knows the river, had once rowed upon it, but its name escapes him now. A silver-haired man enters through the French doors, approaching Mortimer with a smile and an outstretched hand. Mortimer feels that he has seen this man before, that he knows him; but like the river, the man's name escapes him.

"Edward!" the man says, clasping Mortimer's hand. For a moment, Mortimer attempts to put the name, Edward, to the man, but there is no spark of recognition. Then he remembers; Edward is his name, not this man's.

The man gives Mortimer's hand a gentle shake. "It's me, Edward. Stanley, Stanley Bishop."

He tries this name, and somewhere within his cluttered and clouded thought processes there is a spark of something that, if not quite recognition, is at least not the confused darkness within which he now dwells. "Stanley?" he asks.

"Yes," the man tells him, sitting down on the chair opposite, but only after first pulling it close to Mortimer's chair.

"I've come to tell you of the plan."

"The plan?"

"Yes, Edward, the plan. It's all arranged. The learning materials we prepared are ready, safe. When the time comes, I will be long gone, but my son Peter will be reaching his prime. He's five now; I will raise him as best I can, for as long as I have on the earth. When the time capsule and its contents are revealed to him, he'll be ready. Only the final portion of your plan remains."

Mortimer is confused. "Final?"

"Yes, Edward, the final portion. The ritual to be performed upon your death, to capture your soul, and store it, until Peter is ready to call you back, renewed and reborn, in that far off time of nineteen-hundred and sixty-seven, that time of rocket-powered aircraft that shall span the globe."

"Ritual?"

This other man, this Stanley, leans in close, close enough for Mortimer to see the individual white whiskers from which his moustache is composed. "The remaining members of the Society stand ready to perform the final ritual, Edward. But we grow old, and weak, and one-by-one we are succumbing to the madness. We must perform the ritual now, or we may not be able to do it at all. Do you understand, Edward? Do you understand what I am saying?"

Mortimer does not understand. "Ritual?"

"We need to do the ritual now, Edward. We cannot wait." The other man stands, pushing his chair back, and then nods to one of the Bolshevik-not-quite-servants who has materialised beside them, as is the wont of his kind. "Come on, Sir Edward," the attendant says, gently but firmly pulling Mortimer to his feet. "Come with me. We'll take care of you."

"The final years of your life are clouded," Sam continued. "By the madness into which you had degenerated. But the plan had been agreed before the madness, its details determined, the necessary items created. Upon your death, the remaining members of the society performed a ritual to capture your soul and bind it into an enchanted container, to be placed into a time capsule that would be delivered to Stanley Bishop's son Peter, at the appropriate time. A time capsule that would contain the instructions of how to retrieve your soul and decant it into a suitable human body."

The rat began to furiously type at his keypad. A few seconds later, his synthetically voiced replay added, "A suitable Aryan body."

Sam dropped his head to his hands. "If it's not enough to be having a conversation with a sentient rat in possession of a reincarnated human soul, it has to be a sodding anti-Semite." He took a deep breath, then waved a clearly frustrated hand in the direction of Mortimer's cage. "Whatever. The point is that when you found yourself back on this earth, you found that your reincarnation had been performed not by Stanley's son Peter, but by Peter's son, Jason, and the body into which he'd restored your soul was not a human one, but that of a rat — something which very much had not been part of your plan. You were supposed to be in charge, but you'd instead ended up their prisoner. And then they forced you into helping them, passing on your magical learning, teaching them how to do things such as capturing a demon and binding it to tattoos as an enchantment to protect against the effects of magic."

He gave the rat a stare as though daring it to type a reply, but after several seconds of locked eye contact, it gave a resigned nod. Sam had, by now, reached the end of his summary, the end of the tale that Mortimer had told them. "What you haven't told us is what you wanted to do with the power of the network. You must have had some plan other than simply to create it. What was it you wanted to do with it? What did you want to use it for?"

His question was still hanging in the air when a text appeared on Rav's phone, from Jenny Seagram: *"been to see ricky call me when you wake up"*. He glanced back at the others. "I need to make a call, guys." He let himself out into the featureless, beige corridor outside the room, and called her back.

"What's up, Jenny?"

"Sorry, I know it's late. I didn't wake you up, did I?"

"No. I was up anyway. How's Ricky doing?"

"He's not good, Rav. I've just bought someone in to West Mid, and I thought I'd check him out. He's totally lost it. It's like nothing I've ever seen, like nothing any of the psych nurses have ever seen. It's, well… I know this is going to sound mad, but it's like he's possessed. He keeps on screaming in a voice that isn't his, mad stuff, weird stuff. Stuff about a lay, whatever that is, and about a Michael, and a skull, and a circle around the world. Look, it's not like there's anything you can do. But I know he's a friend of yours, and I thought you might like to know."

"Yeah, yeah," Rav answered, distracted by the implications of what she was saying. "Thanks."

She hung up. His thoughts drifted, and when he came to, he had no idea how long he'd been in the corridor, leaning against the wall. He let himself back into the room, just in time to catch the final words of a synthesised statement from Mortimer.

"—and enslave them."

"What was that?" Rav asked.

Jackson answered. "He said his plan, back when he first came up with the scheme, had been to use the ley network to cast a ritual — protected by the tattoos and using a powerful magical artefact as a focus — that would enslave those who ruled the country, so that he might through them rule it himself."

Rav advanced upon the cage. He had already been pretty pissed off at the whole situation, but the news about Ricky was pushing his anger up to a righteous fury. "And is that what Jason Bishop plans to do now that he's got the skull? That's the powerful magical artefact, right?"

The rat sat back on his haunches and splayed out his front paws in a "Who knows?" gesture.

Rav leaned in close. "Did you teach them what they needed to know to cast this ritual?"

The rat paused for several long seconds, then slowly typed in a reply.

"Yes."

A further thirty minutes of quizzing the rat had established one potentially useful fact — that for maximum effectiveness the enslaving ritual would need to be cast within a few miles of the ley line — but little else.

The rat might have been lying, but Rav's gut feeling was that he was telling the truth when he claimed to not know who or what the Bishops' target was. It wasn't so much that he trusted Mortimer, but it had already become clear that if there was one thing the reincarnated occultist hated more than non-whites, Jews, priests, socialists, feminists, homosexuals, Muslims, Catholics, musicians, artists, Americans, and the non-artisan working classes — it was the Bishops. Put simply, Rav was figuring that if the rat knew the details of the Bishops' plan, he'd have spilled the beans, for no reason other than to shaft them.

The first glimmers of the approaching sunrise were emerging through the hotel room's thin curtains, so they decided to try to get some sleep for what was left of the night. The Professor, insistent that Rav take his bed, settled into the armchair.

For Rav, sleep didn't come easy, and when it came it was a troubled sleep filled with tangled dreams of Ricky and Scarlet, and of the Bishops, and of a giant racist rat. But when he finally awoke, a plan came to him, crystal clear and fully formed.

The Professor was already up and dressed, sitting straight in the chair, the blanket that had served as his cover neatly folded.

Rav swung his legs off the bed, ran his hands though his hair, allowed the thought he'd had upon waking a few seconds more time to bounce around his brain, then with a degree of resolve that was frankly unfamiliar, delivered it. "I need to get the tattoo."

The Professor blinked. "I beg your pardon, Ravinder?"

"Whatever it takes, blackmail, threats, bribery, whatever, I need to get Killen to give me the tattoo, like he did for Ricky, and on the chest too, not the arm. Like he did Ricky."

"But why? And why the chest, given that such a location will cause you to descend into madness?"

"Because we need to know what they're doing. Right now, we've got nothing, except a location about five miles wide and two hundred miles long, and meanwhile, they're ready, with everything they need. That phone call I got last night was from Ricky's social worker. The tattoo must be talking to him, because he's been talking about the ley, and the skull, and stuff like that."

The Professor gave him a look that paired a set of raised, querying eyebrows with a worried sigh. "And your thought is that if you have the same tattoo as Ricky, in the same location, then the tattoo, or to be more accurate, the demon, might talk to you as well?"

"Yeah. I figure the demon must be aware of their conversations or thoughts or something. Even if it's only fragments, maybe we'll get a clue we can work with."

"And what if we can't, Ravinder, what then? And even if we can, surely your fate will still be to fall victim to madness?"

Rav shrugged, a gesture that came from somewhere between courage and fatalism. "If we succeed, and stop them doing this, then maybe we can figure out how to free the demon. And once the demon's gone back to wherever the hell they got it from, which is Hell, I guess, then the tattoo will just be a tattoo, right?"

"And if we don't succeed?"

"Maybe I'm better off mad."

Chapter Thirty-Four

It was four days now since Rav had "persuaded" Killen into doing the tattoo. At first, he'd had no sensation except for the discomfort of his newly inked flesh. But as Friday night turned into Saturday morning the tattoo had started whispering, the whispers turning increasingly urgent as Saturday turned into Sunday, and Sunday turned into Monday, until by Tuesday morning he was sharing his mind with a constantly screaming banshee of fury. Raw, unfettered, incoherent rage sloshed around his skull like the contents of a bathtub during a particularly violent earthquake. Constant. Unceasing. A tsunami of pain for which there was no off switch.

Sleep became first difficult, and then impossible. Fatigue began to bear down upon him, further decreasing his ability to fight the madness into which he was descending. He'd gone to his doctor to get signed off work sick, hoping that by doing so he might be able to save his job if, when, he finally got beyond this case. But truth be told, he was so genuinely unwell that no acting had been required to convince Doctor Kowalski that he was suffering from a stress-induced breakdown.

The Professor, Mindy, Jackson, and Sam: each in their way had tried to aid him. But there was no help for this, and no cure but to find and defeat the cultists. And for that, he needed the tattoo to give him something they could work with, something that counted as a clue, something other than random chaotic anger. But no such clue came. His four companions were attempting to pursue other avenues of research. But those other avenues produced no results either.

During one of his long insomniac nights he'd even tried reading the Hindustani, which he'd bought with him as part of their ongoing case documentation. He'd hoped that it might perhaps give him some insight into the case or, failing that, be so boring it might put him to sleep. But over a couple of long sessions he'd managed to read it the whole way through and gain no insight. The Professor had been correct when he'd declared it a truly terrible book.

And then, late on Tuesday evening, midway through News at Ten, something came. A fragment, a thought, an image surfing on a wave of the enslaved demon's anger that hit Rav's memories and clicked into a pre-existing entry in those memories' data banks: one of the greens at Hounslow Heath Golf Course.

After a quick confab in Mindy's room, they decided that given the urgency of the situation, they had no choice but to travel to Hounslow Heath immediately and figure out what to do when they got there. The rat looked up from his internet browsing for a moment as they made their preparations.

"We won't be long, Mortimer," Mindy told him cheerfully, as though he were a beloved family pet, and not a racist and misogynistic piece of shit Nazi.

Jackson paused from grabbing his jacket to take a peek at what Mortimer was currently browsing. From the look of anger that flashed across his face, it clearly wasn't good. "That's disgusting!" he told the rat. "It's sexist and exploitative of women."

The rat gave a contemptuous shrug in return.

"Leave it," Rav told Jackson. "We've got bigger things to worry about." He certainly did, starting with the angry demon that was slowly demolishing his sanity from the inside, brick-by-brick, neuron-by-neuron. As long as the rat wasn't looking at— he paused in the doorway and looked back at Mortimer. "No children or animals, okay?"

Somewhere in the overhead darkness, turbofans whined as an airliner slid down the flightpath towards Heathrow Airport's southern runway. Jason Bishop paused his chanting until the noise faded away. After the years spent working towards this moment there was no point ruining it now because a few crucial syllables had been lost in the scream of a titanium turbine blade.

Lying on the blanketed picnic table that formed their makeshift altar was his wife Phoebe, her slim form encircled by the twenty small, simple devices that would shortly be being dropped off at a nearby airfreight company, where they would be dispatched to addresses ranging from New Zealand to Chile. All that was necessary now was to cast the ritual that would enchant into them the brilliant, elegant networking spell that John Rhys Netherford had devised some eighty years before.

Phoebe, like Jason himself, was naked, except for certain items of enchanted jewellery, and her legs were splayed, ready for Jason to enter her at the climax of the ritual, an act of sexual magic that would be as satisfying as it was effective. Jason could feel himself hardening, but he remained focused, speaking the syllables of a language dead for several millennia, secret knowledge passed down through mystic tomes and hidden traditions. Around them, nine robed and hooded members of the Society chanted an accompaniment, a chorus to his lead.

His words merged with theirs, merging in turn with the lustful anticipation sparking between him and his wife. He felt the energy surging through him, a presence in the air around him, as though the fabric of space-time itself was warping to their collective will. He could feel the ritual taking form, shaping, almost ready for him to— He felt a presence. An interloper who'd arrived out of the surrounding gloom at some point; someone not of their group who Should. Not. Have. Been. There. Bishop ceased chanting, and turned his head towards the unwanted intruder, finding his eyes falling onto a shabby looking man who stood a little way outside of their circle. The man was dressed in a dirty hoodie and tracksuit bottoms, pulled down to reveal a semi-erect penis.

"Don't mind me," the man said. "I'm only watching."

Phoebe lifted her head and shot the man a glare so fierce that had this been happening in daylight, it would most likely have left him with a nasty case of PTSD. "We are not dogging," she hissed. "We are trying to perform a satanic ritual. Now fuck off!"

It'd been years since Rav had played golf on the Heath; he'd only ever been an occasional player at best. The course had since shut down, but when Jackson drove through a set of smashed gates into what had been its car park, they found it nonetheless full of vehicles. They found an empty spot a little way down from the tatty Portakabin that had once been the clubhouse, and got out.

A seedy-looking man in a hoodie and tracksuit bottoms appeared out of the darkness, lurching towards them. He pulled a set of keys from a pocket and pressed the unlock button, causing a parked Vauxhall to flash its lights and beep.

"I wouldn't go down to the fifteenth if I was you," the man said as he climbed into his car. "They're a right anti-social bunch." He started the engine, then put his window down. "I only wanted to watch." Then he drove away, his tyres crunching over the gravel into the gloom beyond.

"That was a bit weird," said Jackson. "I guess he was talking about our mob, right?"

Rav didn't answer. He was too busy trying to mute the screaming inside his skull, or at least quieten it sufficiently that he could manage to string some coherent thoughts together. After a few moments, he managed to point in the direction of the fifteenth hole. "It's that way."

They set off, walking carefully, led by Jess. She was pulling hard on her lead as though she had a destination in mind and a strong desire to go there; it occurred to Rav during a rare moment of silence from the demon that she might perhaps be sensing magic up ahead. He was about to mention that to his colleagues, but then the demon started screaming again.

They staggered forward in the direction from which the seedy looking man had stumbled. Rav was trying to focus, to shut out the screaming and remember the route, but in a world rendered to a monochrome blur by darkness and with memories several years old, he was coming up blank.

They passed across what might once have been a green, and narrowly skirted the velvety black maw of a shadowed bunker before passing through a scattered clump of trees onto a parallel fairway.

From ahead came the sound of chanting. Jess pricked up her ears and altered her course to head towards the noise. They continued on, the chanting increasingly loud.

"Probably a bit late to say this, but we do have a plan?" whispered Jackson.

It was indeed too late, for the fates chose that moment to open a gap in the clouds overhead, allowing a shaft of moonlight to illuminate the scene beyond, and to accompany that gap, said fates chose an audio accompaniment of a long cry of exaltation, a cry of such animalistic qualities that it might possibly have been the sound of a non-hominid ejaculating had it not been accompanied by a scream of "I'm coming!"

And then the demon roared.

Chapter Thirty-Five

Rav came to with what would have been the mother of all hangovers, had alcohol been involved at any point. His hands were shaking and every inch of skin was pouring with sweat. His stomach was turning cartwheels, while his bowels were not so much quivering as pulsing, in a manner reminiscent of a low-budget horror flick five seconds before an entire fifth of the special effects budget is about to be blown in a one-second moment of awfulness. And he was attempting to process this using a brain that felt like it had been scooped out of his skull like ice-cream out of a tub. He really didn't feel too good. From somewhere inside his being, the demon raised a whimper, then shut up, as though even that supernatural personification of evil was feeling a bit spent. Then hands were helping him up from the grass upon which he now realised he'd been laying.

"Are you all right, Ravinder?"

He gave the Professor a shaky nod and concentrated on sitting upright for a few seconds before experimenting with opening his eyes.

They were still at the golf course; how much time had passed, he'd no idea. Through the dim moonlight he saw Jackson and Mindy approaching, Jess at their heels, all three of them dripping wet. Jess gave him a glance that suggested curiosity, if not actual concern, then shook herself dry, showering him.

"Thanks, Jess," he managed through a parched and sore throat.

"It all got a bit confused after you fainted," the priest explained. "We ran in to try and stop them, and Jess managed to get her teeth around Bishop's arm, but then one of the others cast that freeze spell on me. I toppled into the pond behind the green."

"Me and Jess went in and got him," Mindy added.

Sam had appeared from out of the gloom. "Yeah, it pretty much all turned to shit." He smiled ruefully. "Sorry, as a scholar of the Talmud I should probably be giving you a more nuanced description, but…" He spread helpless hands and shrugged.

"So did they, like, get away?" Rav managed to choke out.

"I'm afraid they did, Ravinder," the Professor replied. "They had a circle of devices around the erm, copulating couple—"

"Bishop was shagging someone," Jackson interrupted. "That wife of his, maybe."

"Yes, exactly. I will write up the details in my post-event report, but the summary is that they managed to scoop up the devices and depart. And given that we appeared to arrive at the ritual's, how shall we say, conclusion, I fear that the devices have been successfully enchanted."

Sam gave a little cough. "Yeah. We started off trying to stop them, but when they zapped Jackson, the Professor and I threw ourselves into the far bunker, to be totally honest."

Rav couldn't blame them. To even contemplate the powers the Hidden Mysteries Society might have at their disposal was hard. It was as though they were all characters in a Netflix drama, but the cultists were in possession of the remote control, able to binge, pause, or rewind as they wished. How could they fight opponents who could paralyse them, or bind them to their will, or cause their senses to lie to them? Such people cannot be attacked head-on; they can only be approached indirectly to be defeated by stealth or misdirection.

Of course, right now, that was as academic as a box of Open University course material, given that Bishop and his crew had got away with the devices they needed to bring the ley network up, and with Rav and his team having no idea where the cultists were going to use them, and on whom.

Jackson reached down to him. "Come on. Let's get back to the hotel. We can figure out what to do tomorrow."

The demon had been mercifully quiet when Rav had crawled into his budget single bed, so much so that if anything, it was the noise from the nearby flyover that had been keeping him awake. But having fallen asleep, it was only to have a wakening demon in his dreams, dreams that became ever more confused and unpleasant. By the time he woke up at what the blinking red lights of the cheap bedside clock-radio told him was a little after six, he'd: been incinerated by a cyber-dragon in a post-apocalyptic Westeros; drowned in a methane-sea on the Saturnian moon, Titan; spent a tense several days investigating a murder in a nineteen-fifties meat packing factory with the assistance of the factory's sweet old tea lady, a story which had ended with his being fed feet first into an industrial-sized meat blender by said sweet old lady who, it transpired, was the murderer; and spent several hours tied to a chair while a generic burger-chain-advertising clown that was best described as Ronald McDonald played by Jared Leto stuffed burgers into his mouth while screaming "First Division" over and over.

Awake, and shaken, Rav padded over to the toilet, trying not to wake the Professor, and emptied his bladder, thinking over the dreams. The demon was shouting again, manageable for now, but still an unpleasant thing to be sharing one's headspace with.

"First Division," Rav thought as he idly aimed his spray at a speck of crap clinging to the toilet's rear surface.

"First Division! First Division! First Division!" chanted the demon.

He padded back into the room to find the Professor sitting up, wiping sleepy eyes awake.

"The demon's chanting First Division," he told the Professor. "What's that supposed to mean? Football?"

"Why would that phrase suggest football to you?"

"Because the Football League's top division used to be called the First Division?" Rav sat down on his bed. "Why? What does it suggest to you?"

"Well, there's the First Division Association, which is a trade union-like organisation representing the senior echelons of the civil service."

"What, senior civil servants? Like the ones at the top?"

"Yes. Exactly." An expression of realisation rolled across the Professor's face. "Of course. Mortimer's plan was to enslave those who rule the country. And it's an oft-repeated maxim that it's the civil service that actually runs the country, and not the government."

"Yeah. And now the Bishops aim to turn its leaders into magically enslaved puppets." Rav stood up. "Get dressed. I'm going to wake the others up."

The pentagram was crudely drawn in rough chalk on faded tarmac with an arm that still hurt to buggery. But it would do. Jason Bishop spoke the last words of the summoning ritual and a presence appeared within the pentagon that lay at the pentagram's heart. The presence couldn't be seen, but it could be sensed, if one had the touch and the knowledge, and Bishop had both. He paused for a moment. Then spoke. "Asag, I who have summoned you, I who is your master, I who have bound you to my will, command you to speak."

There was a moment's pause, then a reply came, not spoken, but sensed by Bishop nonetheless. "YES?"

The reply came grudgingly and had the feel of a glacier gliding over gravel, but it had come. And that was what counted. The demon was still his. Yeah, sure, to anyone watching, he would simply be a man standing motionless in the unused carpark of a derelict factory. But this was not for anyone watching. This was for him. This was for him to know. To know what the hell was going on. To sate the anger that burned within him; anger that would have burned strong even if he hadn't twice been at the wrong end of a savaging from a beast who'd both times cut through his magical defences like they'd not even existed.

He gathered himself before speaking.

"Do you serve us, demon? Do you serve those who bear the bonds of your allegiance upon their skin?"

Again a pause, before a grudging, grating reply, a reply forced by magic against the demon's straining consent. "I DO."

Something about the reply, something about its delivery, sparked a flicker of suspicion within Bishop's soul. For a few seconds he allowed his intuition to roam. The tattoo. What was the demon trying to tell him about the tattoo? "The markings on skin to which I have bound you. Can you feel them?"

"I CAN."

"How many can you feel?"

"THIRTEEN."

Thirteen. Two more than the number of tattoos that had been applied to the eleven members of the Hidden Mystery Society's inner council. He'd had his doubts about that bullshitting buffoon Danny Killen; those doubts had clearly been correct. Retribution in that direction would come, and would be delivered in the manner of Samuel L. Jackson's Ezekiel 25:17 — but that could be deferred until later.

He had a more immediate problem. He'd long since realised that the tattoo created a sense of shared consciousness among its bearers; he'd considered it a useful side-effect to the primary purpose of protecting the bearers from the effects of the sorcery they wielded. And that protection was still very much needed; to attempt to cast a ritual powered by the full magic of the ley network without the protection of the enslaved Asag would be an act of suicidal madness. But it was clear now that it was the tattoo's shared consciousness that had led his enemies to the site of the enchanting ritual, at the fifteenth green.

That interruption had very nearly disrupted the entire plan; had it arrived but thirty seconds earlier, it would have.

This leakage of information had to stop.

He turned his attention back to the demon, still held in its prison of chalk. "The last two tattoos, the most recent ones."

"YES?"

"Unlink yourself from them. Talk to them no more. I, your master, command it."

Again, a pause, longer this time. But then— "I HAVE SEVERED THOSE CONTACTS. I SHALL TALK TO THEM NO MORE."

"Good." Bishop raised his hand, ready to wave the demon away from this realm, back to the spiritual cage in which he had it bound. But then a thought occurred to him.

"Have you told them anything else, anything since the golf course?"

Pause.

A continuing pause.

Then a final, grating, admission.

"MIGHT HAVE."

The Professor was a man of strong opinions when it came to the qualities required for a meal to be described as "breakfast", and after six days in the euphemistically named Quality Inn, he was still unyielding in his conclusion that whatever words might be used to describe the offerings available from its so-called breakfast buffet, "breakfast" was not one of them. Weak tea, dribbled from an ugly urn. Unappealing jams whose taste owed more to the work of chemists than farmers. Gristly sausages, dripping with fat. Cheap, white bread toasted in an industrial appliance where the only choice was between one run through the conveyor or two, with one producing little more than a faint touch of scattered gold and two producing a carbonised slab.

One day, some sort of culinary equivalent of Stockholm syndrome might set in, but on this day, as with every one of the previous six, the Professor settled despairingly for serving himself a bowl of muesli and a selection of nearly fresh fruit. That sad act done, he returned to the corner table where the others were engaged in a breakfast meeting. Rav, who was apparently feeling much better if the way he was attacking his breakfast was any indication, had his laptop open, and was tapping away, in between shoving a steam of mashed slabs of sausage, egg, and beans into his perpetually chewing maw. The Professor settled in across from him, and began picking at his muesli, making sure to keep an eye on the laptop and an ear on the discussion.

A map of Southern England was up on the screen, a slanting line cutting across it from Penzance to Great Yarmouth. "Okay," said Rav, pausing to wipe from his screen the splash of tomato sauce he'd just spat across it. "That's the St Michael's ley. Where was that conference again?"

Jackson had his own laptop open. "A bit outside Norwich."

Rav appeared to be using his thumb and forefinger to estimate a distance on the map. "That's got to be fifteen, maybe twenty miles from the ley line."

The Professor forced his way into the conversation with a polite cough. "I'm sorry, which conference is this?"

"The First Division Association are holding their annual conference in a hotel near Norwich, starting tomorrow afternoon, and running through to Saturday evening. There'll be around two hundred attendees, including the Cabinet Secretary, the head of the civil service. Way too much of a coincidence to not be what we're looking for."

"Quite," agreed the Professor.

"So this conference has to be it. It fits too well to not be what they're doing. But it's not on the ley line. Which means—"

"—they've got to transport the attendees to the ley line, right?" said Mindy. "They need to be on the ley line when they cast whatever ritual they're going to use to enslave the attendees, and they're going to need the people there to cast it on, right?"

"That's my reading of the situation," said Sam.

"Aha!" said Jackson. "I've found the conference programme. There are various talks on Thursday afternoon, then for Thursday evening, tomorrow night that is, there's an off-site event with entertainment and refreshment at a mystery location."

"That's got to be it."

"This is tricky," said Sam. "They're going to perform the ritual at a location that could be anywhere along a whole section of ley line and we have no idea where that will be, which would seem to make preventing that ritual taking place somewhat difficult. We could try to disrupt the conference itself, on the Thursday afternoon, but short of burning down the hotel, I'm not sure how we could prevent the evening's event."

The Professor shook his head. "I fear even that wouldn't work. They would likely invoke the Dunkirk spirit or some other rhetorical call to continuity and proceed with the event."

Rav slapped the table. "Coaches!"

"I'm sorry?" said Jackson.

"They're not going to ask everyone to drive to this mystery location. People want to relax, and there's not much mystery if you're told where you're going, and besides, people will want to have a drink and some people might have come by train. They'll hire coaches to take everyone there and back."

"You thinking we should try and stop the coaches, or something?" asked Jackson.

Rav shook his head. "No, because it's the same problem, ain't it? If we try and stop them, they can work something else out, call the police, take a different route. And it don't help that they know what we all look like, and there's the magic shit they can do. We need something more subtle, where they won't know that it's gone wrong, even after it's gone wrong." He stopped speaking, his eyes darting from side-to-side in thought. Then a sly smile settled on his face.

"Do you have a plan, Ravinder?" the Professor asked.

The smile turned into a full-on grin. "Think I might."

Chapter Thirty-Six

Thirty-something hours later, the plan was rolling. Rav took a last look around the room, checking that every detail was correct. Mobile disco, thankfully not manned by him this time. Tables set with soon-to-be-filled champagne flutes. Welcoming canapés. A bar, fully stocked with booze and equipped with two Australian barmen. And a giant banner welcoming the First Division Association. Checks made, he walked out into the sunshine, passing a suited-and-booted waitress on the way.

The knot of tension clutching at his stomach wasn't easing. The room was ready, as it damn well should be given the day-and-a-half of planning that had gone into it, and it wasn't that he lacked confidence in the plan. He didn't. It was his plan after all. But it was a long shot of a plan, full of double-apexed corners with treacherous cambers and minimal run-offs.

Adding to his many doubts was the fact that the tattoo appeared to have stopped talking to him. But since there wasn't much he could do about that, he was trying neither to dwell on it, nor consider what it might mean. (And it was nice to not be on the edge of madness, even if he dared not hope that the reprieve might be permanent).

All of which meant there was little for him to do now other than wait here, so that if — no, *when*, he reminded himself — when the coaches arrived, he could usher the attendees into the party room before any accompanying Hidden Mysteries cultists realised this was not their intended destination.

The attendees would be excited, hungry, bored of sitting on coaches, and looking for a good time, and he'd have a room filled with booming music and a shitload of free food and booze. All he had to do was get them in there, and it would be the devil's own job for anyone to get them out.

They just had to get here. And right now, there was nothing he could do to help that.

Hiding in the cramped, windowless toilet of a hired coach wasn't the way the Professor would have preferred to ride into battle, but once the mechanics of the plan had been outlined, it had been clear that it was the best option. It was a simple scheme, devastatingly so. Aided by Google, they'd phoned every single coach company in London, the northern Home Counties and southern Midlands, working from a script devised by Jackson and Ravinder that had them posing as the Hidden Mysteries Society. Social engineering, the two younger men had termed it. They'd provided the numbers, the Professor had managed the list, and Sam and Mindy — taking it in turns to masquerade as the beleaguered personal assistant of the man who'd hired a fleet of coaches for the Norwich North Conference Hotel for Thursday evening and then forgot the details — had made the phone calls.

It was Mindy who'd struck lucky, her silver tongue convincing the secretary on the other end that she genuinely was the man's assistant, carefully teasing his details out of the woman so subtly, and returning them back so effectively, that by the end of the call the woman on the other end would have sworn that it was Mindy who'd given them to her, not she who'd given them to Mindy. And that was when the second stage of the plan came into effect.

Not to cancel the coaches; that would simply invite the Hidden Mysteries Society to hire a fleet of replacement minicabs, cost be damned.

No, this plan was far more subtle. The original booking had no destination specified, with the coaches being hired by the hour, for a total distance not exceeding forty miles ("You guys were still arranging the location," the secretary had reminded Mindy), with the drivers being informed of their destination on their arrival at the Norwich North Conference Hotel.

That's actually why I'm calling, Mindy had said. *You see, the man who'll be there to give the location, it's his birthday, and we've got a surprise party lined up for him. So tell your drivers to smile when he gives the location, and instead drive to the one we've given you. And of course, if anyone else other than me phones up, don't mention this. We wouldn't want to spoil the surprise, would we?*

And so they'd effectively hijacked the coaches the Hidden Mysteries Society had hired, with a cover story that would keep them from finding out, at least not until it was too late.

There was still the possibility that something might go wrong. Some things cannot be left to chance. The autopilot cannot always be trusted; sometimes a human being must take the helm. Which was why the Professor was hiding in the toilet of the final bus, with Jackson, Sam and Mindy in the three buses ahead, having been picked up from a lay-by in an extra stop Mindy had requested. Travelling openly on the buses was a non-starter, but at least this way, they could be there if needed.

The bus lurched.

This really was a most unpleasant way to travel.

After a journey that seemed interminable, although it couldn't have been more than fifteen or twenty minutes, the coach slowed to a halt, accompanied by the sound of gravel crunching beneath its wheels. The Professor waited, trying to steady his breathing. There was the sound of footsteps, and a brief outbreak of snatched conversation. Not as many footsteps as he would have expected, perhaps, and not as much chatter, either — but then he wasn't best-placed to hear such things. Then came a tapping on the door, a tapping that both acknowledged the engaged sign, and ignored it.

The muffled voice of a man made its way through the half-inch of Formica and chipboard. "Mate! I'm desperate!"

The Professor thought quickly. When he'd raised the question of what might occur were one of the conference attendees to wish to use the toilet, Rav had assured him that the journey would be of a short enough duration to render this scenario extremely unlikely. That his private doubts as to the wisdom of this assumption had proven true was of little consolation to the Professor. What to do? To refuse to leave the toilet would arouse suspicion. Better to leave discreetly, try to hunker down in a rear seat, and hope he would go unobserved by any cultists.

"One moment," he called softly. He waited a few seconds, then slid the bolt across. The door was immediately pushed open, nearly taking his face off in the process. A man in a security guard's uniform stood in the aisle before him; the view through the windows beyond was not the manicured grounds of a hotel he'd been expecting, but a dense forest. A large, calloused hand reached out, grasped the lapels of his linen jacket, and hauled him from the confines of the toilet. It took the man only a few seconds to drag him down the length of the coach — watched all the while by the apparently bored driver — and throw him through the open door to the dirt and gravel track beyond.

The other three coaches were parked ahead, with Sam, Mindy, and Jackson being similarly removed from their coaches, Jackson putting up more of a vigorous struggle than his companions, but ultimately achieving nothing save a couple of viciously sharp kicks in the ribs. Thick forest surrounded them, with — at the far end of the track —

the main road that they'd presumably turned off barely visible. A chill crept down the Professor's body as the hard shock of capture transitioned into the cold realisation of defeat.

Something had gone wrong. Something had gone terribly wrong.

Rav had been standing outside the hired party room for some twenty minutes when a car sped through the main gates and barrelled across the car park before skidding to a halt — nineteen-seventies cop show style — in front of him. Four men dressed in security guard uniforms burst out of four simultaneously opening doors and grabbed him, aided by a momentary paralysis on his part that gave them a second or two's head start. Rav wasn't sure they were professionals, but what they lacked in polish they made up for in raw, terror-inducing menace, and Rav quickly found himself wedged into the back seat between two sets of vice-like shoulder blades.

The man to his right twisted toward him, jabbing a finger in his chest with enough force to hurt his ribs.

"We're going for a drive. If you make a sound, if you make any movement, we will muller the shit out of you. Got it?"

Rav nodded. He did get it. He very much got it.

What the hell was going on?

What the hell had gone wrong?

Chapter Thirty-Seven

Rav had been allowed to remain in the back seat of the car long enough only for them to get away from the party room without any of his hired waiting staff noticing his abrupt departure, and then make it to a secluded roadside lay-by, where the guards then proceeded to blindfold him and gaffer-tape his mouth shut before shoving him into the boot. After a claustrophobic journey, whose duration Rav was utterly unable to estimate given the stress, exhaustion, and terror he was suffering, the car skidded to an abrupt halt. He heard the click of the boot opening and felt the welcome touch of a fresh breeze upon his face, then rough hands grabbed him, dragging him from the boot and dumping him on the ground.

"Get up!" a gruff voice ordered.

Rav staggered to his feet and allowed himself to be led away, across crunching gravel, over some sort of threshold, and then down a flight of stairs. Somewhere within him, a still-running autonomous thought process made a note. Basement. A dozen or so paces later he was bought to a halt by the hand that still grasped the back of his jacket. He sensed someone reaching around him, and then the gaffer tape was ripped away along with the hair growth that his face had been working on all day in preparation for tomorrow's shave.

"Jesu—" he cried, not quite managing to suppress his shout of agony.

He received in reply a lazy chuckle from behind and then he was shoved hard through what was presumably a doorway, given the sound of the door slamming shut behind him. There was the sound of two bolts slamming home, then nothing. He waited a cautious moment, then carefully lifted up the blindfold.

"So they got you too, mate?" said Jackson.

The priest was sitting across from him on a long, low leather-covered bench, flanked by Sam and the Professor on one side and Mindy on the other.

"Yeah," Rav told him. He took a look around. The room measured perhaps eight metres by five, with a ceiling covered in moulded polystyrene tiles and walls painted a deep shade of red and decorated with gold braided hangings and bizarre geometric patterns. Black-and-white checkerboard tiles stretched from wall to wall, broken by scattered shag pile rugs and the occasional...

Piece of equipment?

At first glance it had looked like a home gym, but a second, head-tilted-forward and eyes-focused examination had revealed certain very un-gym-like touches. A swing-like affair of rope and leather. Strange, angled, contoured benches. A rack of whip-like implements on the far wall. Chains. Hand cuffs.

Jackson smiled. "Yeah, we're in a, erm… dungeon."

"Just when I thought this case couldn't get weirder." Rav found a sort of vertical couch to lean against and turned his attention back to his four colleagues. "Did you guys get jumped?"

"Yeah," Jackson said. "The buses went to some woodland track instead of to the hotel. Some security guards got on, knocked on the toilet doors, and when we came out, they grabbed us and shoved us into the back of a van." The priest shifted slightly, wincing as he did so.

"Give you a bit of a kicking, did they?" Rav asked.

"Yeah. I think I put up more of a struggle than they cared for. How about you?"

"Bastards grabbed me so quickly I didn't get the chance to give them an excuse to do me over. Dragged me into a car and brought me here. Most painful bit was when they ripped the gaffer tape off my mouth." Rav took a look around and realised someone was missing. "Where's Jess?"

Mindy shrugged a very awkward, guilt-laden shrug. "Still on the coach, I guess. She was in the toilet with me, but when the guy grabbed me and hauled me out, she stayed in. Guess he wasn't looking down. And I guess she decided it was best to keep out of things."

"Nice. So much for canine loyalty."

"I think that's a bit harsh, Ravinder," said the Professor. "On the two occasions you've cared for her, she's been attacked by both vampiric pigs and actual vampires, been cast into a raging sea, had her fur shorn, twice, been involved in two separate confrontations with a wizard, been exposed to evil magic, undergone an emergency evacuation from an aircraft, and been thrown out of an upper storey window by you yourself. One can hardly blame her for deciding to put her own interests first."

The Professor's words stung, the more so because they were true. Rav turned his attentions away from his erstwhile canine employee, and onto matters more related to their current predicament. "Any idea where the hell we are?"

"There is something strangely familiar about this place," said the Professor, "but I find myself unable to put my finger on it."

"Anything you want to tell us, Professor?" asked Mindy, a slight smile playing across her previously grim face. "Didn't figure you for a visitor to places like these."

The Professor sighed. "Please, Parminder, I was an undergraduate in the early seventies. Of course I've visited sex dungeons. But that's not why this is familiar…"

Rav turned his attention back to the door. It was a thick, stout wooden affair, with heavy cast-iron hinges, and wouldn't have looked out of place in a genuine dungeon, the sort where the beatings handed out were for punishment rather than pleasure. "We're a bit stuffed, aren't we? I wonder how they rumbled us?"

After the shock of Mindy's abrupt removal from the toilet, Jess had commando-crawled away and hid under a seat. She was, as they say, not in a good place. What she needed was some top-quality canine psychiatry to treat the doggy PTSD she was coming down with. And had she been living somewhere like Brighton or San Francisco, that might have been an option. But since she wasn't, she'd no doubt be forced to simply get on with things, as was inevitably the case.

Jess was a simple creature with simple desires: food, a warm place to sleep, regular walks with balls to chase, and no encounters with evil abominations who wished her extreme harm. Bitter experience and repeated disappointment had taught her that her stays with Rav inevitably led to too little of the former, and too much of the latter. And while dogs are famed for their loyalty, loyalty is not blind obedience — nor is it dumb stupidity. A dog is as capable as a man of balancing threat and danger on one hand (well, paw), and loyalty and opportunity on the other, and arriving at a decision that could be summarised as, "Bollocks to this, buddy, I'm out of here!"

And then a little while later, at a point where Jess's thought processes were already a good way to reaching just such a decision, events descended upon her in the form of a stream of people piling onto the bus. She tensed up, alert, sensing, snout already searching for an escape route. Was a bad day about to somehow get worse? But then she realised something.

These were happy people.

Excited people.

Good people.

A face appeared before hers, soothing words being spoken, accompanied by a gently stroking hand.

Perhaps this day was about to get better.

As time wore on, the Professor found himself summarising the various factors that collectively defined their confinement. The room in which they were located was formed of plastered concrete; they'd tried chipping away at it, but that was an endeavour that proved fruitless. The door was solid and bolted from the outside. Rav and Jackson had earlier spent a furious ten minutes kicking and barging it, with the same fruitless result they'd achieved with the wall, save for being told to stop "pissing about" by one of the security guards. They'd then spent a further ten minutes attempting to convince him they were not the eco-anarchist protestors he'd been led to believe, and that he was actually in the pay of a group of cultists engaged in a highly illegal plot, but that too received only swearing in response.

The floor was formed of heavy tiles, which — with no tools to hand — were effectively sealed in place. They'd tried climbing on one of the dungeon pieces and ripping off a ceiling tile, but that had revealed yet more concrete. And being, as they were, in a basement, there were no windows, with the only illumination coming from two sets of bulbs that hung from the ceiling some ten feet above them. Spent, they'd retreated to the long bench by the door, but the subsequent brainstorm had quickly blown itself out.

If this had been The Great Escape, the Professor had pointed out, there might have been a stove beneath which they could dig. And as Rav had then observed, had this been an American TV series of his acquaintance called Prison Break, a toilet would apparently have occupied a similar role. But they had neither a stove nor a toilet. A growing awareness in the Professor's nether regions told him that the latter fact might shortly be promoted from a mere lost opportunity to a specific problem. This was a concern. It was one thing to vandalise their habitat by chipping away at plaster and ripping off ceiling tiles. But urinating on the floor was an act unbecoming of a gentleman, even an illegally kidnapped and imprisoned one.

Then there was the sound of bolts being slid back, followed — a moment later — by the staccato creaking of the door's hinges as it opened to reveal a smiling James Fox.

Rav's studies of the French language had been so disastrous that his command of said language had failed to reach even the "schoolboy French" stage. But he did have a brain stuffed with various chunks of pub quiz trivia, and among them was the knowledge that the French have a phrase, *l'esprit d'escalier*, which refers to the predicament of thinking of a killer insult or reply several minutes after you needed it. This was a predicament that Rav had found himself in on many occasions, but not now, for as soon as Fox appeared in the doorway with a smile that practically begged to be punched, the line Rav needed to deliver popped into his brain, all ready for delivery.

"Mister Henderson," he said. "I was wondering when you'd turn up."

For an instant, Fox's smile disappeared. But then it snapped back into place. In the manner of every cheap pulp movie villain ever, Fox had clearly come here to gloat and he wasn't going to let a snappy comeback disrupt his plan. He advanced a couple of paces into the room, followed by two of the security guards who'd brought Rav here. The guards flexed their fists; whatever verbal bon mots Fox was about to say, they were clearly well prepared to add additional, non-verbal, punctuation.

"Gentlemen, lady, please don't get up."

Rav hadn't been planning on getting up, partly because that looked to be something that might provoke a beating, and partly because it was a courtesy he felt disinclined to extend. Fox paused for a moment, perhaps expecting some sort of response, then continued when that response failed to arrive. "I've come to thank you, gentlemen. And lady."

Again, he got no response.

"Quite frankly, we'd almost given up hope. It was so frustrating. We'd had all our ducks lined up, as it were, except one — the skull. The item that we needed to provide the focus of the grand plan we'll soon be realising. When we were just that bit too late in acquiring the skull, it seemed like we were stuck in something of a cul-de-sac. We found ourselves hitting a brick wall on every side. Then you and the Professor arrived, asking after the tablet, and I suddenly thought, who knows? Could I kill two birds with one stone? Get you two off our trail as regards the tablet, and perhaps also have you succeed with the skull where we'd failed? It was a roll of the dice, granted. After all, the two of you are..." He paused to add a touch of cruelty to his smile, before resuming, "I'll be generous and call you amateurs. As the days passed, and the date of the conference approached, it seemed we would have no option save to postpone, to try again another day. Then my phone rang, and it was you Rav, to tell me you'd found the skull. And to cut short what might otherwise turn into a tiresomely long story, I thought I ought to come down and personally express to you all my gratitude for giving us the final piece of our little puzzle. So gentlemen, lady, thank you."

Rav said nothing, not wanting to give him the satisfaction.

For a moment Fox turned away, a move that might have indicated a prelude to leaving had he not performed it in such an exaggerated, overly theatrical manner. He held the turn for a beat, then swivelled back. "I expect you're wondering how we rumbled your little plan?"

This was a question that had occurred to Rav, but he was damned if he was going to give the bastard the satisfaction of admitting it.

"After the near debacle at the golf course," said Fox, "we discovered that our little pet demon Asag had been communicating with others, others who we realised were likely to be you gentlemen. We made sure to instruct Asag to terminate those communications forthwith, of course. But then it occurred to us that you'd also stolen Mortimer, and that the senile old shit would be only too eager to talk."

He smiled a tight smile, one that suggested not so much happiness as a revenge not yet carried out. Then he shook himself back to the moment.

"Anyhow, having considered the possibility that you might be quite aware of our plans for the imminent event, we got the Inner Circle together and had a little brainstorming session. We realised that if we were you, and we'd discovered the conference and its purpose and knew that the ley was involved, we — you, that is — would deduce that transport would be required to transport the attendees, transport that needed to be hijacked ahead of time."

"So you figured out we'd start calling coach hire companies," Rav said, tired of having Fox talk at him.

"Quite! Our first step was to call the actual coach company and warn them that anarchist eco-protesters were planning on disrupting the conference, so they should instruct all their staff to be vigilant against any suspicious phone calls, and to be sure to deny all knowledge of the event. Then all we had to do was get ourselves a landline number, diverted to one of our mobile phones, knock up a quick website, do a bit of Google advertising to get our number up on your lists, and wait for someone to call with a vague enquiry about an event at the Norwich North Conference Hotel."

"So when I talked to the secretary," Mindy said, "I was actually talking to one of your people?"

Fox smiled, a full-on grin this time. "Exactly. It was Phoebe all along, happily letting you give out all the salient details of your plan. Making an extra stop beforehand to pick up four "additional party organisers". The alternative address where you were going to set up your diversionary party." He looked straight at Rav. "Which is how we knew where to find you, Mister Shah. Then all we had to do was phone the actual coach hire company again and tell them to make two extra stops prior to the hotel, the first to pick up the four additional party organisers, and the second to have them removed. Obviously, we didn't quite put it that way. And I think that pretty much covers it all!"

He let out a long breath.

"Anyway, as I said, I wanted to say thank you. Now I must go. Work to do. Toodle-pip!"

Chapter Thirty-Eight

In the dungeon, time passed, marked for Rav only by his increasing levels of boredom and frustration. At some point hunger might arrive, and possibly the need to take a piss, but however much time had actually passed, neither of those points had yet been reached.

Then the Professor sprang to his feet. "I have it!"

Rav roused himself. "Have what?"

"I recall from where I recognise this location. It's those geometric markings that give it away. Have you noticed that the shapes they describe are non-Euclidean – impossible, that is? This is Bechdel House, the home of the famous German modernist architect, Herman Bechdel. He was famous for his use of geometric designs that described shapes impossible in real life, and for what could politely be described as sexual non-conformity. In his own house, which I recall being in East Anglia, he'd put it all into practice. And he was also famous for one other thing…"

"Which was?"

The Professor was already walking away, eyes scanning. "Secret passages."

Jess was happy. She wasn't quite sure yet who her new mistress was, but when she spoke, it was in tones that mixed firmness with kindness and suggested a better life, one that might involve a proper dog bed instead of a blanket, and luxury dog food instead of dry kibble, and walks, with balls to chase, and no violent encounters with evil abominations.

She wanted this.

Jess snuggled up against her new mistress and looked up at her with eyes packed full of the best pleading signals several millennia of top-quality Darwinian evolution can buy.

She really wanted this.

Finding the secret passage had proved relatively easy. It wasn't movie-easy, where the protagonist walks straight up to a statuette suspiciously mounted on a table as a beer pump handle would be mounted on a bar, pulls it toward them, and is rewarded with an entire section of wall sliding aside. On the other hand, it wasn't Times crossword-hard, where you can expend two hours of struggle only to achieve the answers to three down and six across, with six across later proving to be embarrassingly wrong. (That's if you're Rav, that is; it was his experience that the Professor could polish the whole thing off in little more time than it took him to drink a cup of tea and eat its accompanying biscuit.)

But after ten minutes of the four of them tapping and prodding, it'd been Mindy who'd found a section of dado rail that could be removed with a tug, exposing a hidden switch which, when flicked, allowed the adjacent section of wall to be pushed back to reveal a passageway leading to the side.

Passage found, Rav waited for someone else to volunteer themselves to enter and — when no one did — decided he might as well give it a go. He eased himself through the narrow gap between the wall proper and the pushed-in wall and edged into the passageway, finding himself in a pitch dark interior, which was a bit of a downer given that they had no light sources on them, their phones all having been confiscated. But as he advanced slowly forward, his eyes became accustomed to the gloom, and he managed to make out a switch attached to the wall. He flicked it down; dim lights set along the passageway's ceiling lit, revealing a few metres of narrow corridor with a metal spiral staircase at its end.

He poked his head back out. "I found the light switch. There's some stairs at the end. I say we go for it. No point staying here."

Offstage, behind a set of thick velvet curtains, Jason Bishop waited. He didn't mind waiting. After all, it was granting him an opportunity to savour the magnitude of what he was about to accomplish. A prize that his grandfather, Stanley, had reached for, only to be frustrated by the limitations of his era's technological capability. A prize that his vain, stupid, hedonistic father had been gifted, only to spurn. And now a prize that he was about to seize. Destiny awaited him.

On the other side of the curtains, in the cavernous main lounge of this modernistic country house they'd hired for no reason other than that it was on the ley line and was available, were a good chunk of the people who actually ran the country. The permanent secretaries of the departments of defence, justice, treasury, agriculture, foreign affairs, education, work and pensions, and the home office, plus their assorted deputies. And the prize of them all, the Cabinet Secretary, the head of the civil service. In less than thirty minutes they would all belong to him.

Body and enslaved soul.

Henderson was warming them up; he could hear the man's confident voice booming through the curtains.

"Close the curtains," he was saying. "Dim the lights. All waiting staff depart. Yes, dear, that means you. Off you go. And lock the doors behind you." There was the sound of doors closing, and locks turning. "And now, with discretion assured, so the secrets that occur in this room, remain in this room…"

In his mind's eye, Bishop could see the cheesy, knowing smile that Henderson would be smiling right now.

"Ladies and gentlemen, I give you… The Great Marvelo!"

The spiral staircase had led them up through three complete revolutions, edged by walls of featureless, brutal, unpainted breezeblock, and broken only by the dim, industrial lights. Even for a secret passageway, the Professor found this frankly disappointing, doubly so, considering that this was the private dwelling of the architect himself. It certainly did little to dispel whatever prejudices the Professor might have harboured against the modernist architects of the post-war period of whom Bechdel had been a leading member.

The staircase eventually opened into a short section of corridor that ended at a plain, white dead-end. Rav was pushing and prodding, but the wall appeared disinclined to move. Mounted on a breezeblock to one side of the dead-end was a metal slider. The Professor reached past Rav and moved the slider to the right, just as his colleague launched into an enthusiastic shoulder charge. A section of white wall flew open, sending Rav tumbling into the space beyond.

The Professor followed behind him at a more sedate pace, finding himself in what appeared to be a small, but luxuriously appointed octagonal study lined on four of its eight walls with floor-to-ceiling bookcases, one of which had swung open to allow them entry. Four windows occupied the remaining four walls, each offering a view across the house's roof to the surrounding wooded hills. At the centre of the study was a desk, with a single chair before it. A bank of eight small television screens ran along the length of the desk, each perhaps four inches square, and slightly curved in the way that televisions had once been, and enclosed in the sort of Bakelite plastic that had been the future, back when this house was being built. Each screen had a set of eight buttons below it in two rows of four, labelled, with a singular lack of imagination, "one" to "eight".

Jackson leaned past him to click a button below the leftmost screen. A black-and-white image appeared on its previously blank face, showing an entrance hall-type room from the classic CCTV perspective of an upper corner. A bored looking security guard stood with his back to the camera. The Professor and Jackson's three other companions quickly crowded in.

"That must be the lobby, right?"

"Try another button!"

Jackson began to click through the buttons, number two for the second screen, number three for the third, and so on, with each screen in turn displaying an image of a different room.

"Dining room!"

"Kitchen!"

"Bedroom! Bedroom? Is that even legal?"

"The Professor did suggest he was something of a pervert," muttered Jackson. "Guess he's a control freak with it." He continued clicking.

"Another bedroom."

And then the sixth screen came to life with a view of a sprawling room, crowded with what looked to be a good hundred-plus people sitting on sofas, chairs, and rugs. And at their centre, a figure stood beside a table upon which sat a skull.

"And there we go," said Jackson.

Rav pushed between the priest and the Professor to point at the standing figure. "Is that Bishop? What the hell's he wearing?"

"Hang on, there's a speaker here," said Sam from his end of the table. He jabbed at something, and a voice emerged from speakers set around the table.

Bishop.

"And now finally, we get to the climax of our show, as I, the Great Marvelo, prepare to cast my final ritual!"

A burst of tittering emerged from the speakers, the sort of tittering you get when a crowd knows they're watching something ludicrous, but are sufficiently lubricated by alcohol that they'll enjoy it nonetheless.

"The Great Marvelo?" said Jackson.

Rav snapped his fingers. "They're hiding in plain sight. Think about it. How the hell can you manage to cast a seriously involved magic ritual on people without the people concerned getting so freaked out that they disrupt the proceedings?"

Sam supplied the answer. "Disguise it as a cheesy magic show. Genius."

Rav straightened up abruptly. "We need to get down there, now. Do something, anything to stop it."

Jackson was already moving. "Yeah!" He spun round, taking in the same view as the Professor. Four walls that contained only windows. And four walls that contained only bookcases, albeit one of them being a secret door to a secret passageway that led only to a sex dungeon. "There's no actual proper door."

The Professor cleared his throat. "Perhaps there might be a second secret door?"

The second hidden door had led to a second spiral staircase, which led down through two revolutions before ending against a plain white section of wall of a similar design to the entrance into the study. Forewarned this time, Rav opened the concealed door, and thus was able to ease himself gently out, rather than hurling himself through. Once again, he found himself in an octagonal room, but one of considerably greater scale, stretching up as it did through two complete floors, with a balcony completely encircling it at the first-floor level. A huge chandelier hung from the ceiling; four oak double-doors were set equally around the room. He edged forward, allowing his companions to follow him.

"Pick a door, I guess," he whispered to no one in particular.

A cough sounded from above him. He looked up, and found himself looking at the not-quite-beautiful features of someone his gut instinct told him was Phoebe Bishop. She smiled a smile that emitted kindness in the way a black hole emits light, then tossed something up and out of her hand. It spun lazily in the air as momentum waited for gravity to get its act together, the thousand-fold-fragmented light of the chandelier reflecting off its smooth, white, oval surface.

An egg, Rav realised.

And then it hit the floor and shattered.

The Professor was already turning away as the egg impacted, but his action was too late, and probably futile anyway. Magical energy washed over him, both fire and ice at the same time, his nerves blazing with an agony worse than any he'd ever felt. He wasn't sure that any of this was real, but what did it matter; is pain any less real for existing only within a man's soul?

Then a peal of laughter made him look up, to see India Ponsonby standing on the opposite side of the balcony from Phoebe Bishop. A second egg came tossing out of her hand, falling so slowly and yet so fast, hitting the parquet floor and smash—

The second egg hit the floor, and this one brought not agony, but memories. Images thrust their way into Rav's brain, recollections drawn from across his life, every one of them bad, every one of them bringing its cargo of misery forgotten but not quite unremembered. Madam Clara, screaming. The near-drowning at the canal. The suicide by train he'd witnessed aged ten. Every single act of bullying he'd experienced at infant, junior, and secondary school. Every racist incident. The mugging, aged twelve, that had been the last he'd seen of his first mobile phone, only eight days after he'd received it for his birthday. Falling off his bike aged seven. Breaking his wrist on a school trip aged nine. Every single time he'd tripped and fallen as a toddler. His grandmother dying when he was eight. His grandfather following her a year later. The death of his hamster when he was six. A hundred occasions of utter misery experienced in an instant.

Somehow, through this, he was aware of falling to his knees, screaming; an awareness told him that his companions were similarly suffering. He screamed, and screamed, and screamed, and then a dull wet thud on his back told him that an egg had hit him directly— and the memories and the pain stopped. Snuffed out. He staggered to his feet, but around him, Jackson, Sam, the Professor, and Mindy were still locked in their agonies. As he watched, carefully aimed eggs hit each one of them, but instead of staggering to their feet they slumped, still, to the floor.

Why? What?

Then one of the double oak doors opened and a giant of a man stepped through it, wearing tight black jeans and an even tighter white t-shirt. Rav was in the process of placing him — Ponsonby's dial-a-shag from a week or so ago — when the guy reached behind his back with both hands and pulled out—

Two golf clubs? Woods, not irons?

The guy advanced on Rav, each of his giant paws spinning a club, so fast that they were almost twin blurs, like Tiger Woods reborn as a scaled-up ninja (or possibly, Tiger Woods's former wife after she'd discovered he was something of a bedroom ninja). "You want some?" the bloke asked.

Rav didn't want some. He backed away, desperately looking around the room for something — anything — he could grab, but this was a modernist house with a minimalist interior decor, and thus entirely lacking in the sort of items — standard lamp, occasional table, sword — that one might find lying around in a more traditional country home. The bloke darted in with the golf club his left hand was spinning; Rav ducked away, only to collide with the right hand's club. It smashed into his side; something that felt a lot like a rib cracked, and he let out a cry of pure, honest agony.

The man danced back, smiling, then approached once more, shielded by his twin spinning shafts of doom.

Golf clubs? It was so incongruous that Rav might almost have laughed, were he not so obviously in the final act of a three-act tragedy. From somewhere, utter desperation and raw terror conjured up a desperate gambit: "You know we watched her shagging some other bloke round the back of a restaurant, right?" he found himself asking. From the look of anger that for an instant flashed across the guy's face, he hadn't known, but from the way he then headed forwards, it looked like Rav's desperate gambit had merely increased the guy's desire to murder him.

And then a woman's voice cut right through the entire third act like a Sherman tank manoeuvring through a two-man tent. This wasn't the voice of someone politely enquiring, or insistently asking, or even urgently informing. This was a voice of command. This was the voice of a woman who'd commanded the girls' hockey team not through skill or leadership but through a clear willingness to break whatever legs needed to be broken. This was the voice of a woman born to lead and bred to rule. A posh voice, but not braying. A voice whose tones said that it would speak and you would listen. A voice that was now saying—

"What the damned hell is going on?"

The dial-a-shag took a step-and-a-half backwards, his spinning clubs slowing to a halt. Rav turned, enough to take in the new arrival whilst keeping a wary eye on the two clubs and their psychotic wielder. The voice belonged to a woman in perhaps her mid-fifties, with a face that was stern though not necessarily unattractive, and a neat, functional hairstyle that emphasised the air of brisk confidence she was projecting.

A familiar looking, shorn, brown-dyed Border Collie stood beside her. A whole bunch of security guards accompanied them, the attention they were paying to the woman making it clear that for now at least, they were serving her.

"Lola knew something was wrong," the woman said. "We were spending some quiet time together in one of the other lounges when she sensed something. So I gathered these guards together and she led us here, and then as we got closer, we heard the noise and commotion." She bent down to stroke Jess's head. "She's such a clever dog."

"Lola?"

The woman's harsh face split into a smile as she looked back down at Jess. "She's my dog. I've adopted her."

Rav gave Jess a long, hard look and received in reply a casually disdainful glance that looked so much like the canine equivalent of a dismissive shrug that it probably was the canine equivalent of a dismissive shrug. "Sorry, and you are?"

"Elisabeth Atkinson, Principal Private Secretary to the Secretary of State for Culture, Media and Sport."

The Professor's voice sounded from halfway across the room. "So you would be Bernard to his Jim Hacker?"

Atkinson turned her attention to the Professor. "Why are you lying down?"

"I'm temporarily paralysed from the neck down for reasons that would be too convoluted to explain at this moment."

Now that her attention had been attracted downward, Atkinson realised that the floor was covered with the remains of smashed eggs, with a single dying chicken foetus at the centre of each patch of remains. "What on earth is going on here?"

Rav looked up; there was no sign of Phoebe Bishop or India Ponsonby. Presumably, they'd weighed up the odds, considered the fact that the security guards appeared to have realised that something was up, and had decided to do a runner. That conclusion made, and keeping a wary eye on ninja-golf-club-dial-a-shag-boy, he took the half-shuffle towards Atkinson that was all he was capable of right now and tried to gather what remained of his reserves of charisma. "I can explain later. But right now I really need to get through one of these doors."

Power surged through Jason Bishop; a power greater than anything he'd ever experienced. His awareness had expanded; it was as though

217

his soul now stretched around twenty-four thousand miles of a living ley line, from his location here in East Anglia to sacred locations in New Zealand on the opposite side of the globe. He could live another fifty years and never experience anything that came close to this. Even the most exquisite orgasm was but a pale splash of beige when set against the thousand-coloured tapestry of this experience.

In a circle around the lounge, eight members of the Inner Circle chanted, their voices and his bringing the ritual to its climax, they like he protected by Asag from the forces that would otherwise have torn their souls to pieces. As to the other inhabitants of the room, they were laughing no more. The cover story of the cheesy magic show had served its purpose, allowing him to seal the room, and then keeping them quiescent as the ritual built, drawing them in. They'd even laughed when he'd revealed his "assistant", Horace, laughing at what they thought was a plastic skull placed upon a covered table, giggling at the cheap ventriloquism he'd thrown in.

But that was then, and in the now of several minutes later they were drawn in, their faces blank, their eyes locked, once firmly clutched drinks now dropped upon the carpet. Bishop was guiding the ritual. Raising up, swooping down, shaping, lifting, forces coming together. The ley was delivering power smoother than he'd dared hope, and the skull was focussing it, allowing him to construct a ritual of a scope and force greater than any wizard of any age could even have dreamed of.

Almost there.

A few moments more.

There were one hundred and twenty-seven souls in this room beyond he and his companions, and every single one of them was now locked into the ritual, their mind plugged in to a central channel in which he was about to pour the enslaving spell he'd spent the last ten minutes creating. On the table, surrounding Horace, his victims' photo-ID lanyards were piled, placed there as part of the "ritual" he'd jokingly told them he was going to cast. Named as they were, and emblazoned with an image, those photo-IDs would serve as the controls through which he could henceforth control his enslaved servants. Forever.

Power beyond any reasonable man's dreams was about to be his.

Nearly there.

Now!

Then the doors that were supposed to be locked crashed open and a voice shouted.

"Oi!"

Chapter Thirty-Nine

In his twenty-something years on Earth, Rav had spent a lot of his time considering questions that many might consider niche to the point of absurdity. Who would win in a fight between pirates and ninjas? Ninjas, obviously. Who would win in a fight between ninjas and Vikings? Still ninjas, unless the Vikings were berserkers, of course. Is Die Hard a Christmas film? Yes, and if Bruce Willis says otherwise, he can do one.

One question that had never occurred to him was what might happen if you were to distract a man while he was in the process of casting the most powerful magical ritual ever cast in the whole of human history. However, had that question occurred to him, and had he attempted to form an answer, his best guess would have been that the outcome would not be good. And as it happened, not good turned out to be a very accurate description, if one were using the British-English meaning of "not good" which translates into standard International English as "absolutely catastrophic". One moment, aided by a key he'd borrowed from one of the security guards, Rav was crashing through the doors and shouting "Oi!", the next he was looking at the panic flickering across Bishop's face as the man lost control of the ritual and Rav found himself wondering if he might perhaps have screwed up.

I mean, sure, saving the higher echelons of the British civil service from becoming the enslaved puppets of a selfish, cruel, and shallow middle-class pseudo-hippy from Richmond was all very well, but not necessarily if the result was to instead find yourself at Ground Zero of the magical equivalent of Hiroshima.

A perfectly circular wave of blue-green energy blasted out of the skull in a manner that would have looked like cheap CGI were it not for the fact that: a) it was accompanied by a clapping screech that sounded like the fabric of the universe tearing; b) Rav felt as if his soul was being squeezed out of his brain like juice from an orange; and c) it actually looked like the best CGI money can buy.

Every single person in the room was screaming, Rav included. The wave of energy hit the walls with enough force to blast the plaster off, then bounced back, the now chaotic wave pattern filling the room like ripples in a small pond into which a large rock has recently been heaved. Rav took one heavy-footed step forward, and another, but the nearer he moved to Bishop and the skull, the further away he was. The room was expanding, he realised — no, the universe itself, or at least this local part of it, was expanding, unevenly. Angles that should have been right angles no longer were; in fact, not only were the corners of the room no longer square, he wasn't even sure they were restricted to a mere three dimensions. From somewhere inside of him that was still capable of halfway coherent thinking, the thought occurred to him that had Professor Stephen Hawking still been around, this was one sight that would have forced even he to say, "I. Have. No. Fucking. Idea. What. Is. Going. On."

Suddenly he was standing beside Bishop, and in that instant, he looked into the man's eyes and saw that the ritual still had him, was still ongoing, albeit badly, and in a way he clearly hadn't intended. Then the fabric of space-time warped again, and they were perhaps a mile apart. A shape was at his feet. Small and artificially brown and howling in agony. Jess, he realised, as affected by the ritual as he, because this was no hallucination, this was real — horribly, awfully, and quite possibly fatally so.

The universe pulsed once more, and he and Jess were again standing next to Bishop. Rav raised an arm, only to find his pointing hand stretching a couple of hundred metres past Bishop. "Jeeeeeeeeeeeeeeeeeeeeeeeeeeee," he managed, as time slowed to a halt, leaving him unable to complete the syllable.

Jess was not capable of verbalising her current feelings. But had she been, she might have observed that she now knew what it would feel like to be a can of dog food being first opened, and then having its contents removed. Even with her simplified soul, the sensations she was currently experiencing were beyond mere pain. She would have left the room had she had any idea of where the entrance was; as it was, up, down, forward and backward appeared to have lost all meaning.

Rav was beside her; quite frankly she would have attacked him had it not been for the fact that right now, he was the only thing in her currently observable universe that could in any way be understood by her relatively simple brain. And then he was there. Him. The man. The bad man. The man who'd made Rav fall into the water. The man whose face she'd attacked in the big room. The man whose arm she'd got a hold of at the big park.

She leapt, aiming at his face, but the universe was shifting again, up becoming down becoming up. She caught hold of something and bit hard.

And then the screaming in her skull stopped.

The Professor had blacked out at some point. He came to on the floor, looking up at the domed ceiling. The room was near-silent now, save for soft sobbing and what sounded like people retching. His body felt like it had been disassembled to its component atoms, and then reassembled badly by a nineteen-seventies British workforce on a Friday afternoon after a lunch long on liquid and short on actual lunch. At that precise moment, staying where he was for the next decade or so seemed like an attractive option, but the duty instilled into him by his prep school masters was calling, and he found his elbows levering him painfully upright.

Careful hands helped him to his feet. Mindy. "Are you okay, Professor?" she asked.

He nodded, speech being something that he didn't quite feel capable of, right now. He staggered through the double doors through which Rav had exited, and into a room now host to a scene of subdued chaos and quiet confusion. Rav approached, a dazed-looking Jess in tow, and said something he didn't quite catch. Across from him, Sam and Jackson were already working, moving from person to person, a soft touch here, a quiet word there. Professionals. Doing their job. Elizabeth Atkinson, posse of security guards in tow, appeared to be establishing some sort of chain of command. And more security guards were entering now, the shocked looks on their faces and angry tones in their voices revealing that whatever role they might have been playing, they'd not been privy to the conspiracy's innermost truths. Mindy said something to Rav, and this time the Professor caught it. "What did you do?"

"Nothing, except interrupt Bishop. He lost control of the ritual, the whole universe sort of started turning inside out, and then Jess bit him and that stopped it." He shook his head. "Christ knows what would have happened if she hadn't done that."

Mindy bent down to kiss the top of the dog's head. "Good girl, Jess. Good girl."

The dog gave a protesting whine, then wagged her tail cautiously.

Around them, the security guards were grabbing cultists, angry shouts interspersed with mutterings of, "Look, I don't mind giving anarchist scrotes a slap, but this is bang out of order," and other lines of different wordage but similar meaning.

And then the Professor realised that something, and someone, was missing.

The skull of St Horace.

And Jason Bishop.

Rav didn't need the Professor to say anything. The shocked face and the arm pointing at the area where Bishop and the skull had been, was all he needed.

"Shit!"

"What?" asked Mindy.

"Bishop's gone, and he's got the skull."

"Where the hell's he gone?"

Rav didn't answer, but instead called out across the room. "Jackson!"

A security guard was passing: a shaven-haired, middle-aged white guy of the sort that in Rav's experience could be either the salt-of-the-earth diamond geezer you might accidentally bump into in a DIY superstore, or the salt-of-the-earth diamond geezer who might kick the shit out of you if you were to accidentally bump into him at the wrong end of an away match against Millwall.

"Hey mate, we need a car," Rav said.

"You what?" said the guy, in a tone that was more Saturday afternoon Millwall than Sunday morning DIY store.

"We need a car. And we ain't got one on account of you guys kidnapped us and brought us here on the say-so of the bastards who did this."

Jackson appeared.

"Jackson, tell him we need a car."

The priest shifted to face the security guard, subtly letting his leather jacket fall open to reveal the dog collar inside. "We need a car." Then he turned to face Rav. "Why do we need a car?"

Chapter Forty

Jackson gunned the engine of the borrowed Ford, spinning it into a gravel-crunching, fishtailing arc towards Bechdel House's main driveway. "Where to?" he asked. "We don't know where he went."

Rav didn't say anything, because he knew where Bishop had gone, or at least he knew where he'd be going, and it would take only a few seconds of searching on his phone, which he'd managed to retrieve from the security goons, to establish where that place was. He tapped through to Google Maps, and typed in "tv mast".

A pin appeared, several miles north of the blue dot that marked their location. Rav jabbed a finger at the pin and read the words that appeared: "The Tacolneston transmitter." The car crunched to a halt at the end of the drive. Rav took a glance at the map. "Okay, turn right."

Jackson waited for an oncoming car to pass, spun the Ford out onto the road, then accelerated hard. "And what's that?" he asked, once he got the car settled into a steady fifteen-miles-an-hour over the fifty-miles-an-hour speed limit.

Rav clicked through to the Wikipedia page. "It's a tv transmitter mast. Two-hundred-and-six metres tall. Covers Ipswich and Norwich." He clicked back to the maps. "Left turn at the next roundabout."

"And sorry, why do we think he's going there?"

"Remember the novel Mortimer wrote?"

The flat, featureless East Anglian horizon receded further and further as Bishop climbed ever higher up the tower. A fury burned within him, a fury so righteous and consuming that it was as though gravity itself had released him from its bonds, so easy was the climb. Up and up he went, propelled by the strength of his anger. Earlier, the skull nestling within his canvas backpack had been heavy upon his back, but now he scarcely felt its weight.

Most was lost, but perhaps not all, because the ley network might still be active, and if it was, then revenge, at least, would be his.

Rav was bloody knackered. It was one thing to declare that you were going to climb up two hundred metres' worth of ladder in pursuit of the bastard who was already halfway up; it was another to actually try it, using muscles that in the historical long-term had been disgracefully neglected and in the immediate short-term had been savagely abused.

But he knew he couldn't stop, not with Bishop somewhere ahead of him, and Jackson right behind him.

And all the while, that gut-punching line from the Hindustani's ending was bouncing through his brain.

A long scream slowly faded as the Hindustani fell to the ground a thousand yards below.

He reached for the next rung.

Bishop reached the top of the ladder and pulled himself onto the small platform that sat at the top of the tower. Time was of the essence, he knew that. At best, the ley network could operate for several hours once activated, but with the chaotic end of the enslaving ritual, only the devil himself might know if it still survived.

The ritual he was intending to cast now was only a shadow of the plan he'd meant to unleash. A consolation at best, and perhaps not even that, perhaps no more than an angry lashing out, a desire to do something, anything with the power he'd created. Where the enslaving ritual had been elegant and crafted, this was merely a raw blast of power, focused by the skull and transmitted through the mast's electromagnetic power. For twenty, perhaps thirty miles, the blast would radiate out, incinerating the minds of all those caught within that radius who were not magically protected. And he, as the focus of that blast, would in turn receive the incoming energy from all those shattered souls, altering and transforming him into something that might perhaps be more than human, more than mere, mortal flesh.

He flipped the skull out of the backpack and placed it on a handy pillar that marked the very centre of the tower. He didn't waste time on preparation. There were no acolytes here to be impressed, no flummery that needed speaking. This was a time for raw and direct spellcasting. Bishop might have been vain, but he was no fool, and he possessed enough self-awareness to recognise his vanity and the dangers it could present. But equally he knew that when it came to magic, he was good, and he knew that as a fact beyond mere vanity. He'd taken the skills posthumously bequeathed to him by his grandfather, via a locked trunk in his late father's attic, and had built upon them through a decade or more of study that had taken him to the ends of the earth, from Tibetan mountaintops to dusty Oriental libraries. By the time he'd resurrected Mortimer, he was already the greatest spellcaster who'd ever lived. Whatever path his future might take, this act on this day might prove to be the greatest mark he would leave upon history.

He began to chant: ancient words, power words, words that some said had been built into the universe by its creator — a claim which, given the power they possessed, might very well be true. He'd always known that to wield these powers was to risk his soul, and he knew that the act he was about to perform would take its toll. A part of him would die this day. But another part of him would live, magnificently so.

The ley network opened once more. Raw magical power surged into the tower, running up and down its full length before rippling outwards, riding on the transmitter's broadcast radio waves. An ever-expanding disc of mystical energy that was turning the sky itself to the colour of death.

And then, from the corner of his eye, guided by that small portion of his brain that was not fully occupied channelling the forces of the ley through it, he sensed movement. He turned, but too late. Already, a figure was slamming into him, hurling him against the platform's low, encircling railings. The cold metal dug hard into his hip, and he spun over, into the empty air beyond.

The climb up the tower had combined near-total physical exhaustion with a terror that bubbled barely within Rav's ability to cope. He'd never been that great with heights, but when the height you're talking about is in excess of two hundred meters and you know that according to prophecy, you'll shortly be making the return journey at an acceleration of nine-point-eight metres per second squared, the phrase "fear of heights" fails to adequately describe the situation. Twice making the schoolboy error of looking down hadn't helped, and when the now familiar dark energy had begun to surge up and down the tower, he'd felt he was nearing his limits. By the time he finally reached the platform he was in a pretty bad way.

He hadn't come up with any sort of plan, hadn't thought of anything apart from getting to the top without losing it, and this was perhaps for the best. Killing a man is never easy, and a premeditated decision to do so would be a decision he could never have made. But as he hauled himself onto the platform, saw Bishop facing away from him — his hands wreathed in blue hellfire — and felt the universe itself beginning to scream, some deep-rooted thought lurking down in the primeval portion of his brain realised that he simply had to act. Now. Not think. Act. Bishop had to be stopped, now. Hesitation would be fatal.

It was as though he were a passenger in a body piloted by someone else, watching helplessly, unable to intervene. He felt the scrabbling of trainer-on-metal as he scrambled onto the platform and launched himself forward, turning to bring his shoulder to the fore. He felt the juddering impact as his shoulder slammed into Bishop's chest.

And he watched as Bishop tumbled over the encircling handrails. The energy surging up, down, and around the tower, stuttered, pulsed out in a final massive outburst of energy that rippled in every direction, and then died. Stillness returned to the landscape. Only then did a full, sentient consciousness return to Rav. *I just killed someone*, he realised.

And then Jackson was beside him. "Where is he?"

Rav pointed. "He went over."

"Oh," said the priest, managing to pack a whole load of meaning into that one-syllable word. "Look, I could talk a load of theology, but mate, he needed stopping."

Rav managed a nod, although right now what he really wanted to do was break into a long, shuddering scream. He'd thought he hated Bishop before, but now, for what Bishop had forced him to become, he hated him even more. And then the preceding line from the Hindustani's final chapter played across his mind — "He pulled himself back onto the platform and launched himself at the policeman, the fury of his charge sending the man tumbling into, and then over, the narrow encircling rail."

Operating on instinct, he took a step back, just in time for Bishop to go barrelling past him, the wizard hurling himself though the space that Rav had occupied mere split-seconds earlier. Bishop tried to stop himself, but it was too late: he was committed, his momentum carrying him over the rails for a second time. And this time, he didn't find anything to catch hold of, if the long scream that slowly tailed away was anything to go by.

Rav walked cautiously over to the rail, Jackson beside him, and leaned over. A long way below, the matchstick-like figure of Bishop lay on the green turf, unmoving, limbs brokenly splayed.

"Cool," said Jackson. "Out with justified homicide, in with death by misadventure. Works for me!"

He slapped Rav on the back. "Come on, mate. Let's climb back down."

Chapter Forty-One

The tiny church of St Mungo's lay near the centre of what was already being called the Anglian Desert, a wind-whipped patch of drifting sand that stretched from the edges of Bury St Edmunds in the west to the coastal town of Lowestoft in the east, and from Ipswich in the south to Norwich in the north. A dried-up channel that had previously been part of the Norfolk Broads ran past the church's tiny cemetery. It had been a nearly a week since the five of them, six if you included Jess, had been together. Now Jackson, who of all of them had the best contacts with the authorities, was filling his colleagues in on what had happened — save for Jess, who was choosing instead to sniff her way slowly from gravestone to gravestone, pausing only to cast the occasional wary glance in Rav's direction. (She'd probably have preferred to stay with Elisabeth Atkinson, but since she wasn't his dog to give away, he'd been forced to insist on having her back).

"Okay, so there were a couple of hundred thousand people in the affected area who went to bed with one hell of a headache," said Jackson. "But according to the regional health authority, there appear to be no permanent effects." The priest shuddered. "I don't like to think what might have happened if you hadn't have stopped him, Rav. Hell, even interrupted as it was, it still did this." He waved a hand across the sand-filled graveyard to the dunes beyond.

Rav nodded. There were many things about the events of the past few weeks that kept him awake at night, but the knowledge of what horrors he might have prevented was at least a partial balm to his conscience. (And the hours of overtime he'd been working in a just-about-successful attempt to pull his social work career back from the edge of oblivion had at least served to offer some distraction).

"But what about the desert?" asked Mindy. "Seems like that was a big story for a few days, and then everyone got bored."

"Pretty much. The authorities are saying it's down to global warming." The priest shrugged. "I know in this case it isn't, but given that global warming's a thing, it might actually make people take it seriously."

Despite everything, that almost had Rav smiling. "You trying to argue that turning a thousand square miles of prime farmland into desert's a good thing?"

Jackson shrugged again. "Well, obviously there's economic and social costs, but the local tourist board has already set up a working group to figure out ways of marketing it. You know, adventure tours, quad-bikes across the dunes, that sort of thing."

"I've heard one chap's thinking of importing some camels from Arabia," added the Professor. "He's going to be running expeditions where you ride across the sands from Norwich to Ipswich."

"That'd be pretty cool!" said Mindy. Then her brow furrowed. "Although ain't they supposed to be right angry sods?"

Rav brought the resulting conversational free-for-all to a halt by the judicious use of waved hands and shouts of "Whoa", ironically in much the same way that a camel herder might try to bring order to his recalcitrant animals. "Guys, can we focus? Are we really satisfied that it's over?"

Sam nodded in recognition of a very fair point. "For starters, Bishop's dead."

Jackson nodded. "I managed to blag my way into the morgue while you were being interviewed by the Norfolk constabulary. Amazing what you can do when you've got a dog collar. Anyhow, the bloke was proper dead." He shook his head. "I wanted to make sure, you know?"

Sam continued. "Fox and Phoebe Bishop got away, but the security guards grabbed the rest of the cultists and handed them over to the police. There were enough senior civil servants pointing hysterical fingers to get the police to take it seriously. Of course, when the dust settled, they realised there wasn't really anything they could charge them with that would stick, given that they didn't have any idea what the hell had gone on. But they apparently gave them some pretty stiff warnings to keep their noses clean in future. I think they were mostly middle-class idiots looking for a bit of a thrill. They've had a scare, and some of them took a bit of a beating from the security guards, so I think they'll retire from evil cult stuff."

"What about Fox and Phoebe Bishop?" asked Mindy.

Sam handed the thread of conversation back to Jackson with a nod. The priest resumed speaking. "I managed to talk to India Ponsonby while she was in custody."

"Dog collar again?" asked Rav.

"Yeah. That and a phone call from the Bishop of London to the Bishop of Norwich and a phone call from the Bishop of Norwich to the Chief Constable of the Norfolk police, which was also part of why they accepted our story of what happened to Bishop. Anyhow, she was happy to blab about pretty much anything and everything. Like, apparently Phoebe was shagging Fox behind Bishop's back."

"Nice."

"They've gone on the run, Phoebe and Fox that is. Central Asia, Ponsonby reckons. Turns out that Fox's business was on the edge of bankruptcy and he was already under investigation for the illegal trafficking of cultural artefacts. They're dangerous, but I think Bishop was the main man. With him gone, the whole thing collapsed."

"What about Asag and the tablet?"

"Sam and I found the tablet hidden in a storeroom at Bechdel House. We did a sort of blessing on it that seems to have broken the link and freed Asag to go back whence he came, as they say. Least," he shrugged, "the tablet's no longer reeking of evil."

"We gave it to the police," Sam added. "Who gave it to Interpol. It should be heading back to Istanbul now. We did put in a suggestion that they might want to look into it being an inside job."

Rav mentally ticked through his list of loose ends and found nothing obviously hanging. "So that's that, is it? All done and dusted?"

The Professor coughed. "There was one point that was intriguing me, which was where Mortimer came up with the idea for the ley network. He was clearly a man with talents, but this seemed to me to be a work of genius, anticipating as it did ideas of networking and information technology that would not become common parlance for several decades. John Rhys Netherford may have been such a genius, but remember it was Mortimer who had the idea and then recruited Rhys Netherford, not the other way around."

Sam nodded in agreement. "That thought had occurred to me, too. Especially since this was an idea that came to him late in life, after a long career singularly devoid of any similar works or accomplishments. I suppose we could ask him?"

The Professor smiled. "I already have. I took the liberty of paying Mindy a visit two nights ago."

Mindy had volunteered to have Mortimer, which suited Rav fine. "He's not much trouble as long as you keep his water and whisky topped up and the Wi-Fi turned on," she said, laughing. "I put his cage in the corner of the living room. My mum hates him. Says he looks evil."

"He is evil," Jackson pointed out. "Anyhow, what did he say,

Professor?"

"He was initially somewhat reluctant to talk, but I think he's a tad lonely, which is perhaps not surprising given his condition. The story he eventually told was somewhat interesting. It appears he'd committed himself to a study of the practice of magic, in particular the casting of sorcerous rituals in which a key tool was an ancient ankh he'd acquired in Egypt before the First World War."

"The ankh we found by the canal?"

"Yes, that one."

"The one I took to Madam Clara, that freaked her out, because she said it was evil?"

"Yes. It had already been a deeply magical item with a long history, but its ritual use by Mortimer both increased its power and bound it to him. He used it as a focus in minor rituals, in much the same way the skull — which possessed far greater power — was intended as the focus of the enslaving ritual. It was after just such a use in a minor ritual that Phoebe Bishop mislaid it at the warehouse by the canal. But I diverge from the point, which is that due to its repeated use, the ankh was, in a sense, connected to him."

"Right. And this is relevant because?"

"One other area of Mortimer's studies was the use of clairvoyance and divination through both time and space. Knowing, as he did, the forces he was experimenting with, and having something of a paranoid streak at the best of times, Mortimer used clairvoyance and divination as tools to pre-emptively detect any threats or attacks against him. And it was during these sessions, sometime in the early nineteen-thirties, that he became aware of a force or threat from some four score years in the future that would, at that later date, attempt to frustrate a scheme or venture of his. And that the ankh, his ankh, in its future, was the conduit through which this future threat was even now probing him. But —" the Professor jabbed a finger to emphasise the point he was about to make — "at this juncture he had no idea what that future scheme or venture might be."

"Sorry, you've lost me," Rav said.

"Hang on," said Jackson. "You're not saying what I think you're saying?"

"I fear I am."

"What?" exploded Rav. "Will someone explain to me in words of one syllable what the hell is or was going on?"

The Professor held up a placatory hand. "Let me try to explain. When he became aware of a person or persons in the future who'd gained possession of his ankh and were using it to perform clairvoyance on him, Mortimer began an intensive series of clairvoyant and divinatory rituals to perform the process in reverse, with the intention of discovering who the persons in that future were, why they were trying to stop his plan, and what exactly that plan was. Through those rituals he became aware of you, me, and Jess, and of the ley network that we were apparently attempting to stop."

An awful truth began to occur to Rav. "You're telling me that the sole reason that it even occurred to him to try and build a ley network was because I took his ankh to Madam Clara and asked her to do a reading on it?"

"In a sense, yes."

"This is all my fault?"

"Well, I think cause and effect have become somewhat linked in a closed and contradictory loop in this case, given that the only reason you had the ankh to take to Madam Clara was because Mortimer had first placed it in a package to be delivered to his future successors in order that they could resurrect him and then help him build the ley network, and then secondly because Phoebe Bishop was careless enough to leave it lying in the dirt at the warehouse."

"So it's not my fault?"

Jackson slapped him on the back. "I can't give you absolution, seeing as how Martin Luther got rid of all that stuff as part of the whole Protestant Reformation thing, but if it helps, I don't think it's your fault."

"Right. And then at some point he wrote it all up as a novel?"

"I asked him about that," said Mindy. "He said he needed a bit of extra money, and he figured it would become a classic of the science fiction genre and help establish his credibility with the next generation of cultists." She pulled a face. "Then he went off on a rant about how science fiction of the time was all run by New York Jews and that was why they failed to recognise his literary greatness."

"Remind me again why we're not having him put down?"

"Because he's still in possession of a human soul," said Jackson. "Possibly. In as much as it was a human soul to begin with."

"I suppose I should be grateful that he wrote the novel," said Rav.

"Because it provided a useful clue at the start of the case?" asked the Professor.

"Kind of, yeah, but it's more than that. When I knocked Bishop over the railings, I thought he was gone. I turned my back. I had no idea that he'd caught hold of something and was climbing back up. And then I remembered a line from the end of the book."

"He pulled himself back onto the platform," said the Professor, quoting. "And launched himself at the policeman, the fury of his charge sending the man tumbling into, and then over, the narrow encircling rail."

"Yeah. That was what made me take a step back. If I hadn't have done that, it would've been me who went over."

"So that's why the prophecy didn't come true," said Mindy. "It had been true, up until the point that he wrote it down in a novel. But the act of writing made it no longer true."

"I guess." Rav looked out beyond his companions at the seemingly endless sands beyond, broken only by a village a few miles away, whose inhabitants would no doubt be fighting a battle against the invading dunes. This place was changed, perhaps forever. As was he. Then he looked down at the cardboard box that was placed on the ground beside Jackson. "Maybe we should do what we came here to do?"

The priest nodded. "We should." He reached down, untied the string that bound the box, opened the flaps and pulled a skull out from within. "Come on, Horace. It's time to grant you the rest you deserve." He began to walk towards the freshly dug grave that sat at one side of the churchyard. A middle-aged woman priest with a kindly face stood beside the grave. A friend of Jackson's from back in theological college, apparently, with a church that they figured was appropriately located. Rav didn't know why, but after the millennium-and-a-half of wandering that Horace had suffered, it seemed right that he be returned to rest here, where his journey had ended.

Jackson placed the skull in a sling that had been waiting by the grave then began to lower it into the hole as his fellow priest spoke the words of a funeral service that were vaguely familiar even to a notional Hindu like Rav.

He leaned in to whisper in Mindy's ear. "I need to be somewhere. I'll catch up with you later." He gave Jackson and Sam a discrete nod each. It was strange. For the last few weeks they'd been bound as tightly as any historical brothers-in-arms, but now they were going their separate ways. There hadn't been any deep discussions about it;

just an instinctive, mutual understanding that they led separate lives journeying towards different destinies. One day their paths might re-cross and their comradeship resume, but for now, this was it. It felt weirdly like the goodbyes at the end of a holiday friendship, with commitments made to future contact that were heartfelt in tone but deliberately vague in substance.

A few hours later, his hired Range Rover was nosing to a halt in a narrow, waste-strewn street that lay behind a nondescript row of retail outlets. Black metal fire escapes snaked up over single-storey rooftops to the flats above the shops. At the base of one of them, a familiar figure waited.

Ricky Fletcher. Gaunt, and still haunted looking, but the sanity returned to his features. "Doctor Shah!" he said, extending his hand. "I didn't know if you'd be here."

Rav took his hand. "It's Rav. Just Rav. Jenny — your social worker — she called me. I'd asked her to keep me in touch. You're feeling better, right?"

Ricky nodded. "Yeah. Truth to tell, I've got a big piece missing from my memories. I remember the voice in my head, the tattoo, getting louder and louder until it was all I could hear. But a week or so ago, it just went away, and I came back. Was that down to you?"

"Sort of, yeah. Partly."

A blue Ford chose that moment to nose its way down the street, easing to a halt behind Rav's Range Rover. Jenny got out from behind the wheel, nodded at Rav, then opened the passenger door and reached in to undo some belts. A small figure burst out from underneath her arm and sprinted across the gap that lay between them, hurling itself into Ricky's waiting arms.

"Daddy!" the figure screamed.

Fletcher hugged Scarlet long and hard, before looking up at Rav. "Doctor Shah, Rav. Thank you. This means more than I can ever say. I've got nothing to pay you with now, but I can try and rake something—"

Rav silenced him with a wave of the hand. "It's nothing. I don't need paying. Seeing you two back together is everything I needed."

Jenny tipped her head at Ricky. "Now you understand that you're still under my supervision, given what happened, yeah? I'll be calling in on you from time-to-time. But only to check you're both doing okay."

"You'll be fine with Jenny," Rav said. "She's a good 'un."

Scarlet eased out of Ricky's arms and turned to face Rav. He squatted down to bring his face level with hers.

"Did you make Mister Tattoo go away?"

"Yeah, I made him go away."

She thought for a moment, chewing on her lip, as a tense expression appeared on her face. "Will he come back?"

Rav looked her hard in the eyes. "No. He's gone forever, and he isn't coming back."

She thought on that for a moment more, before pasting onto her face an expression that she obviously intended to be that of a serious grownup. "Thank you for making my daddy better, Doctor Shah."

She stuck out a hand, which Rav solemnly took. "You're most welcome, Scarlet, but you don't need to thank me. It's what I do."

He gave her a final smile, then pushed himself to his feet, nodded goodbye to Ricky, and set off back towards his Range Rover. Jenny fell into place beside him. "What exactly is it that you do, Rav?" she asked. "Other than, like, social work. People don't just get cured like that. What's going on? Is he going to be okay?"

He stopped beside the Range Rover. "Yeah. Don't ask me to explain, but yeah, he's going to be okay. As to what I do, it's a weirder world than most people realise, and people like me…" He looked away for a moment, at a reassuringly normal steel-grey sky. "Let's just say that when weirdness comes knocking, I'm the man you need to call."

THE END

Dear Reader,

Thank you for purchasing and reading *Sticks and Stones*. All of us at Wild Jester Press hugely appreciate it. We hope you enjoyed the read and, if you did, we would ask one small favour of you: that you take some time to write a short review in the online location of your choice.

Online reviews are hugely important for independent and small-press publishers like us. We don't have marketing budgets. We can't pay to be prominently displayed in bookshops. We sell by "digital word of mouth", and reader-produced online reviews are the means by which that happens.

Thank you!

Out now from Wild Jester Press

Looking to read something else by Jonny Nexus? Then check out *The Sleeping Dragon*.

In a fantasy world transformed by mass-produced magic, five individuals find themselves drawn into a mystery five-hundred years old. They are: Blade, an AdventureSport warrior at the tail end of a once glittering career; Presto, a disgraced and unemployed ex-wizard once of the Imperial University; the Storm, the herb-addicted lead lutist of the rock band Northern Fire; Darick, a priest whose career progress is blocked by his possession of actual religious beliefs that his church no longer shares; and Dani, a grifter who lives her life on the margins of a complex and soulless society.

Thrown together by circumstances beyond their comprehension, they find themselves embarking on a quest that will take them from the towering spires of Empire City to the wild and bleak Eastern Territories, and from the decadence and glamour of Upabove to a final confrontation upon which rests the fate of their world.

"...a Tolkien-inspired, Pratchett-esque, science-fantasy tale featuring all of your favourite fantasy character archetypes in a delightfully subversive way." -- *A Hidden Jam*

"As soon as I finished it, I wanted more ... And I wanted to watch it as well - I would love to have this as my next program to binge watch on Netflix. Overall a great book, and I just wish it didn't have to end." -- *Michael Carter, Goodreads*

Alternatively, check out his ENnie-nominated first novel, *Game Night*.

Six Gods Sit Down To Spend An Evening Roleplaying. Badly.

In an anachronistic realm at the far end of creation, five adventurers near the climax of an epic quest, upon which hangs the fate of their world. Sadly for them, however, they are but pieces in a roleplaying game being played by a group of bickering gods.

Epic events will unfold, only to then unravel. Secrets will be revealed and then forgotten. A much-abused reality will warp, mutate, rewind, and – on occasion – capitulate. Stupidity will birth tragedy; mischief will spawn chaos; malevolent arrogance will conjure forth genuine evil.

A story of myth and legend twelve thousand years in the making is heading towards its final chapter.

It's game night.

"The best novel ever written about gaming. One of the funniest novels ever written about anything."
– Steve Darlington, gaming writer

"A Pratchett-esque debut novel of gods, roleplaying, and game-night kerfuffles. Buy Game Night. It's a fun, fresh, irreverent read that'll ring true to any gamer even if, unlike the protagonists, you happen not to be a god."
– John Kovalic, Writer & Artist (Dork Tower, Munchkin)

Printed in Great Britain
by Amazon